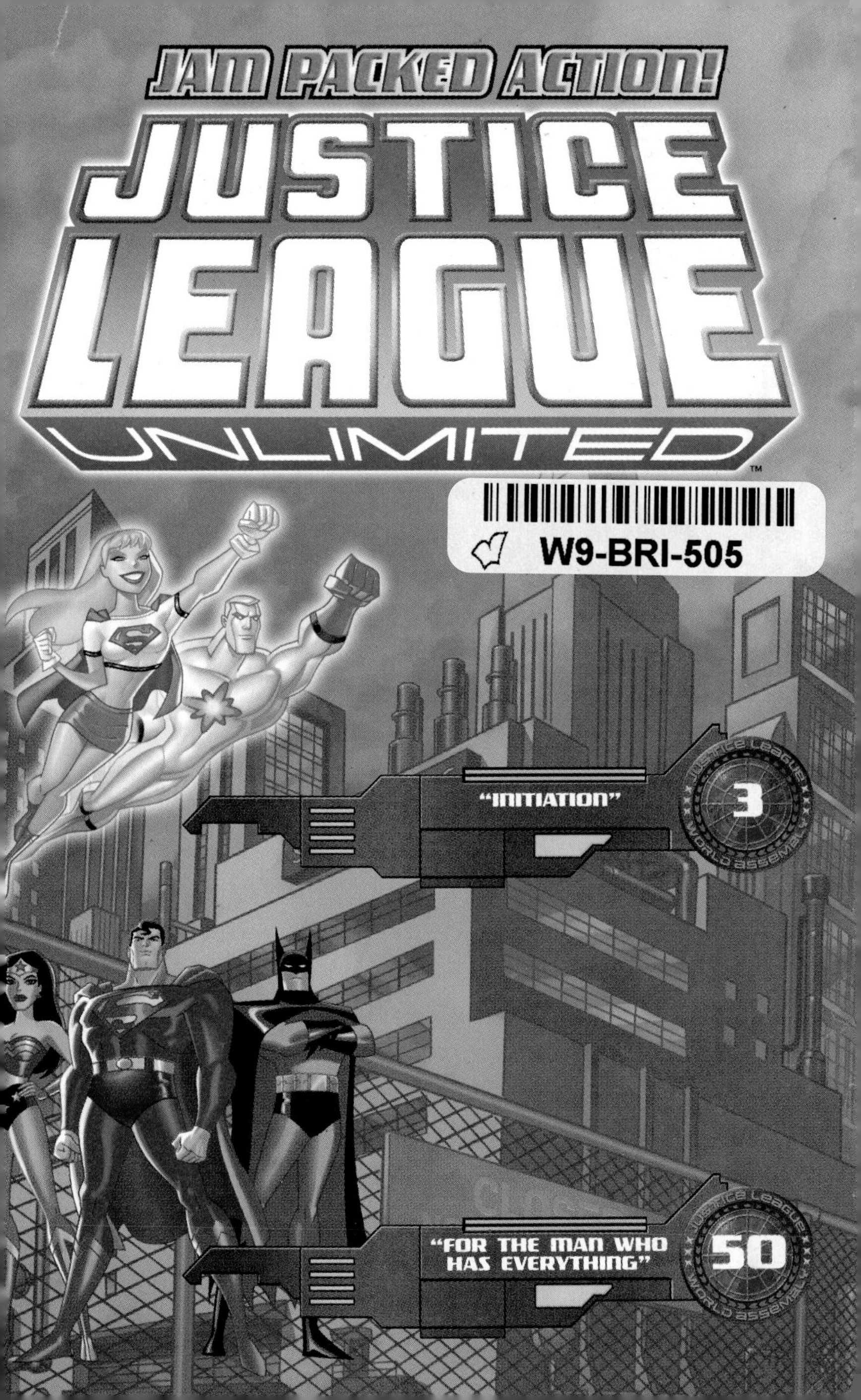
JAM PACKED ACTION!
JUSTICE LEAGUE UNLIMITED™
"INITIATION"
3
"FOR THE MAN WHO HAS EVERYTHING"
50

Dan DiDio, VP—Editorial
Paul Levitz, President & Publisher
Georg Brewer, VP—Design & DC Direct Creative
Richard Bruning, Senior VP—Creative Director
Patrick Caldon, Senior VP—Finance & Operations
Chris Caramalis, VP—Finance
Terri Cunningham, VP—Managing Editor
Stephanie Fierman, Senior VP—Sales & Marketing
Alison Gill, VP—Manufacturing
Rich Johnson, VP—Book Trade Sales
Hank Kanalz, VP—General Manager, WildStorm
Lillian Laserson, Senior VP & General Counsel
Paula Lowitt, Senior VP—Business & Legal Affairs
Jim Lee, Editorial Director—WildStorm
David McKillips, VP—Advertising & Custom Publishing
John Nee, VP—Business Development
Gregory Noveck, Senior VP—Creative Affairs
Cheryl Rubin, Senior VP—Brand Management
Jeff Trojan, VP—Business Development, DC Direct
Bob Wayne, VP—Sales

Script Adaptations by WildStorm
Design by Ed Roeder & Larry Barry
Lettering by Tom Long
Edited by Ben Abernathy
Special Thanks to Amy Wagner

JAM PACKED ACTION!

JUSTICE LEAGUE UNLIMITED™

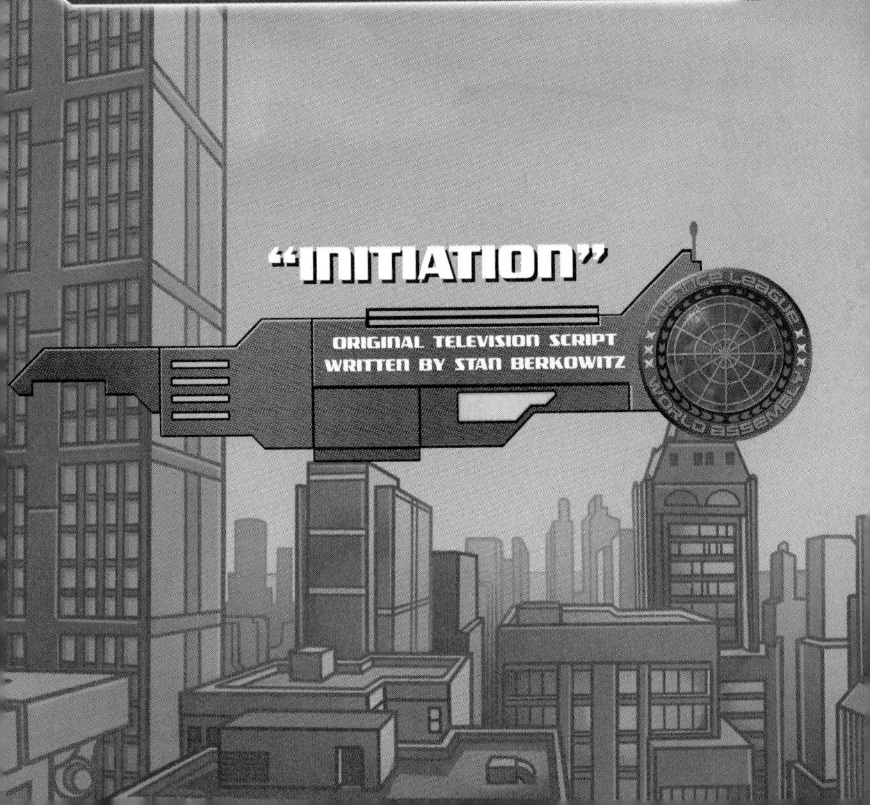

"INITIATION"

ORIGINAL TELEVISION SCRIPT
WRITTEN BY STAN BERKOWITZ

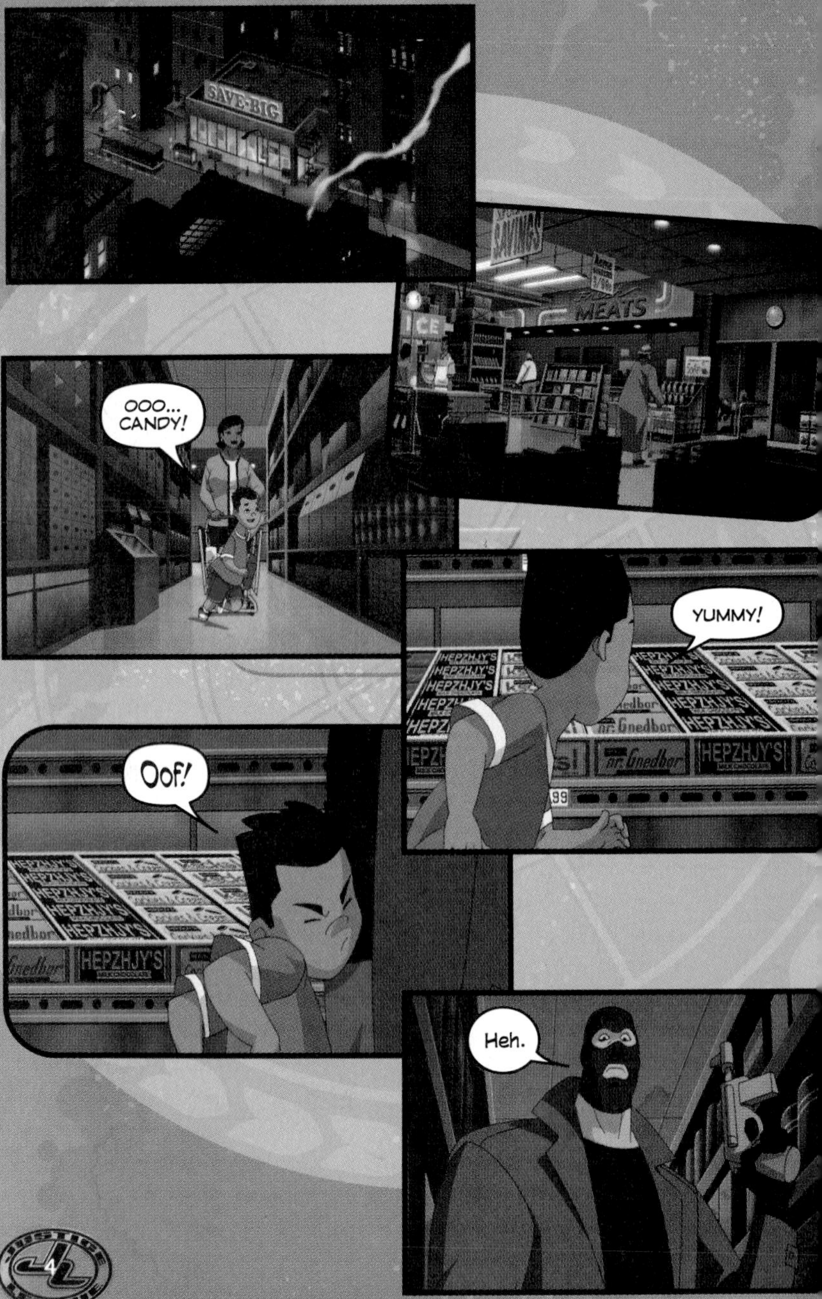
SAVE-BIG
MEATS
ICE
OOO... CANDY!
YUMMY!
HEPZHJY'S
Oof!
Heh.

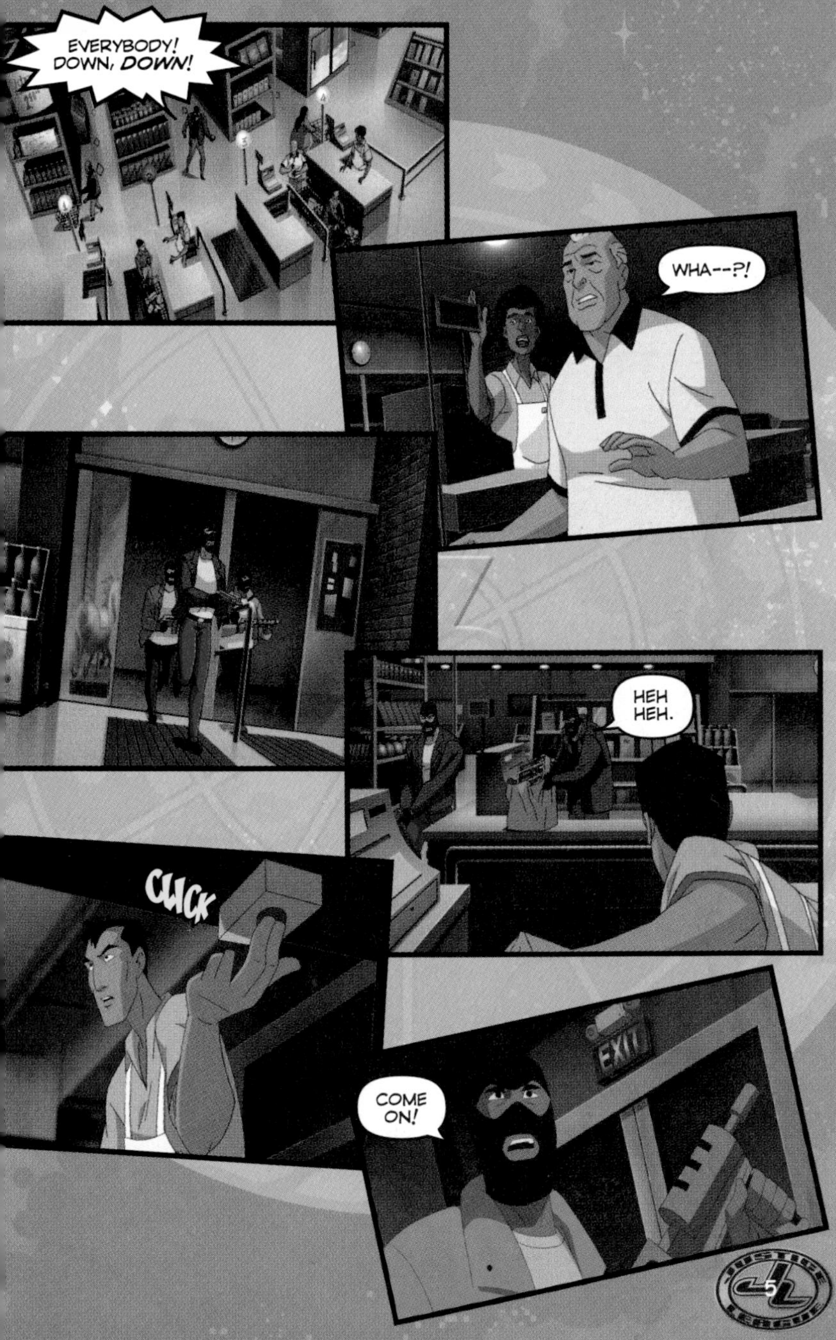
EVERYBODY! DOWN, DOWN!
WHA--?!
HEH HEH.
CLICK
EXIT
COME ON!

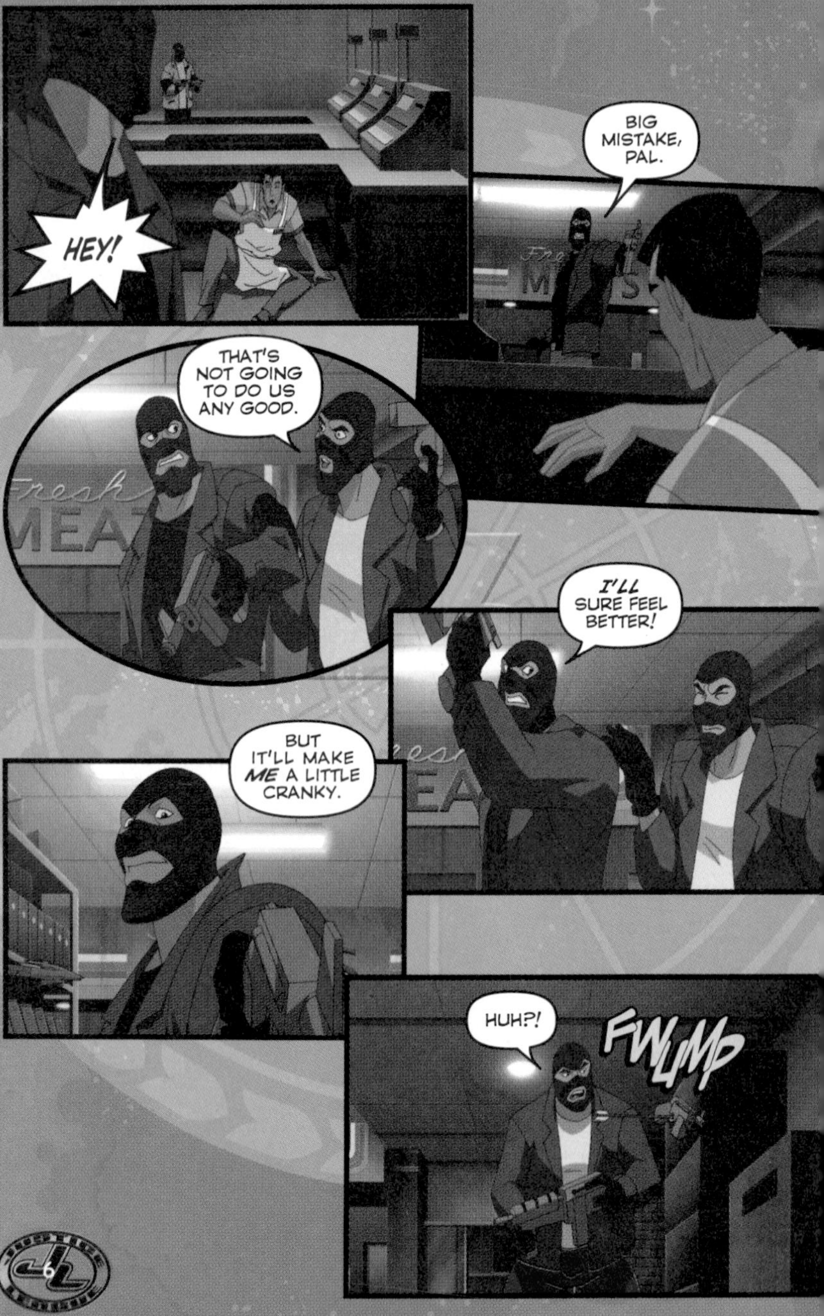
HEY!
BIG MISTAKE, PAL.
THAT'S NOT GOING TO DO US ANY GOOD.
I'LL SURE FEEL BETTER!
BUT IT'LL MAKE ME A LITTLE CRANKY.
HUH?!
FWUMP

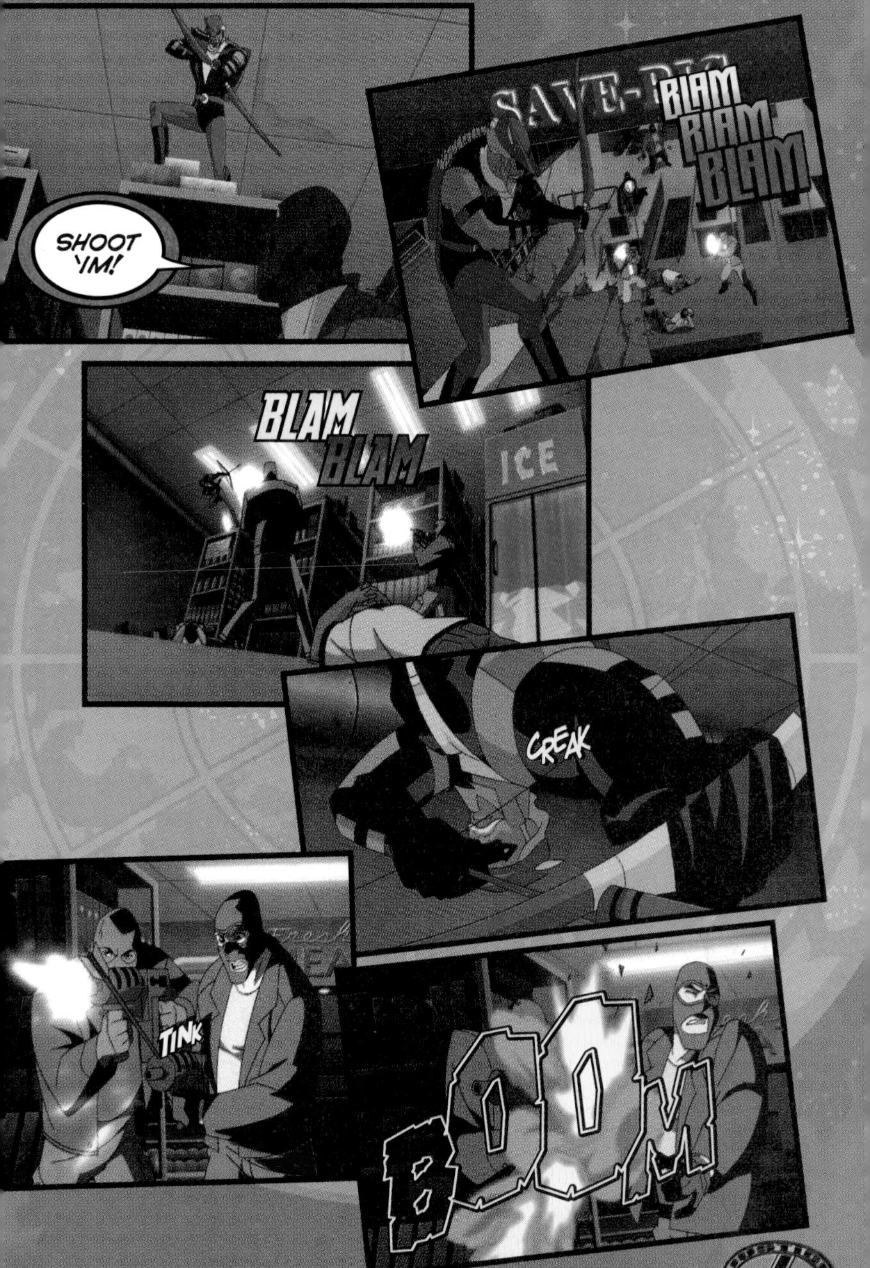
SHOOT 'IM!
BLAM
BLAM
BLAM
BLAM
BLAM
ICE
CREAK
TINK
BOOM

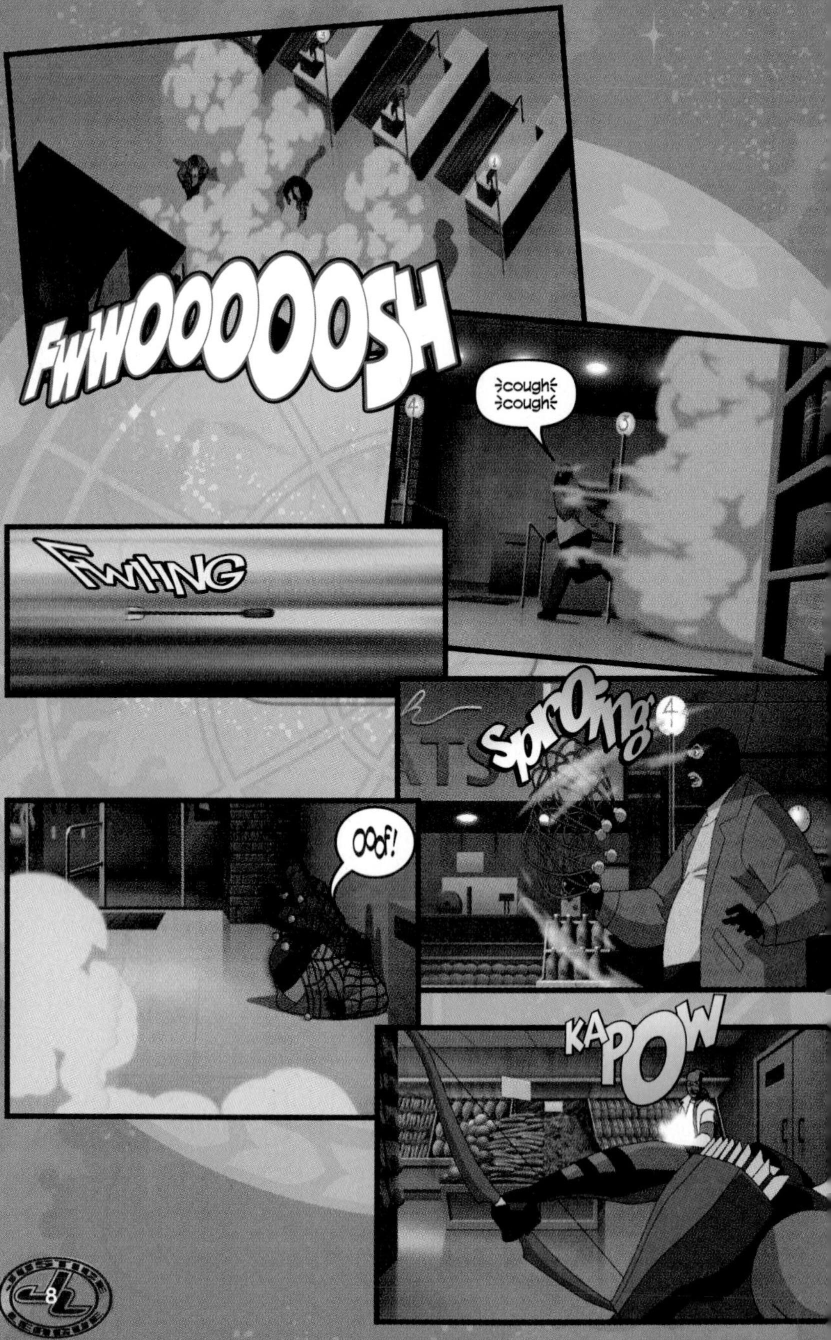
FwWOOOOOSH
cough cough
FWHING
SPROING
OOOF!
KAPOW

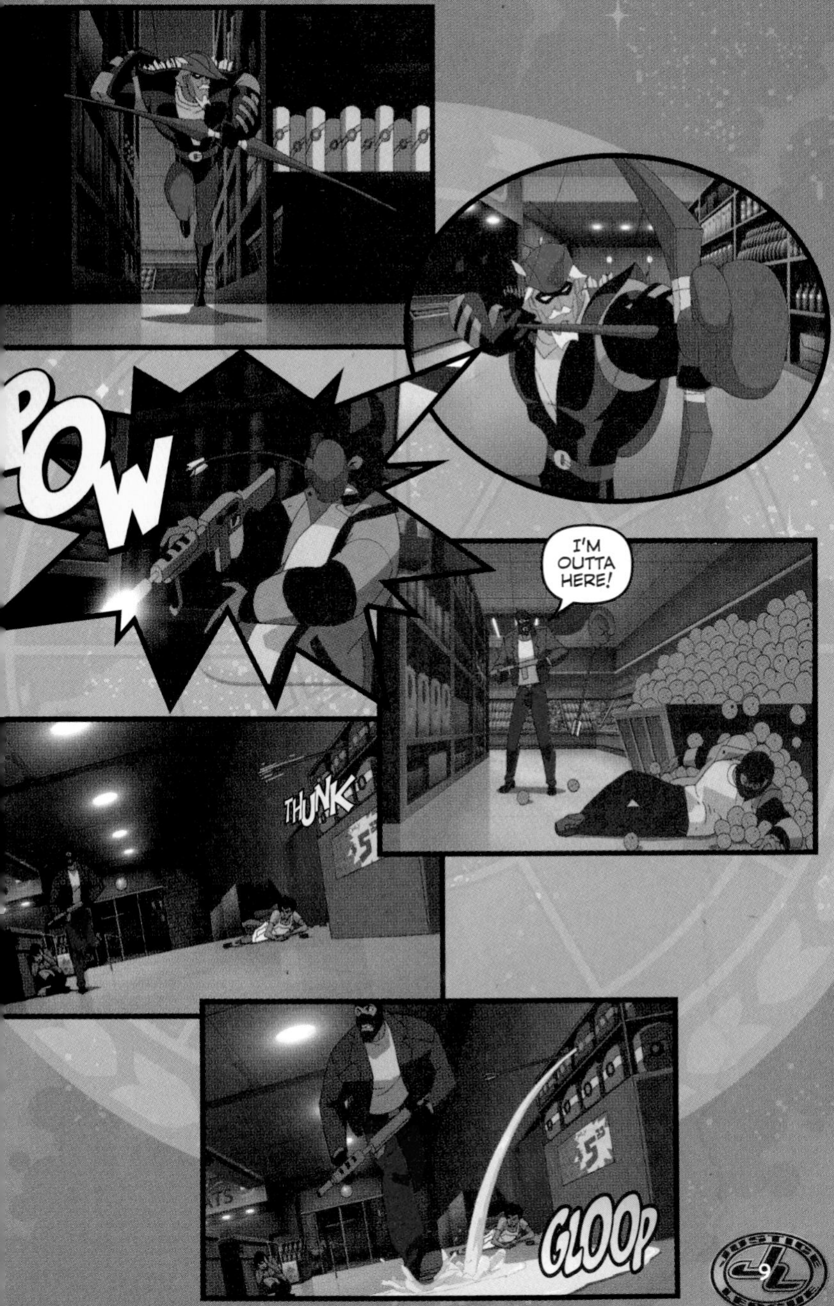
POW
I'M OUTTA HERE!
THUNK
GLOOP

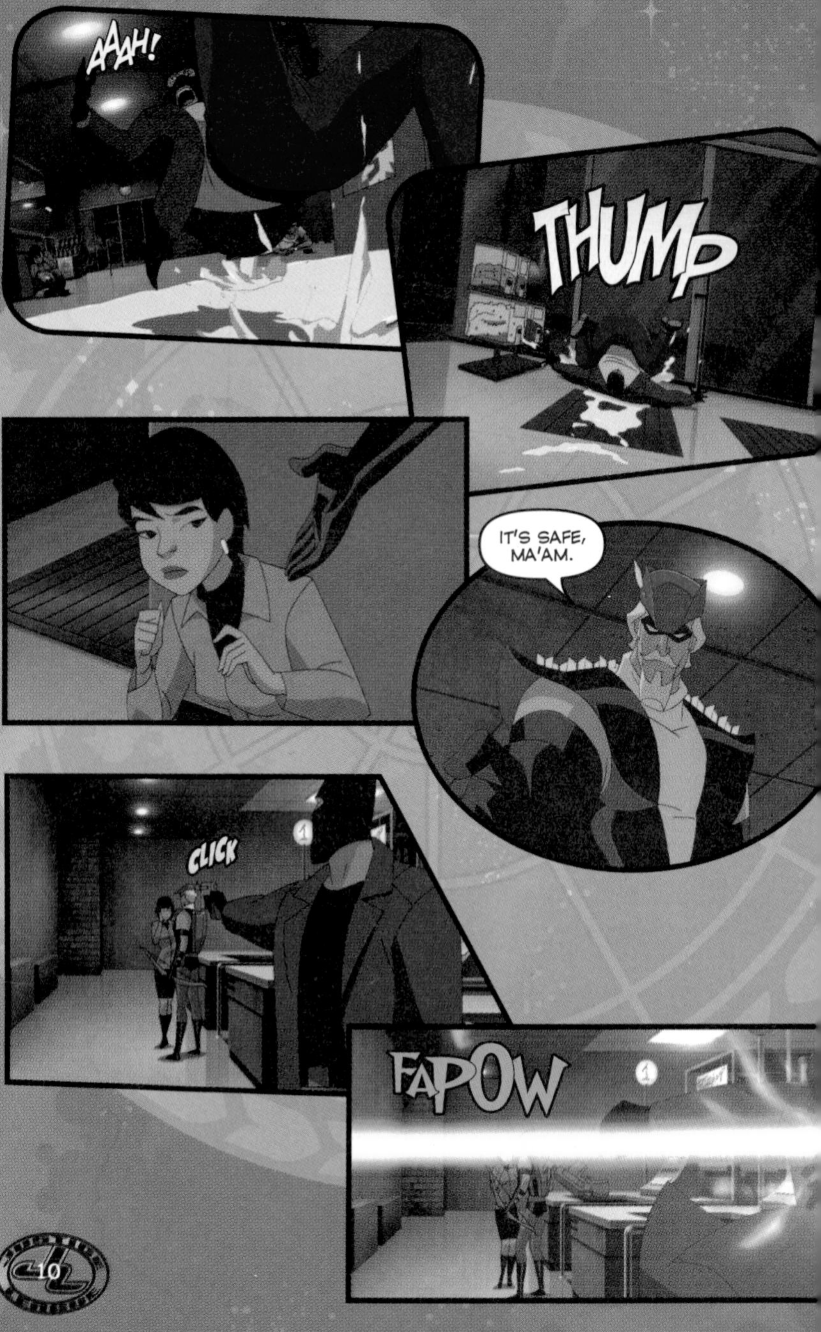
AAAH!
THUMP
IT'S SAFE, MA'AM.
CLICK
FAPOW

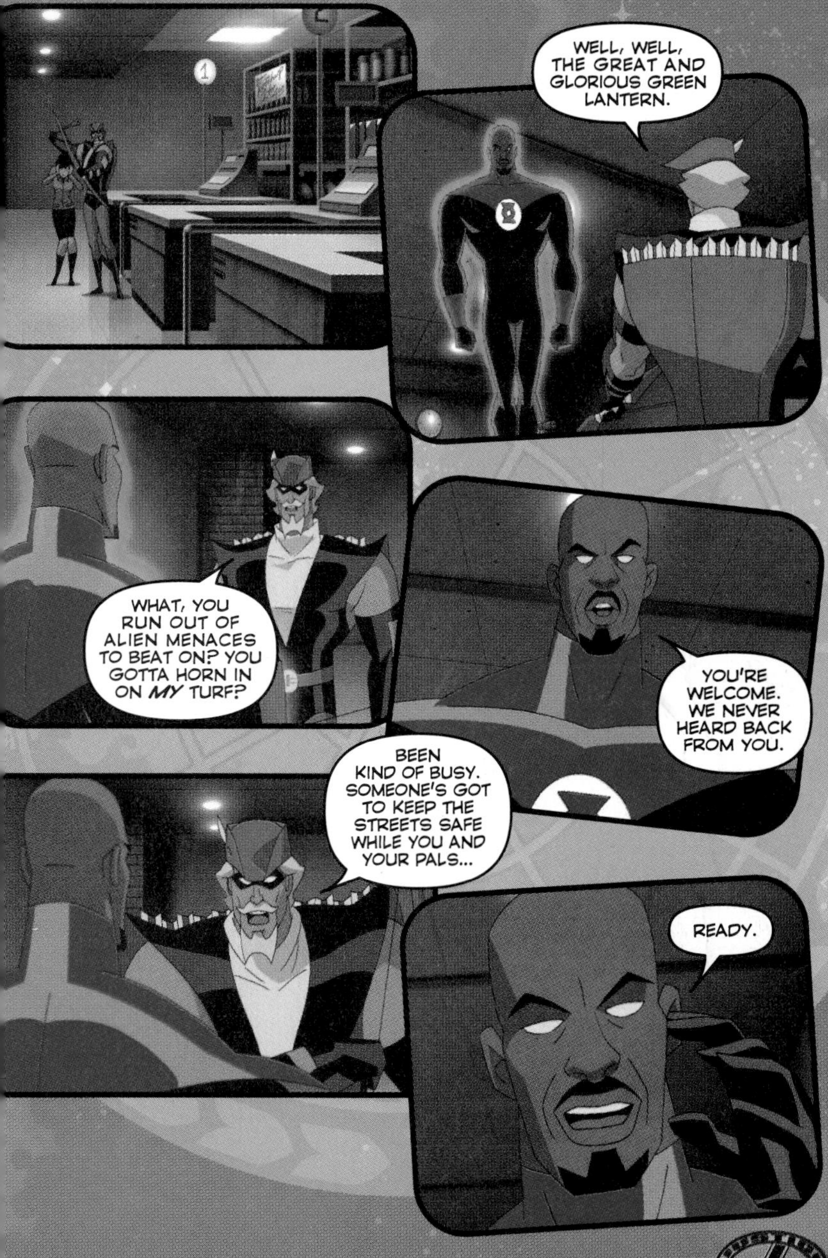
WELL, WELL, THE GREAT AND GLORIOUS GREEN LANTERN.
WHAT, YOU RUN OUT OF ALIEN MENACES TO BEAT ON? YOU GOTTA HORN IN ON *MY* TURF?
YOU'RE WELCOME. WE NEVER HEARD BACK FROM YOU.
BEEN KIND OF BUSY. SOMEONE'S GOT TO KEEP THE STREETS SAFE WHILE YOU AND YOUR PALS...
READY.

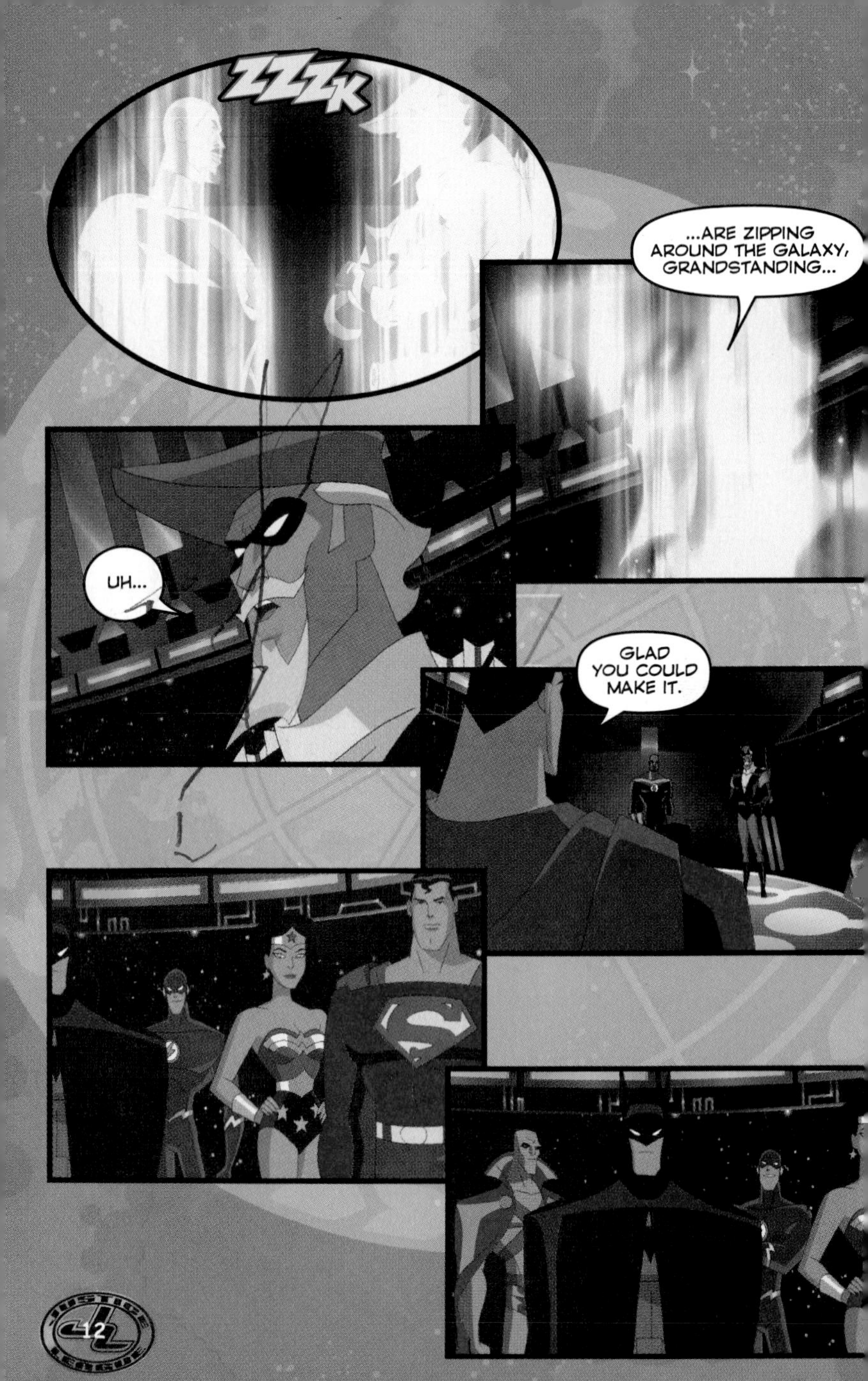
ZZZK
...ARE ZIPPING AROUND THE GALAXY, GRANDSTANDING...
UH...
GLAD YOU COULD MAKE IT.

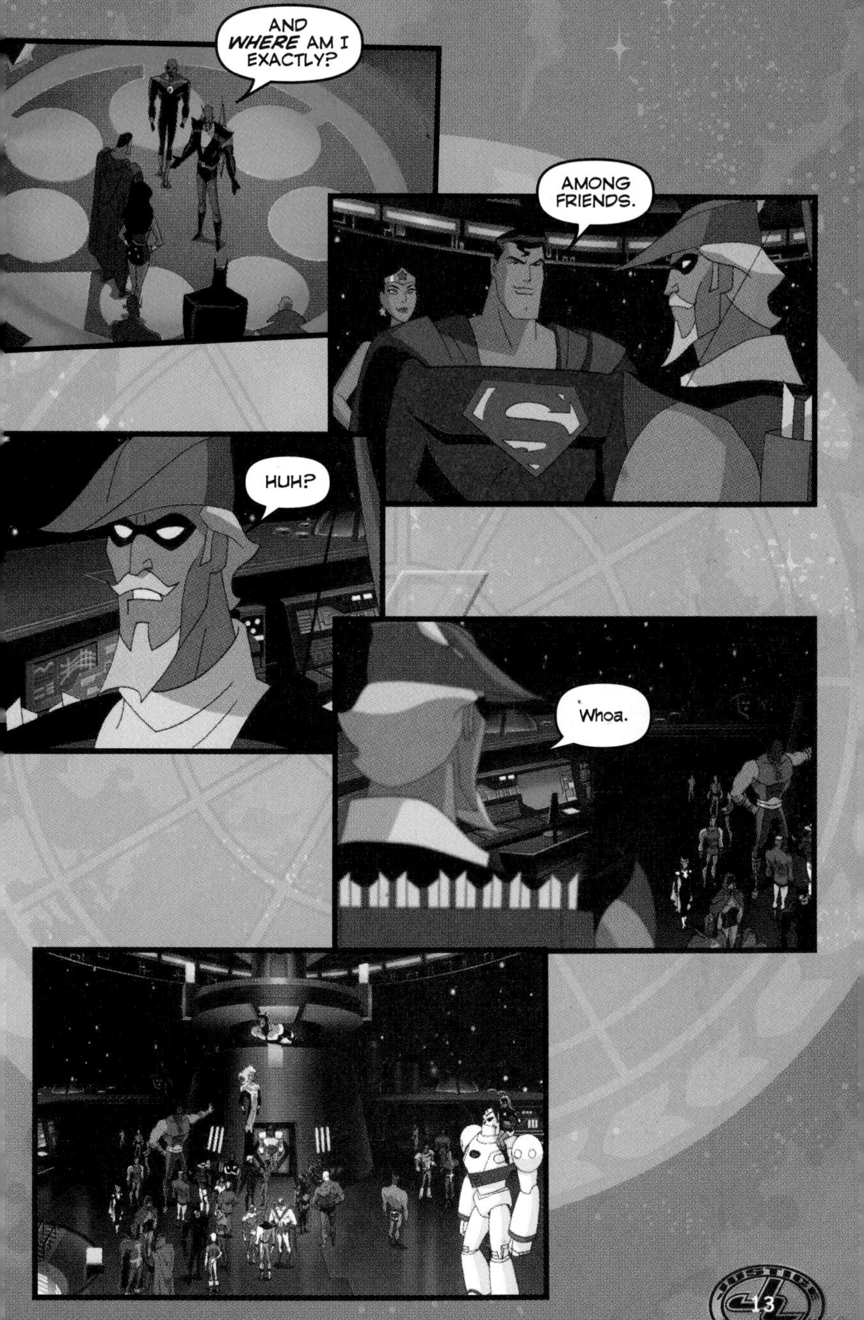
AND *WHERE* AM I EXACTLY?
AMONG FRIENDS.
HUH?
Whoa.

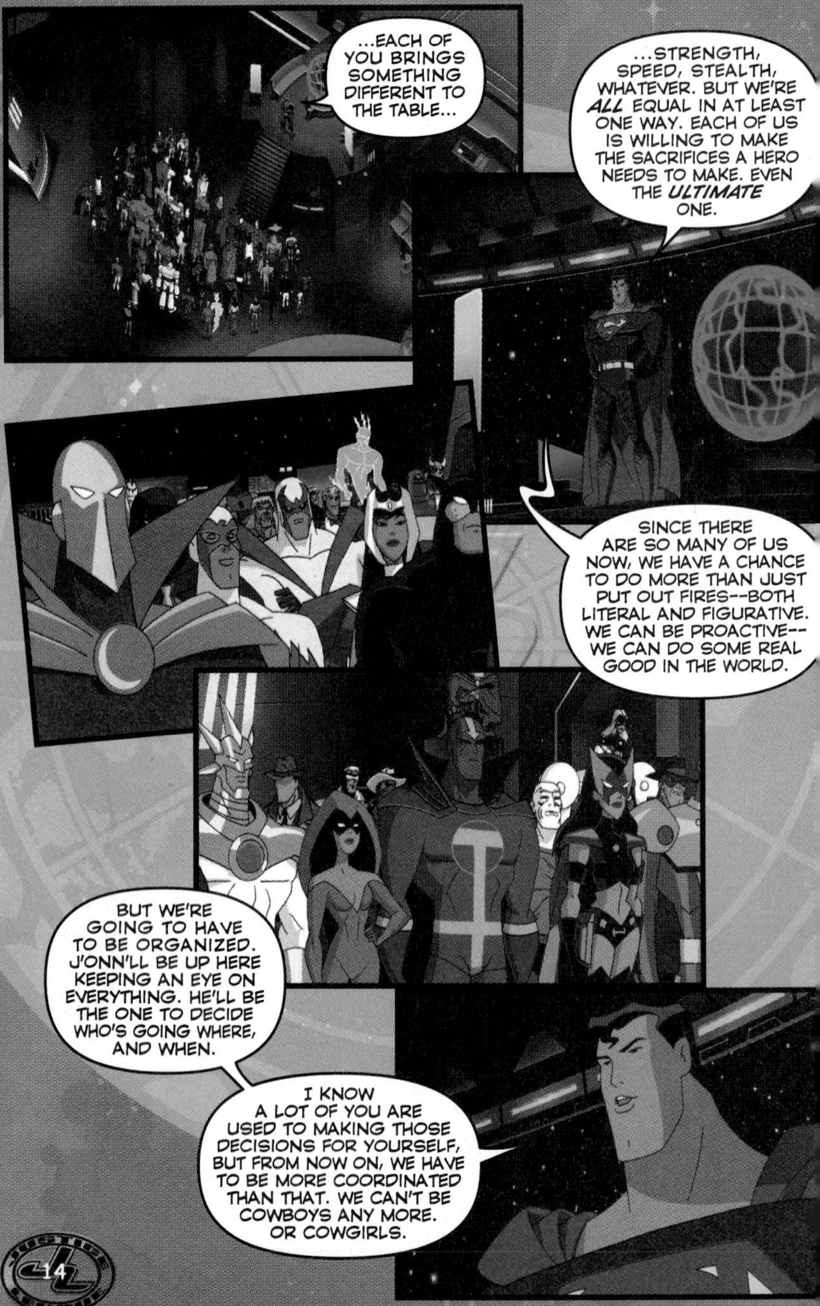

...EACH OF YOU BRINGS SOMETHING DIFFERENT TO THE TABLE...
...STRENGTH, SPEED, STEALTH, WHATEVER. BUT WE'RE *ALL* EQUAL IN AT LEAST ONE WAY. EACH OF US IS WILLING TO MAKE THE SACRIFICES A HERO NEEDS TO MAKE. EVEN THE *ULTIMATE* ONE.
SINCE THERE ARE SO MANY OF US NOW, WE HAVE A CHANCE TO DO MORE THAN JUST PUT OUT FIRES--BOTH LITERAL AND FIGURATIVE. WE CAN BE PROACTIVE--WE CAN DO SOME REAL GOOD IN THE WORLD.
BUT WE'RE GOING TO HAVE TO BE ORGANIZED. J'ONN'LL BE UP HERE KEEPING AN EYE ON EVERYTHING. HE'LL BE THE ONE TO DECIDE WHO'S GOING WHERE, AND WHEN.
I KNOW A LOT OF YOU ARE USED TO MAKING THOSE DECISIONS FOR YOURSELF, BUT FROM NOW ON, WE HAVE TO BE MORE COORDINATED THAN THAT. WE CAN'T BE COWBOYS ANY MORE. OR COWGIRLS.

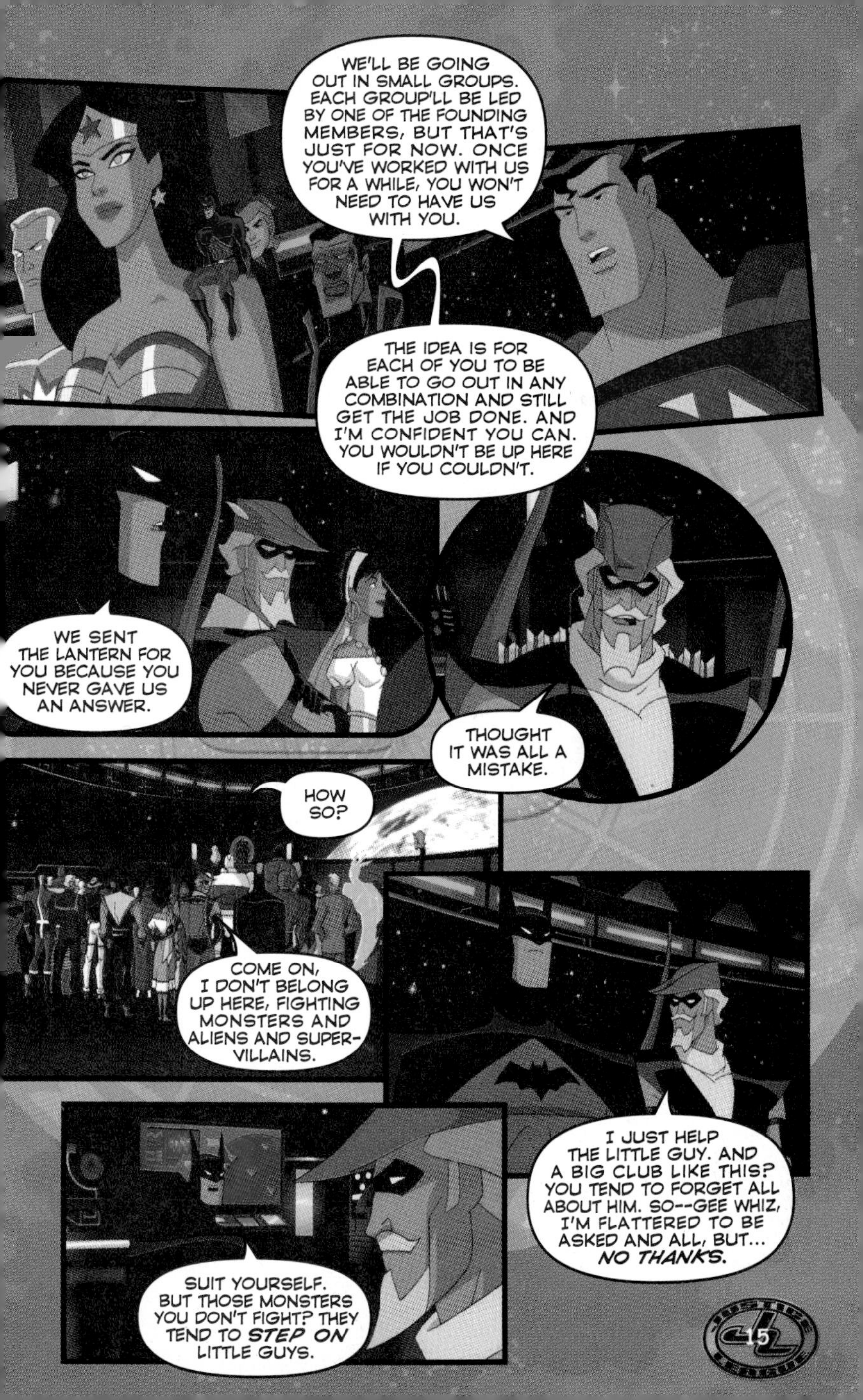

WE'LL BE GOING OUT IN SMALL GROUPS. EACH GROUP'LL BE LED BY ONE OF THE FOUNDING MEMBERS, BUT THAT'S JUST FOR NOW. ONCE YOU'VE WORKED WITH US FOR A WHILE, YOU WON'T NEED TO HAVE US WITH YOU.
THE IDEA IS FOR EACH OF YOU TO BE ABLE TO GO OUT IN ANY COMBINATION AND STILL GET THE JOB DONE. AND I'M CONFIDENT YOU CAN. YOU WOULDN'T BE UP HERE IF YOU COULDN'T.
WE SENT THE LANTERN FOR YOU BECAUSE YOU NEVER GAVE US AN ANSWER.
THOUGHT IT WAS ALL A MISTAKE.
HOW SO?
COME ON, I DON'T BELONG UP HERE, FIGHTING MONSTERS AND ALIENS AND SUPER-VILLAINS.
I JUST HELP THE LITTLE GUY. AND A BIG CLUB LIKE THIS? YOU TEND TO FORGET ALL ABOUT HIM. SO--GEE WHIZ, I'M FLATTERED TO BE ASKED AND ALL, BUT... *NO THANKS.*
SUIT YOURSELF. BUT THOSE MONSTERS YOU DON'T FIGHT? THEY TEND TO *STEP ON* LITTLE GUYS.

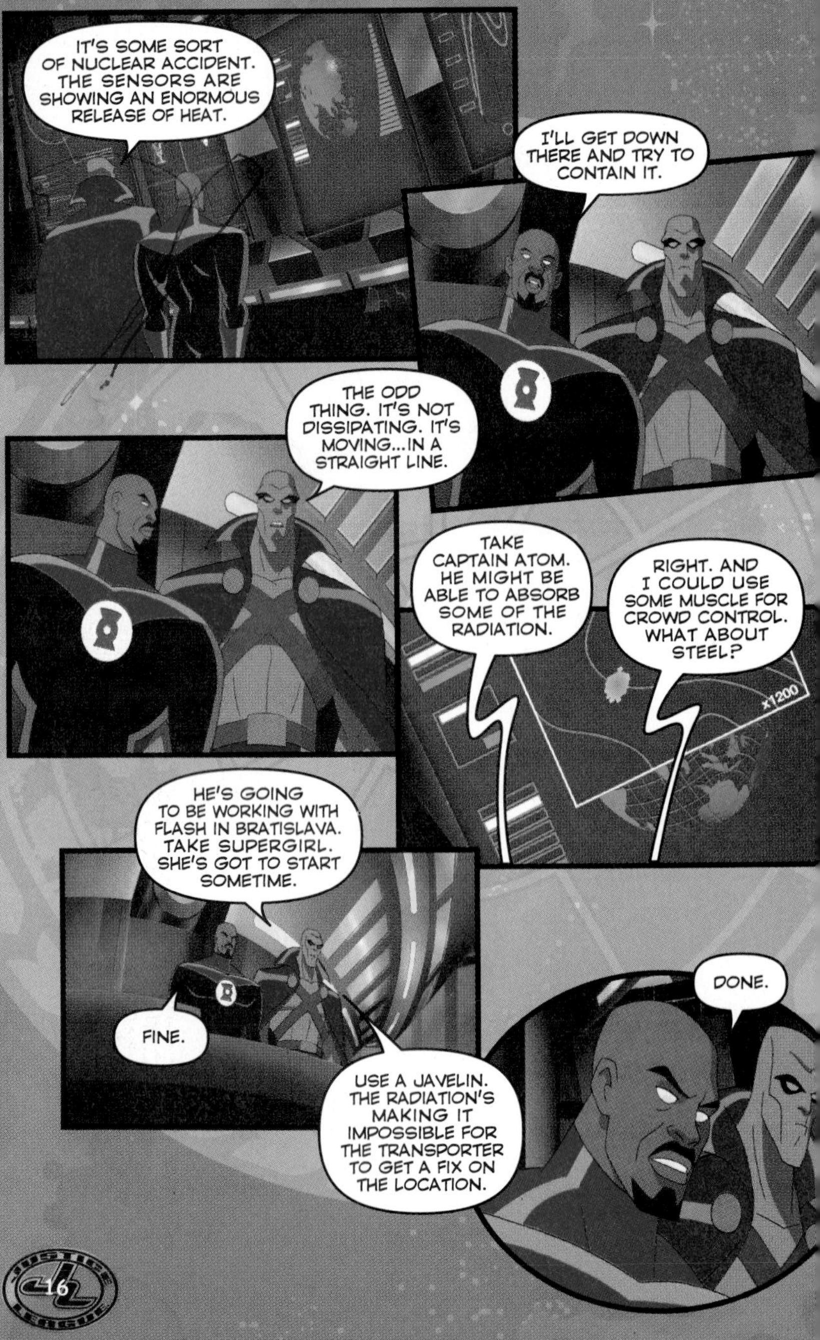
IT'S SOME SORT OF NUCLEAR ACCIDENT. THE SENSORS ARE SHOWING AN ENORMOUS RELEASE OF HEAT.
I'LL GET DOWN THERE AND TRY TO CONTAIN IT.
THE ODD THING. IT'S NOT DISSIPATING. IT'S MOVING...IN A STRAIGHT LINE.
TAKE CAPTAIN ATOM. HE MIGHT BE ABLE TO ABSORB SOME OF THE RADIATION.
RIGHT. AND I COULD USE SOME MUSCLE FOR CROWD CONTROL. WHAT ABOUT STEEL?
x1200
HE'S GOING TO BE WORKING WITH FLASH IN BRATISLAVA. TAKE SUPERGIRL. SHE'S GOT TO START SOMETIME.
FINE.
USE A JAVELIN. THE RADIATION'S MAKING IT IMPOSSIBLE FOR THE TRANSPORTER TO GET A FIX ON THE LOCATION.
DONE.

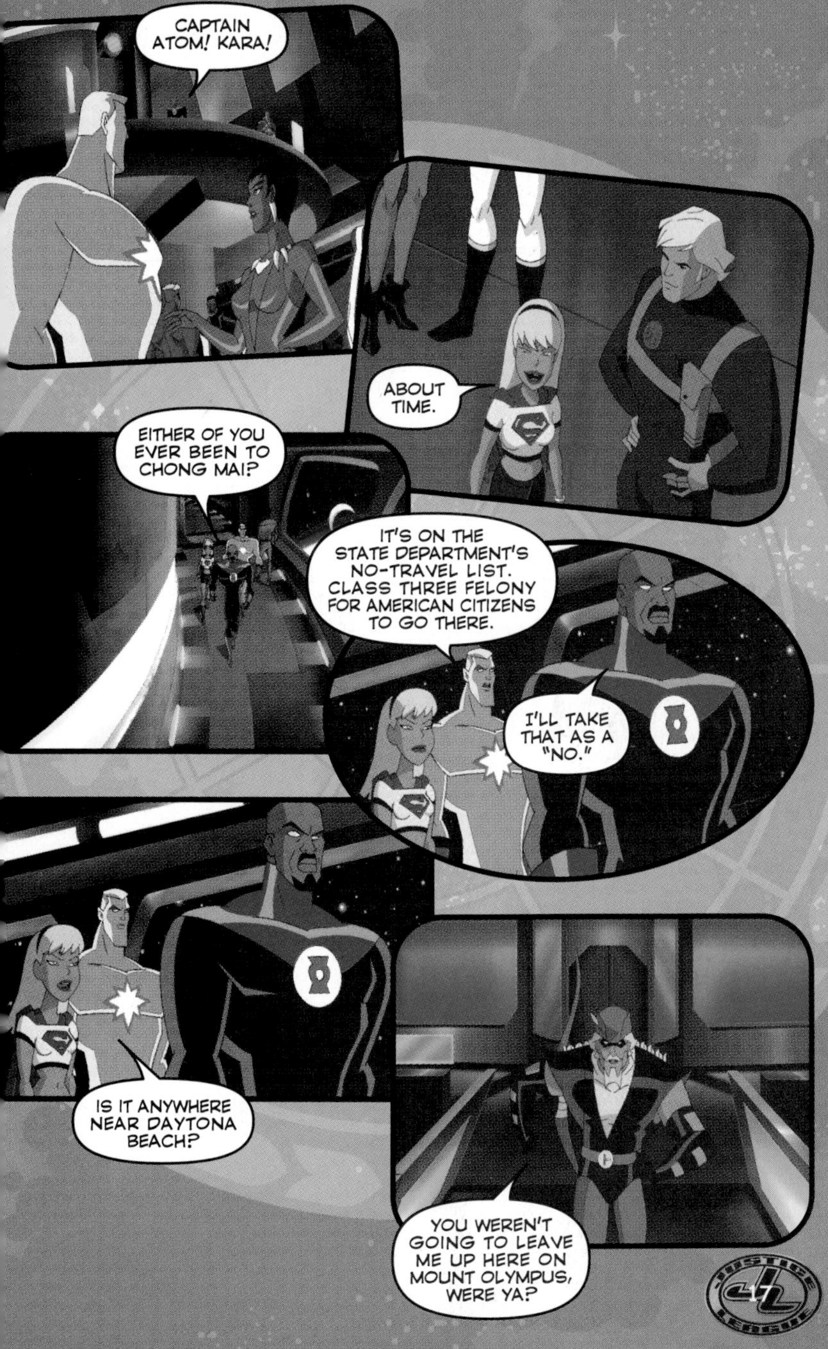
CAPTAIN ATOM! KARA!
ABOUT TIME.
EITHER OF YOU EVER BEEN TO CHONG MAI?
IT'S ON THE STATE DEPARTMENT'S NO-TRAVEL LIST. CLASS THREE FELONY FOR AMERICAN CITIZENS TO GO THERE.
I'LL TAKE THAT AS A "NO."
IS IT ANYWHERE NEAR DAYTONA BEACH?
YOU WEREN'T GOING TO LEAVE ME UP HERE ON MOUNT OLYMPUS, WERE YA?

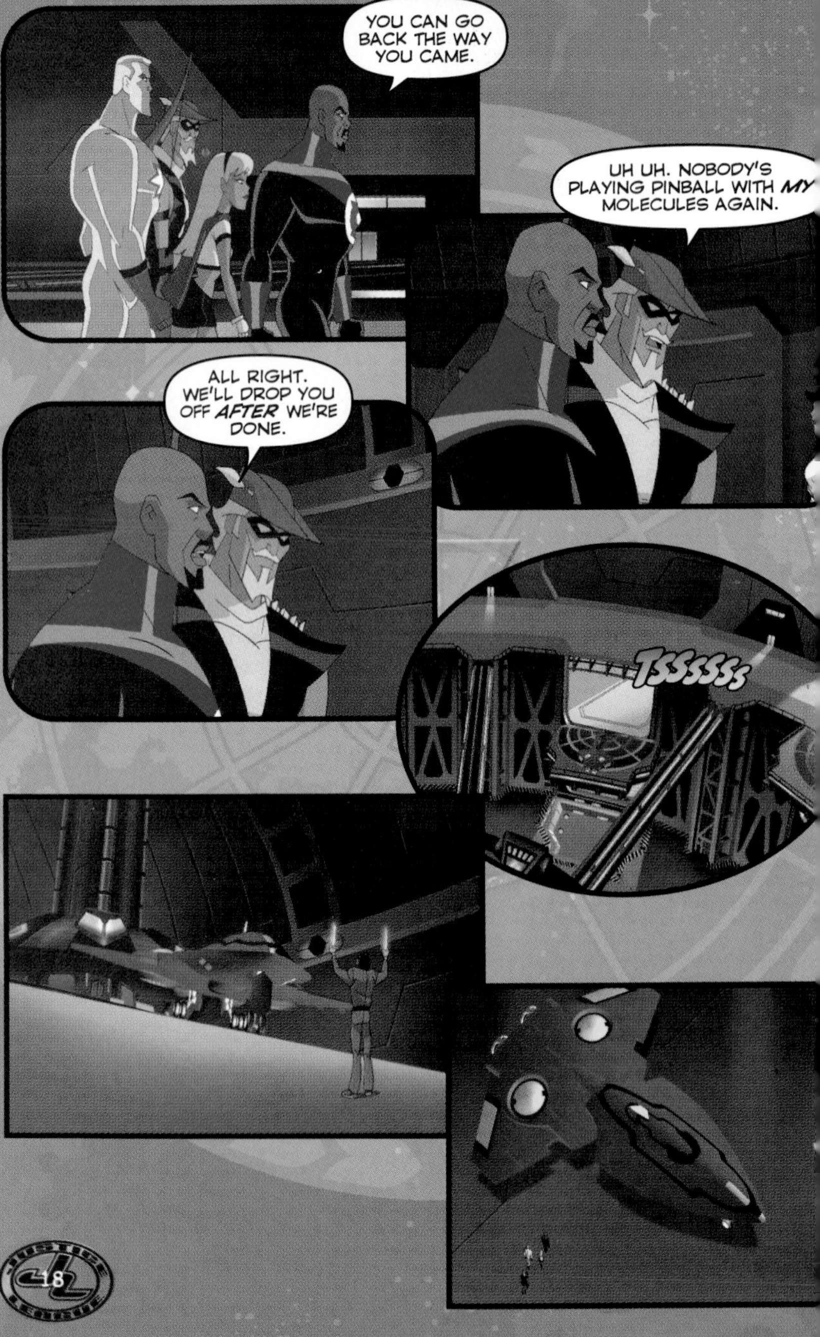
YOU CAN GO BACK THE WAY YOU CAME.
UH UH. NOBODY'S PLAYING PINBALL WITH *MY* MOLECULES AGAIN.
ALL RIGHT. WE'LL DROP YOU OFF *AFTER* WE'RE DONE.
TSSSSSS

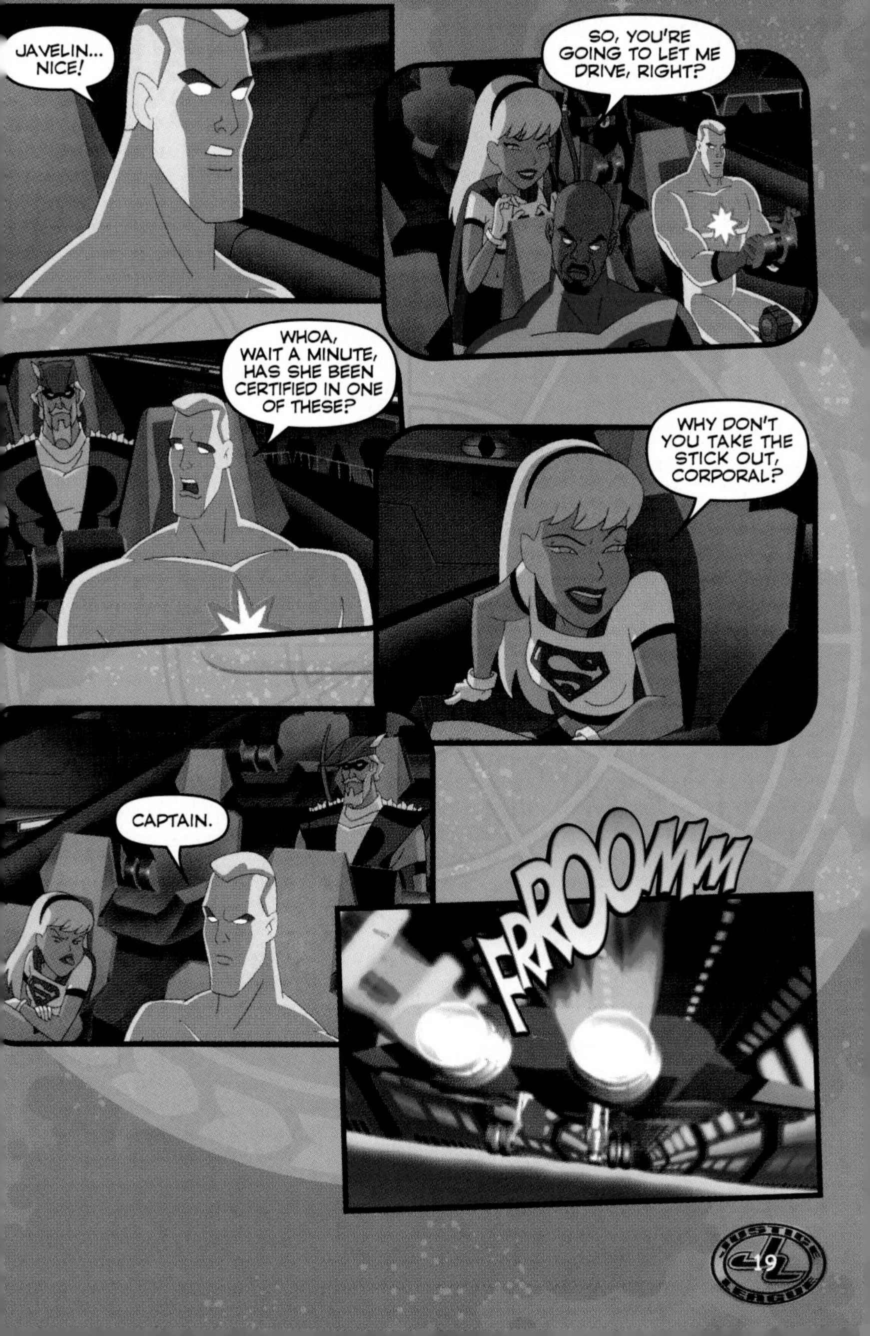
JAVELIN... NICE!
SO, YOU'RE GOING TO LET ME DRIVE, RIGHT?
WHOA, WAIT A MINUTE, HAS SHE BEEN CERTIFIED IN ONE OF THESE?
WHY DON'T YOU TAKE THE STICK OUT, CORPORAL?
CAPTAIN.
FRROOMM

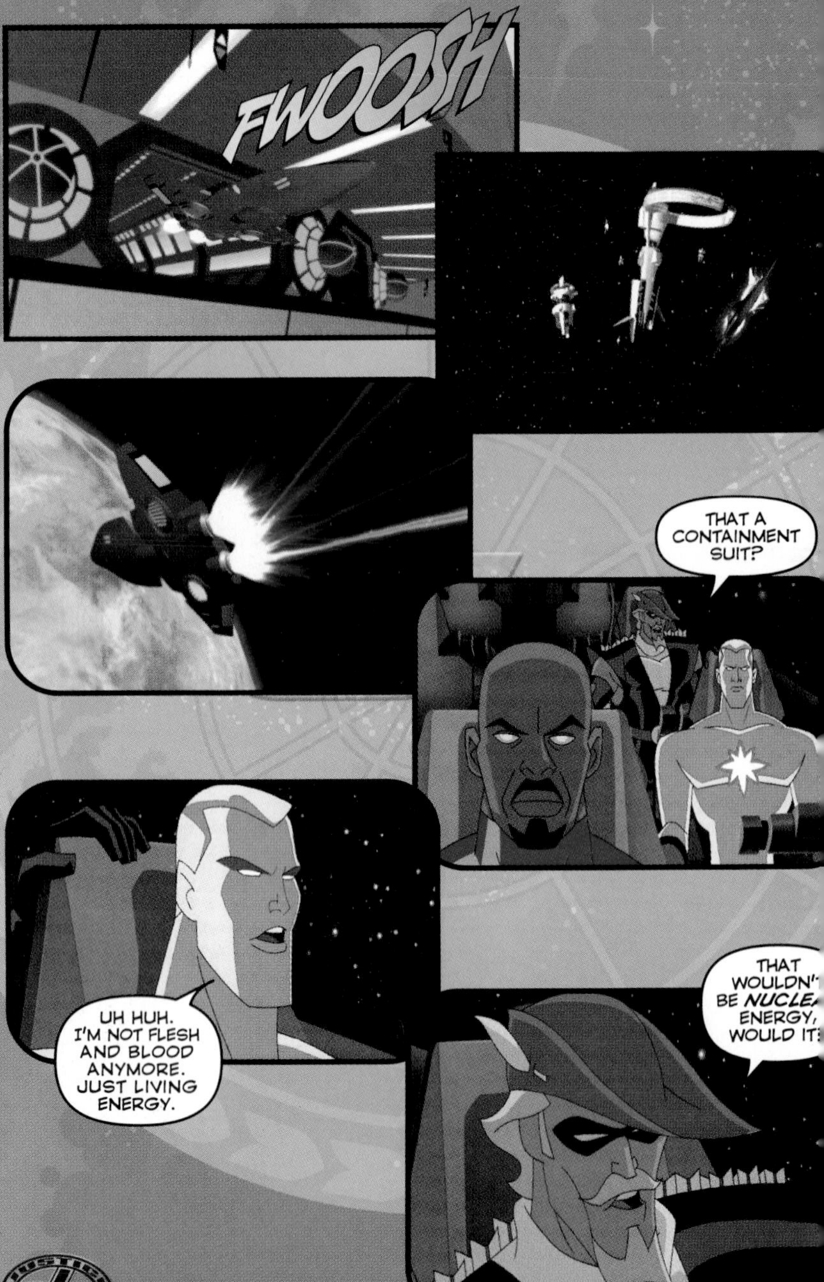
FWOOSH
THAT A CONTAINMENT SUIT?
UH HUH. I'M NOT FLESH AND BLOOD ANYMORE. JUST LIVING ENERGY.
THAT WOULDN' BE NUCLE ENERGY, WOULD IT

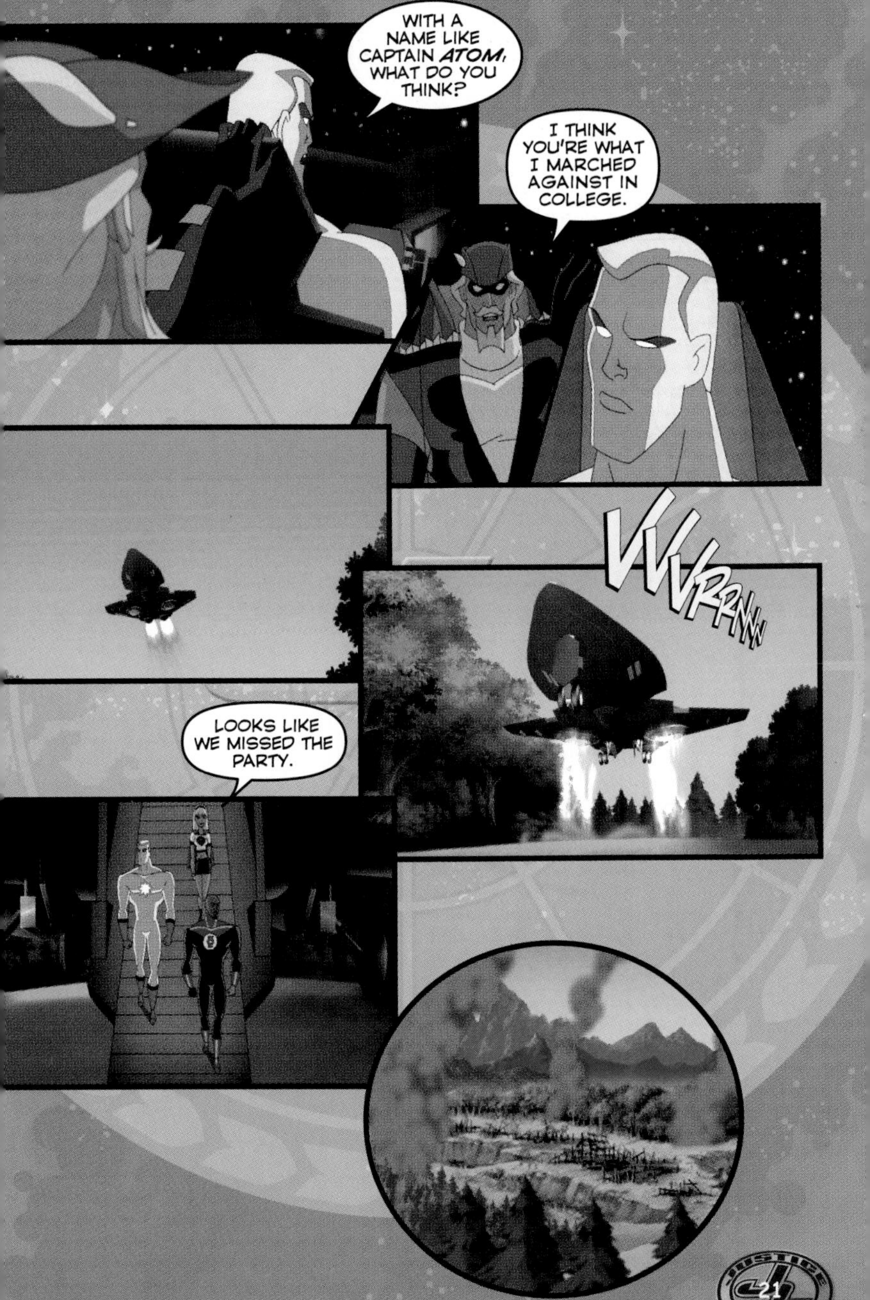
WITH A NAME LIKE CAPTAIN ATOM, WHAT DO YOU THINK?
I THINK YOU'RE WHAT I MARCHED AGAINST IN COLLEGE.
VVVVRRNNN
LOOKS LIKE WE MISSED THE PARTY.
JUSTICE LEAGUE

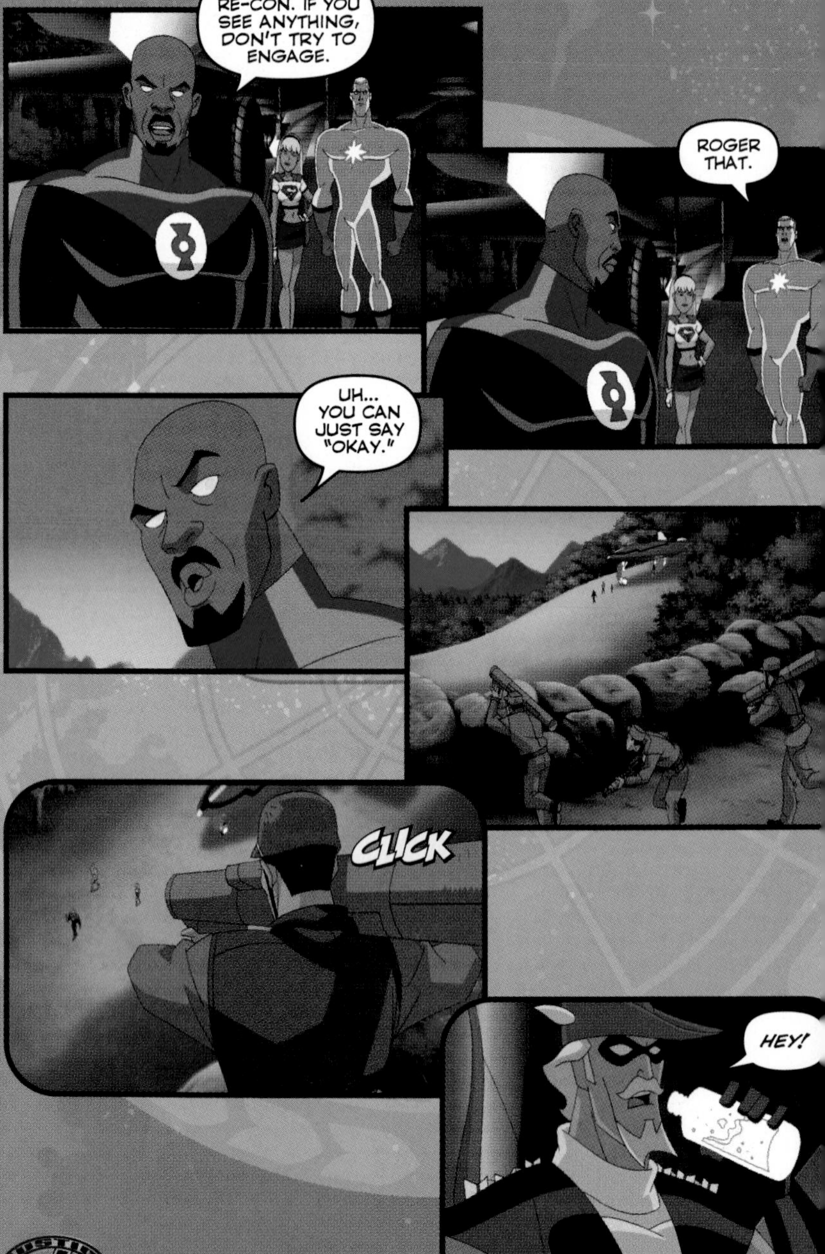
WE'LL DO RE-CON. IF YOU SEE ANYTHING, DON'T TRY TO ENGAGE.
ROGER THAT.
UH... YOU CAN JUST SAY "OKAY."
CLICK
HEY!

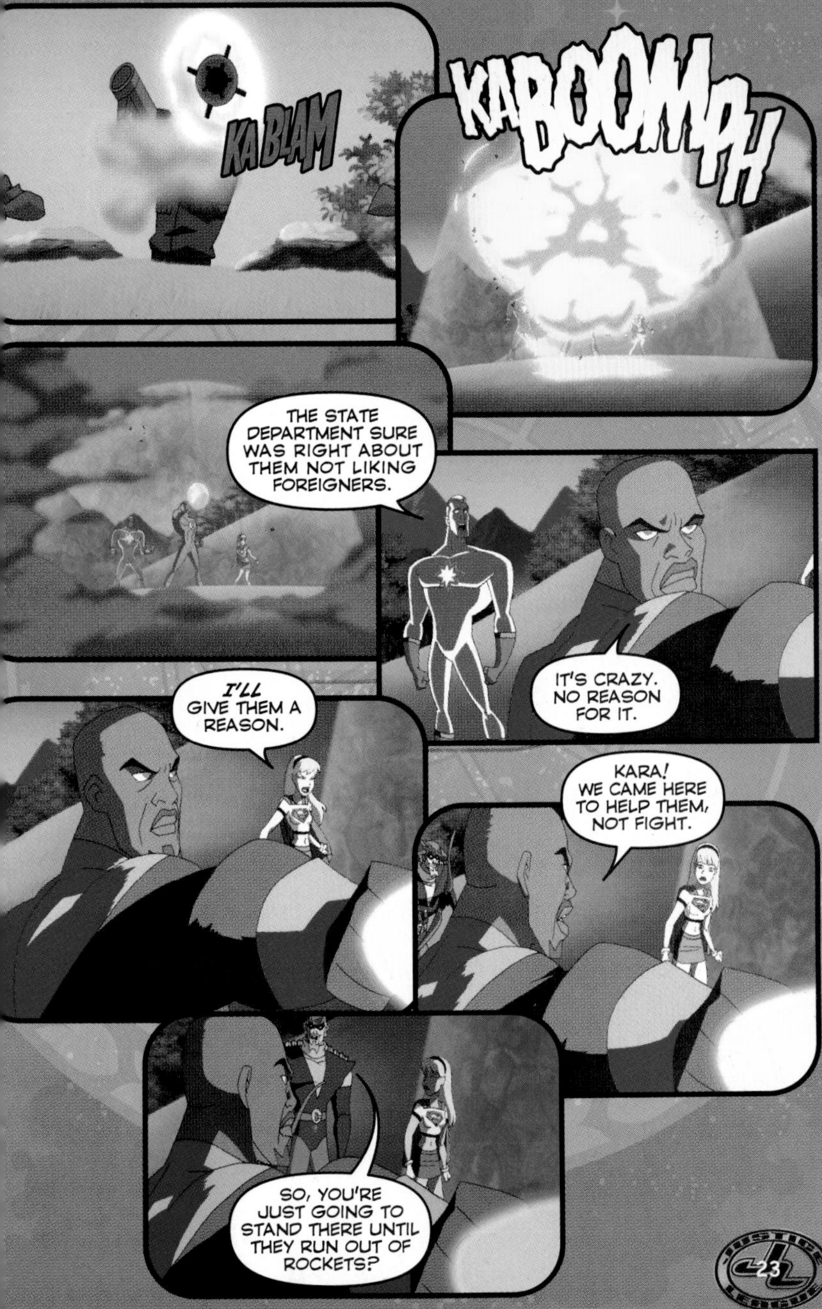

KA BLAM
KABOOMPH
THE STATE DEPARTMENT SURE WAS RIGHT ABOUT THEM NOT LIKING FOREIGNERS.
IT'S CRAZY. NO REASON FOR IT.
I'LL GIVE THEM A REASON.
KARA! WE CAME HERE TO HELP THEM, NOT FIGHT.
SO, YOU'RE JUST GOING TO STAND THERE UNTIL THEY RUN OUT OF ROCKETS?

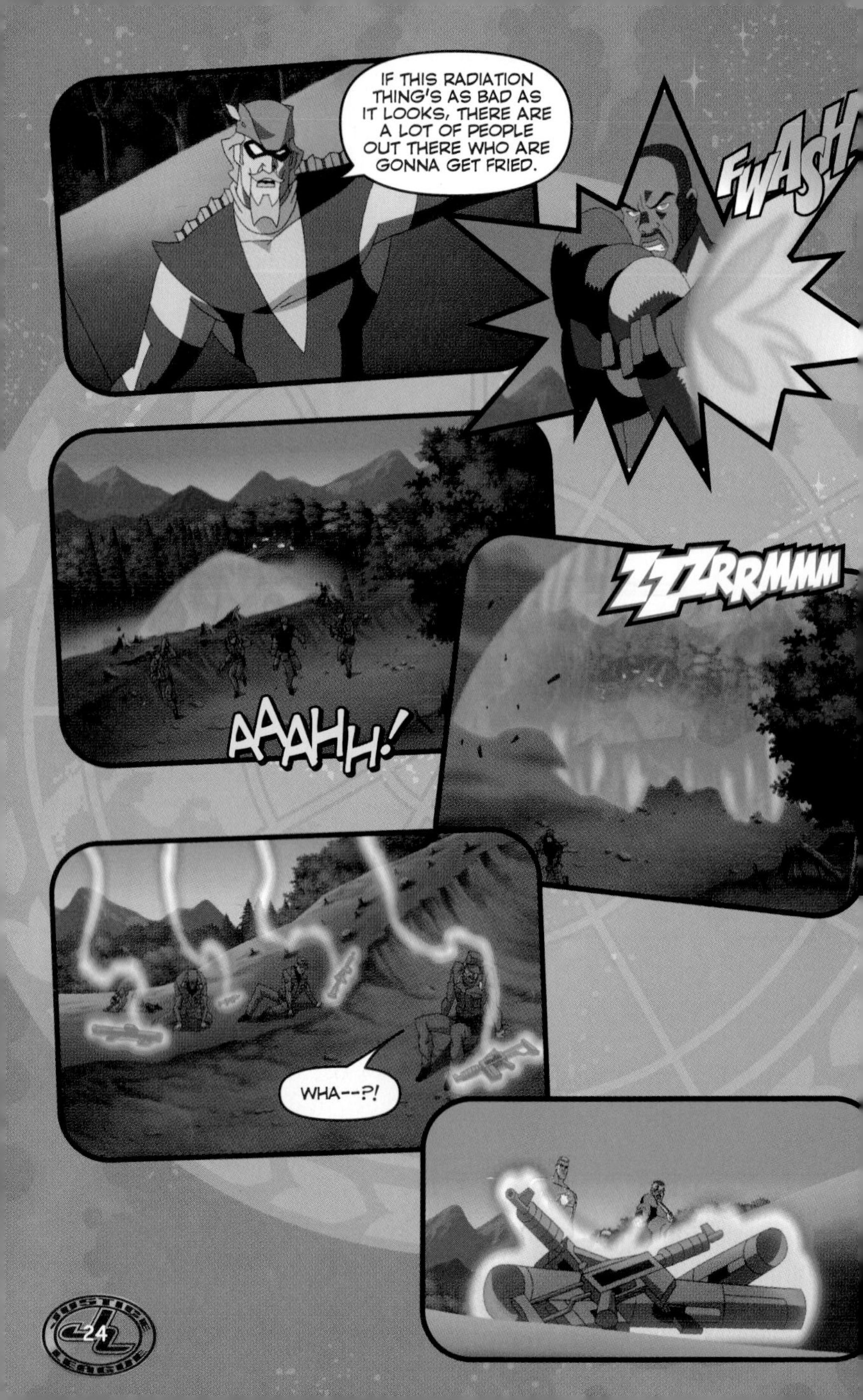

IF THIS RADIATION THING'S AS BAD AS IT LOOKS, THERE ARE A LOT OF PEOPLE OUT THERE WHO ARE GONNA GET FRIED.
FWASH
AAAHH!
ZZZRRMMM
WHA--?!

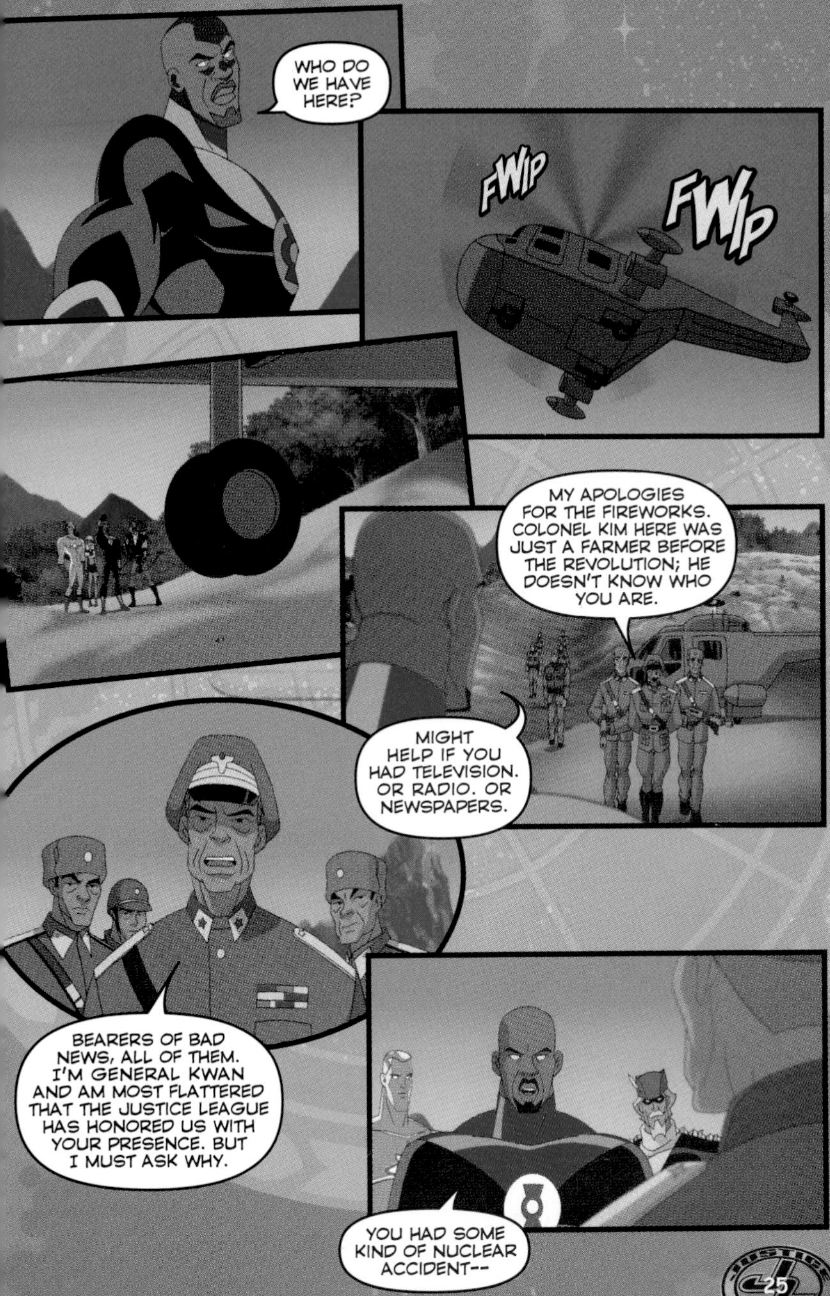
WHO DO WE HAVE HERE?
FWIP
FWIP
MY APOLOGIES FOR THE FIREWORKS. COLONEL KIM HERE WAS JUST A FARMER BEFORE THE REVOLUTION; HE DOESN'T KNOW WHO YOU ARE.
MIGHT HELP IF YOU HAD TELEVISION. OR RADIO. OR NEWSPAPERS.
BEARERS OF BAD NEWS, ALL OF THEM. I'M GENERAL KWAN AND AM MOST FLATTERED THAT THE JUSTICE LEAGUE HAS HONORED US WITH YOUR PRESENCE. BUT I MUST ASK WHY.
YOU HAD SOME KIND OF NUCLEAR ACCIDENT--

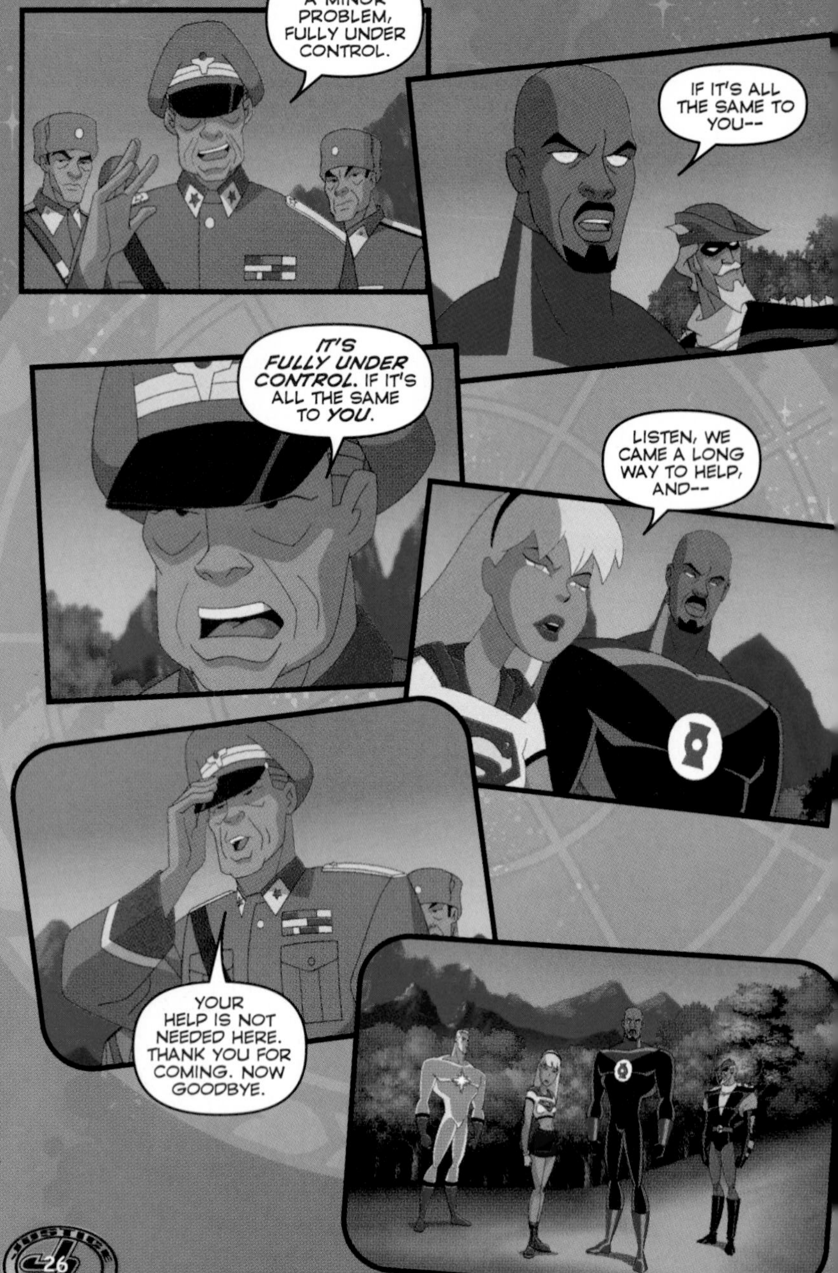
AH, THAT. A MINOR PROBLEM, FULLY UNDER CONTROL.
IF IT'S ALL THE SAME TO YOU--
IT'S FULLY UNDER CONTROL. IF IT'S ALL THE SAME TO YOU.
LISTEN, WE CAME A LONG WAY TO HELP, AND--
YOUR HELP IS NOT NEEDED HERE. THANK YOU FOR COMING. NOW GOODBYE.

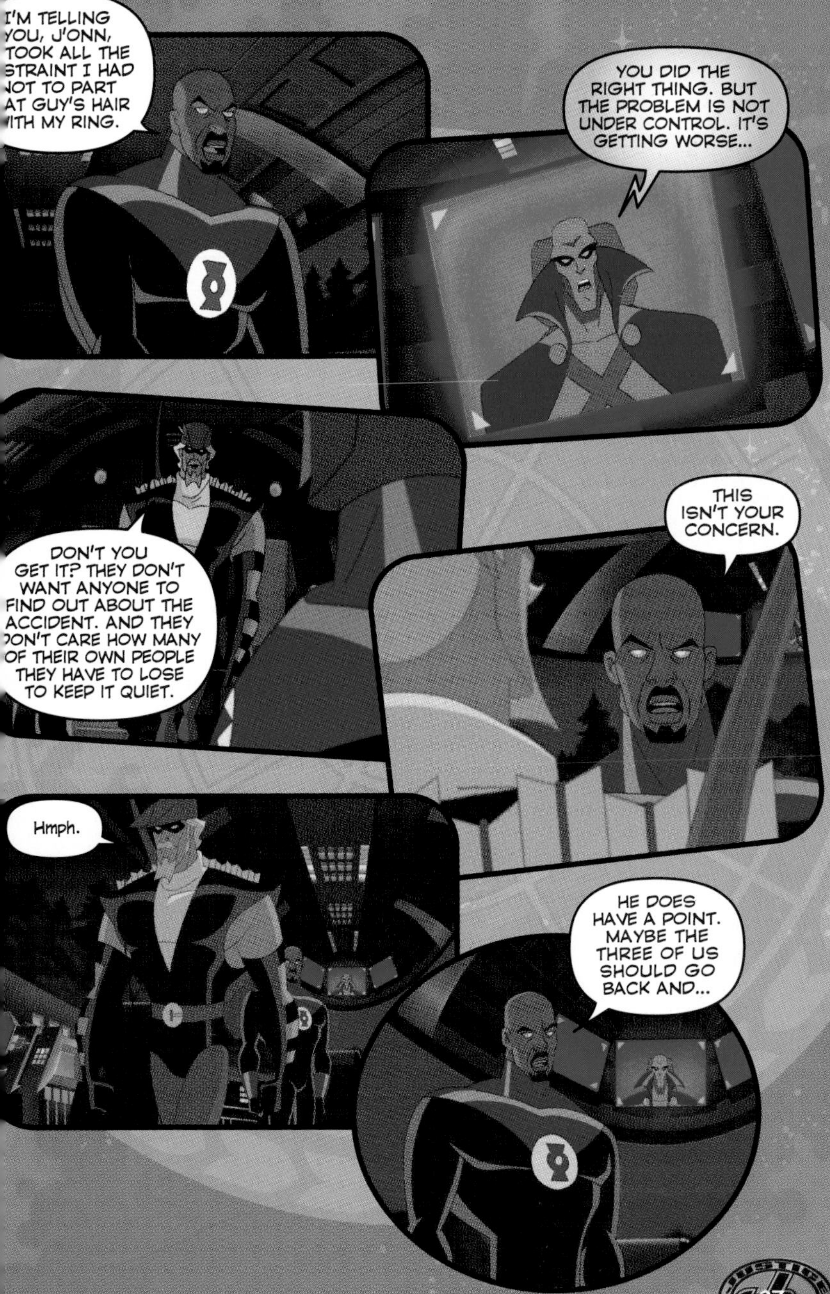
I'M TELLING YOU, J'ONN, TOOK ALL THE STRAINT I HAD OT TO PART AT GUY'S HAIR ITH MY RING.
YOU DID THE RIGHT THING. BUT THE PROBLEM IS NOT UNDER CONTROL. IT'S GETTING WORSE...
DON'T YOU GET IT? THEY DON'T WANT ANYONE TO FIND OUT ABOUT THE ACCIDENT. AND THEY ON'T CARE HOW MANY OF THEIR OWN PEOPLE THEY HAVE TO LOSE TO KEEP IT QUIET.
THIS ISN'T YOUR CONCERN.
Hmph.
HE DOES HAVE A POINT. MAYBE THE THREE OF US SHOULD GO BACK AND...

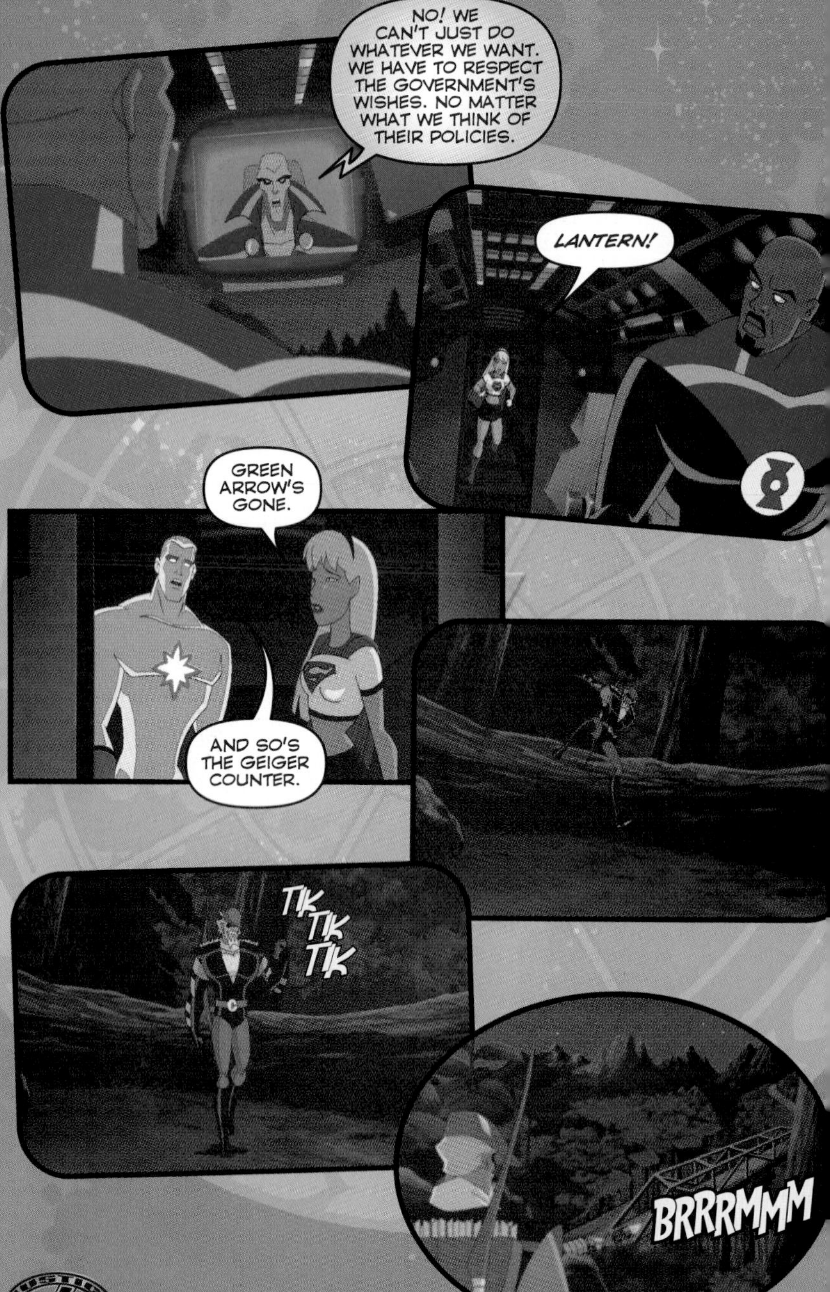
NO! WE CAN'T JUST DO WHATEVER WE WANT. WE HAVE TO RESPECT THE GOVERNMENT'S WISHES. NO MATTER WHAT WE THINK OF THEIR POLICIES.
LANTERN!
GREEN ARROW'S GONE.
AND SO'S THE GEIGER COUNTER.
TIK TIK TIK
BRRRMMM

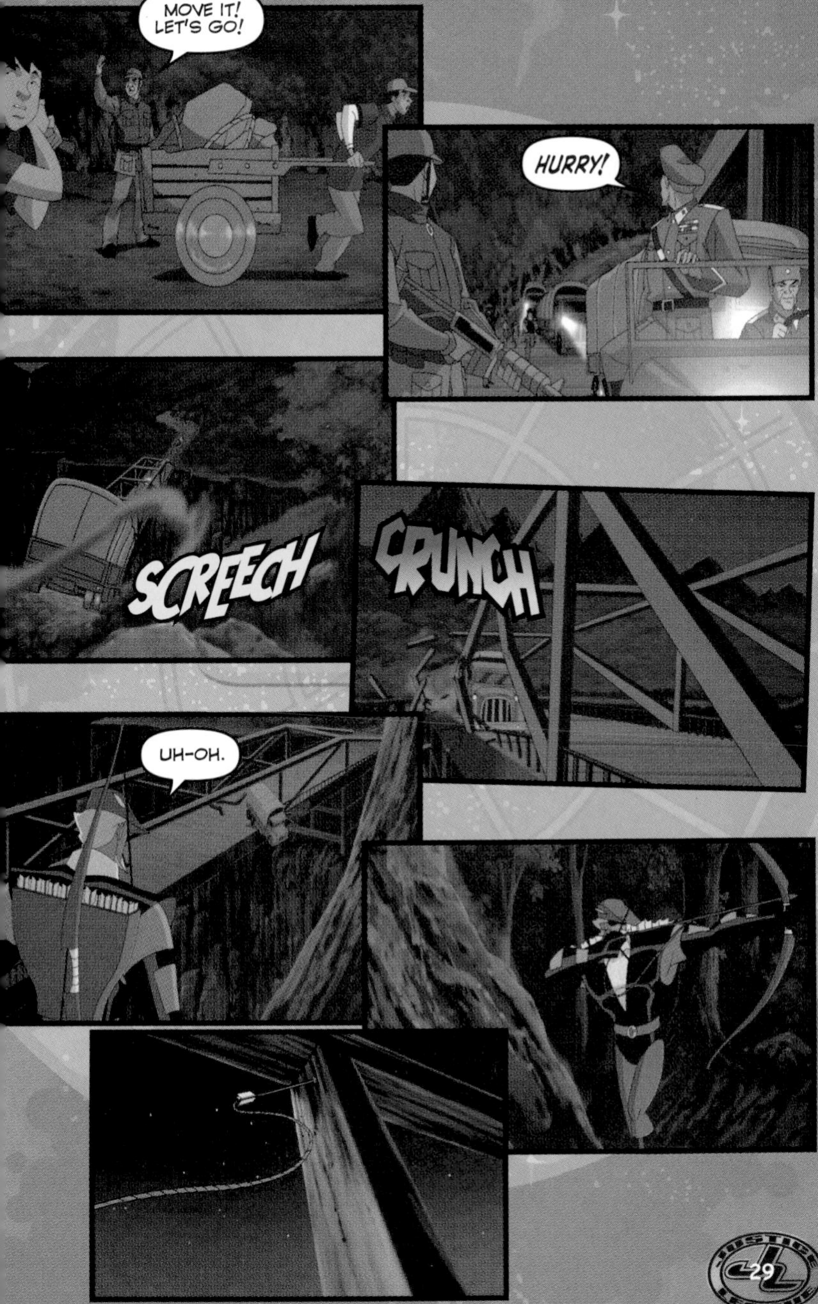
MOVE IT! LET'S GO!
HURRY!
SCREECH
CRUNCH
UH-OH.

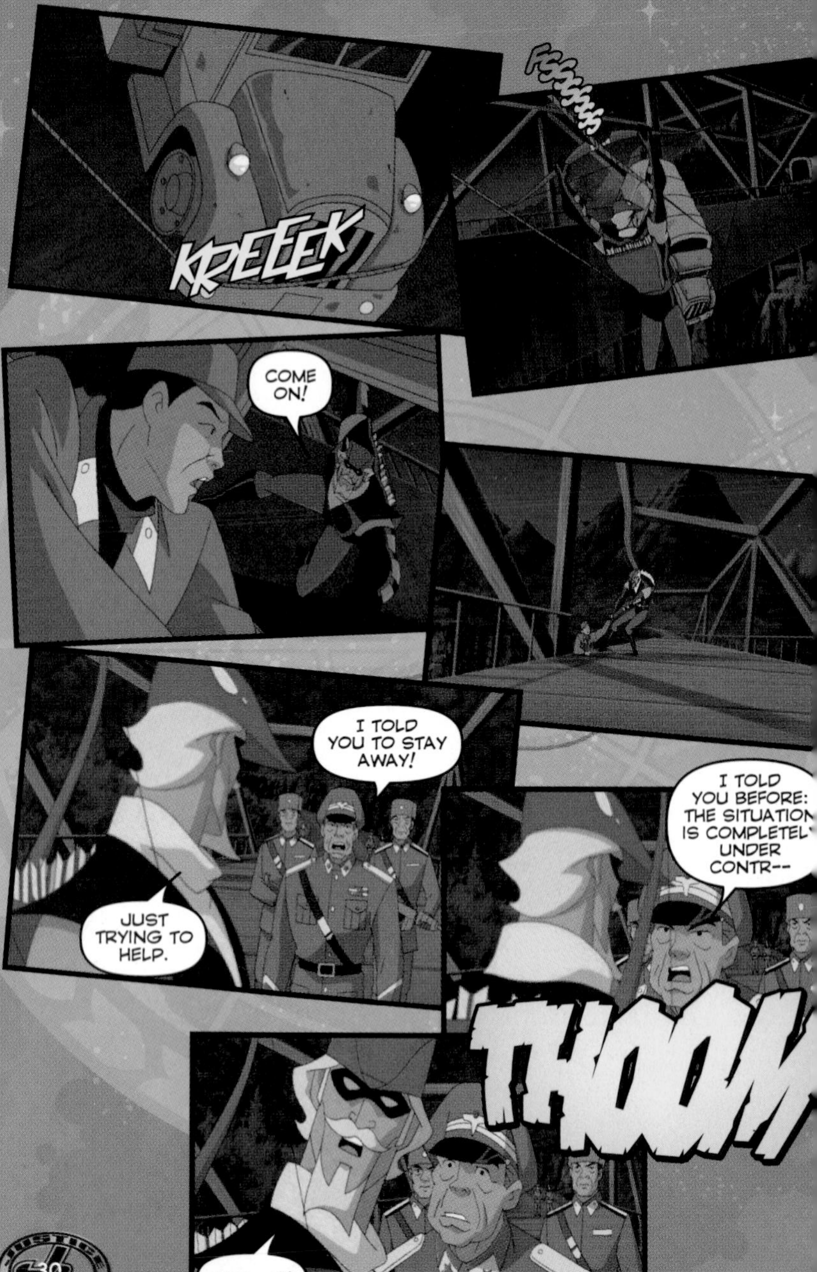
KREEEK
FSSSSHHH
COME ON!
I TOLD YOU TO STAY AWAY!
JUST TRYING TO HELP.
I TOLD YOU BEFORE: THE SITUATION IS COMPLETELY UNDER CONTR--
THOOM
WHA--?!

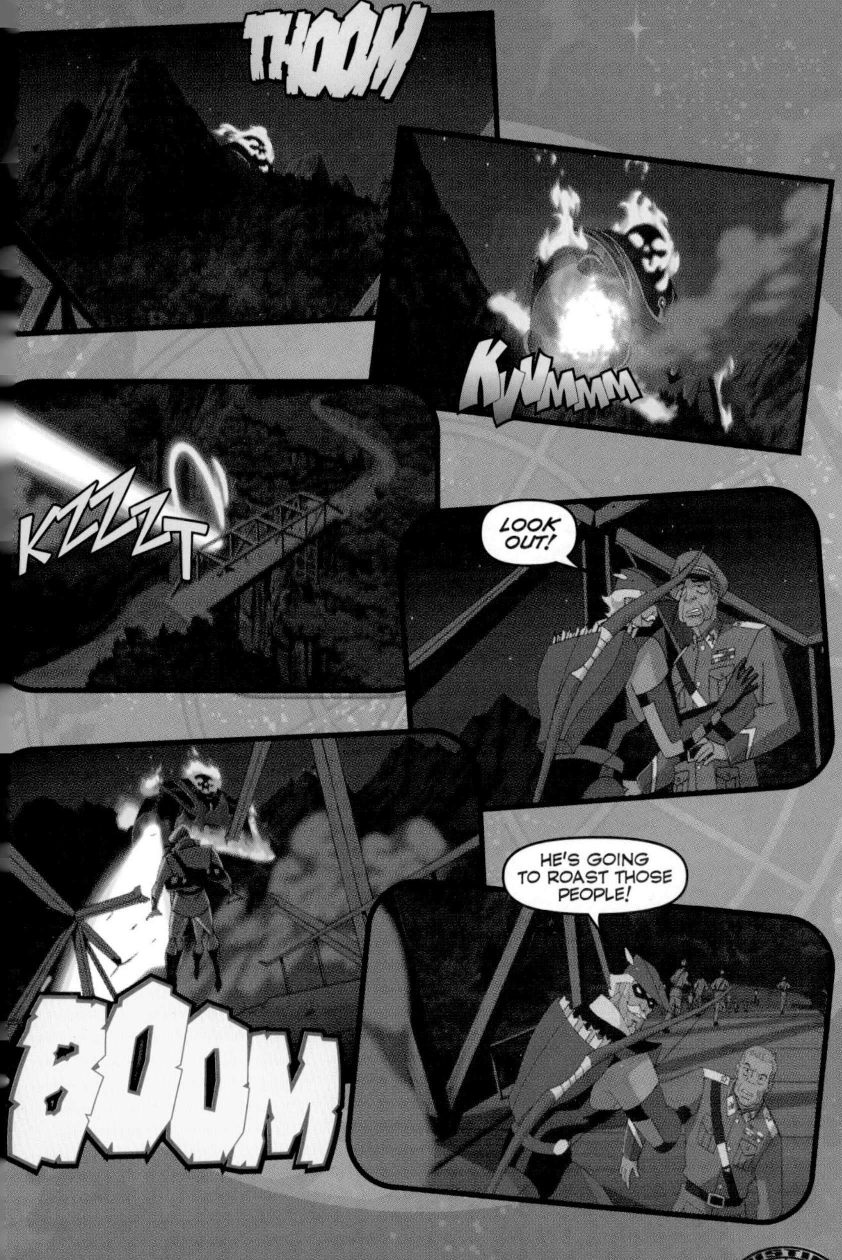
THOOM
KVUMMM
KZZZZT
LOOK OUT!
BOOM
HE'S GOING TO ROAST THOSE PEOPLE!
JUSTICE LEAGUE

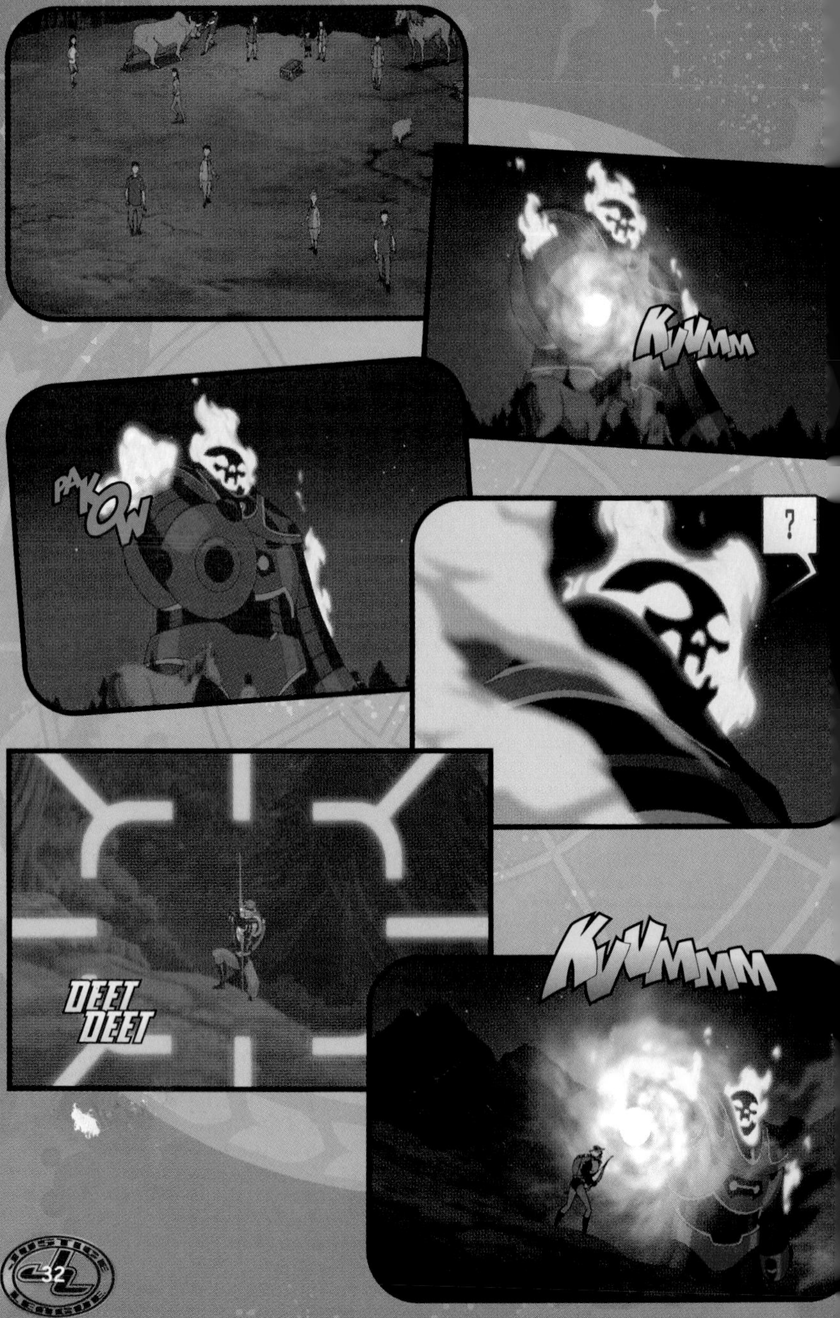
KVUMM
PAKOW
?
DEET DEET
KVUMMM

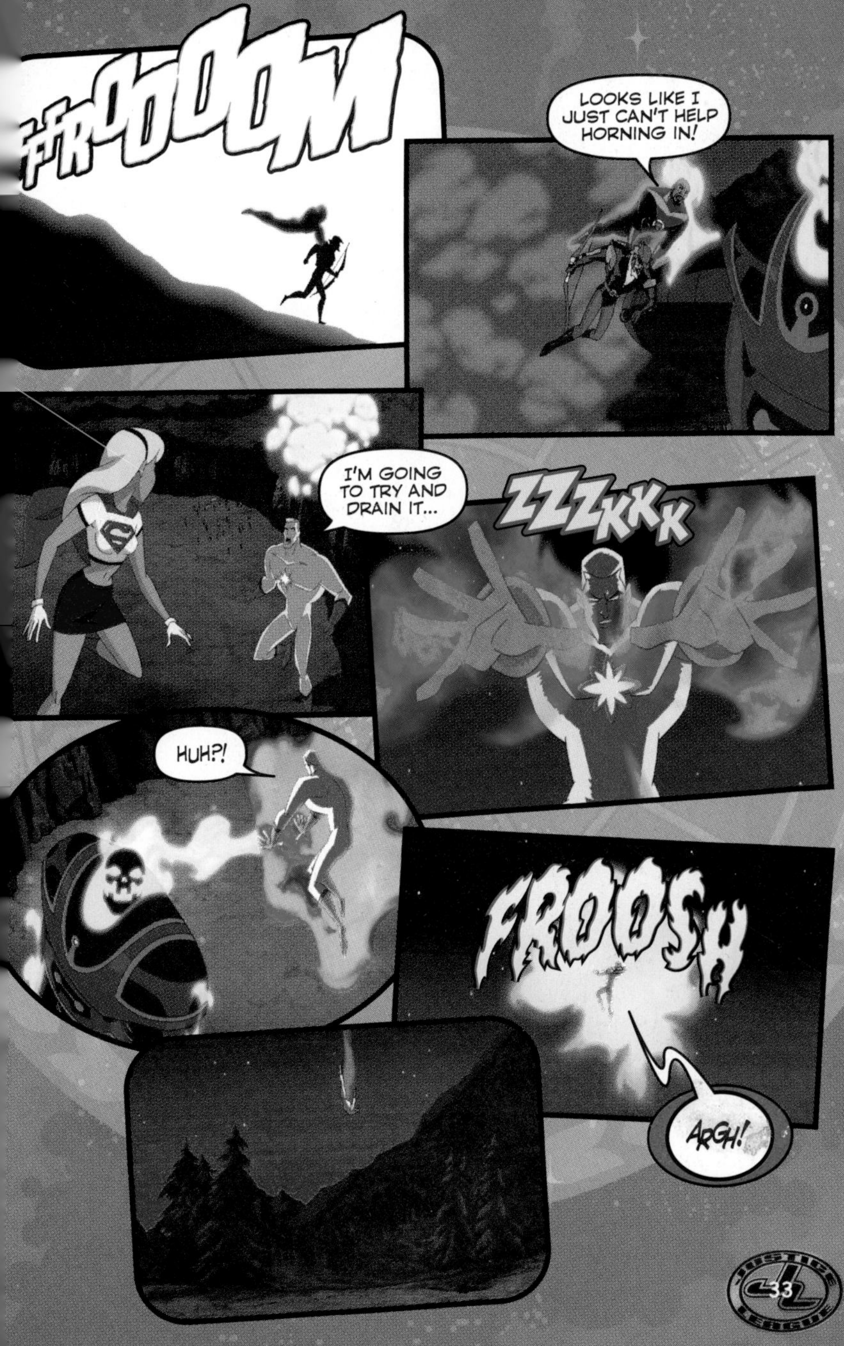
FROOOOM
LOOKS LIKE I JUST CAN'T HELP HORNING IN!
I'M GOING TO TRY AND DRAIN IT...
ZZZKKKK
HUH?!
FROOSH
ARGH!

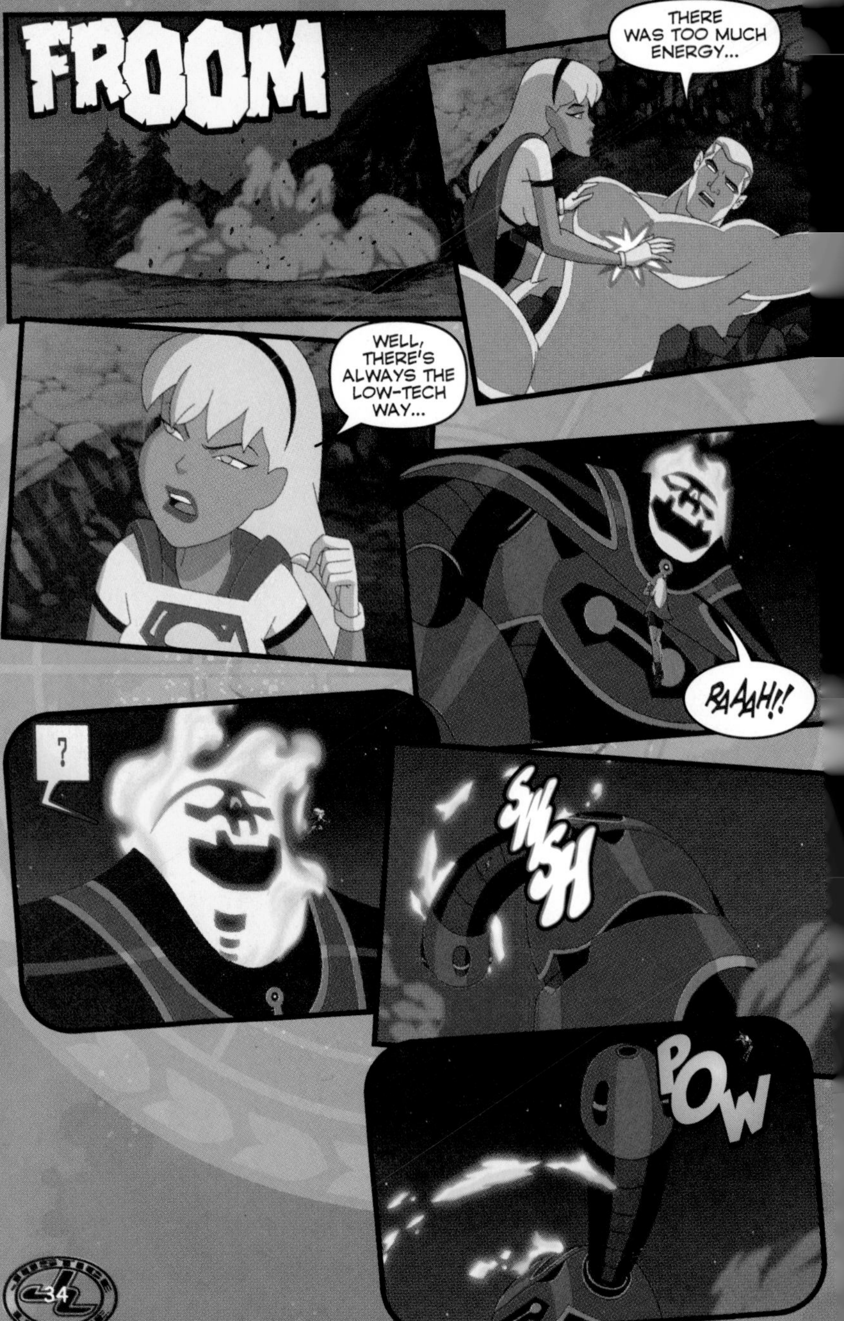
FROOM
THERE WAS TOO MUCH ENERGY...
WELL, THERE'S ALWAYS THE LOW-TECH WAY...
RAAAH!!
?
SWISH
POW

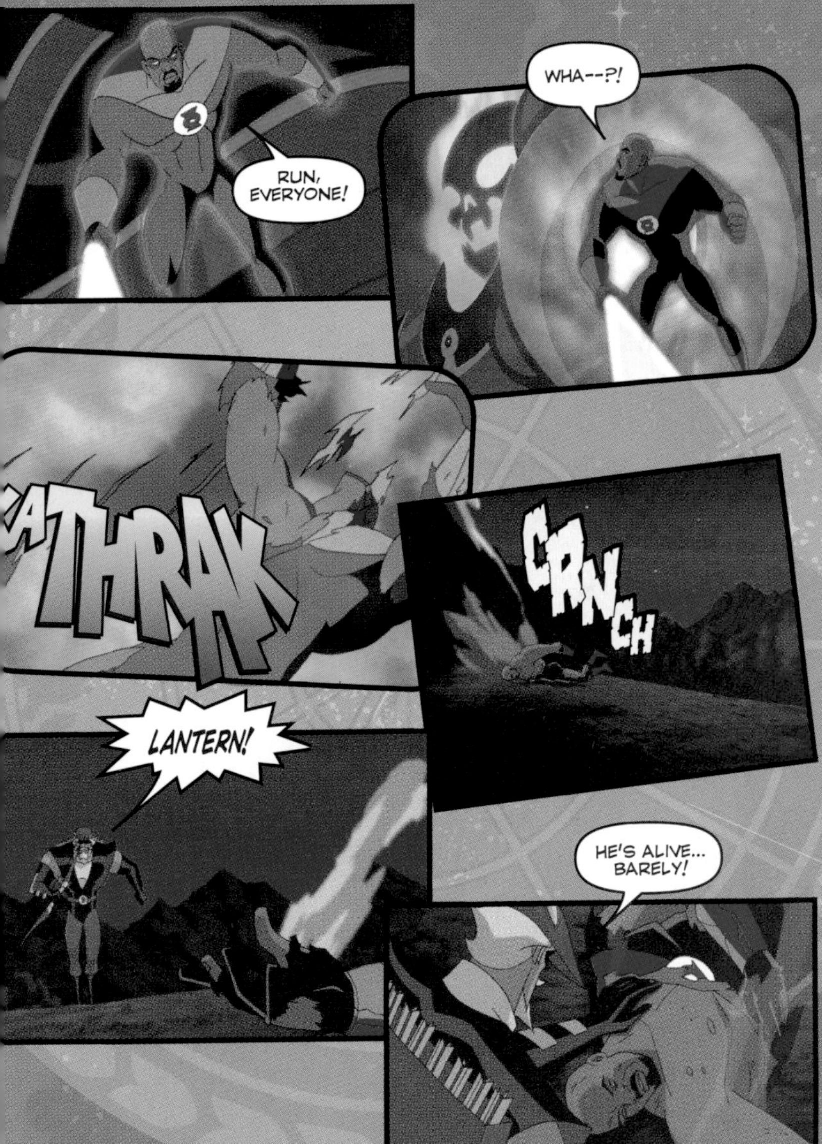
RUN, EVERYONE!
WHA--?!
THRAK
CRNCH
LANTERN!
HE'S ALIVE... BARELY!

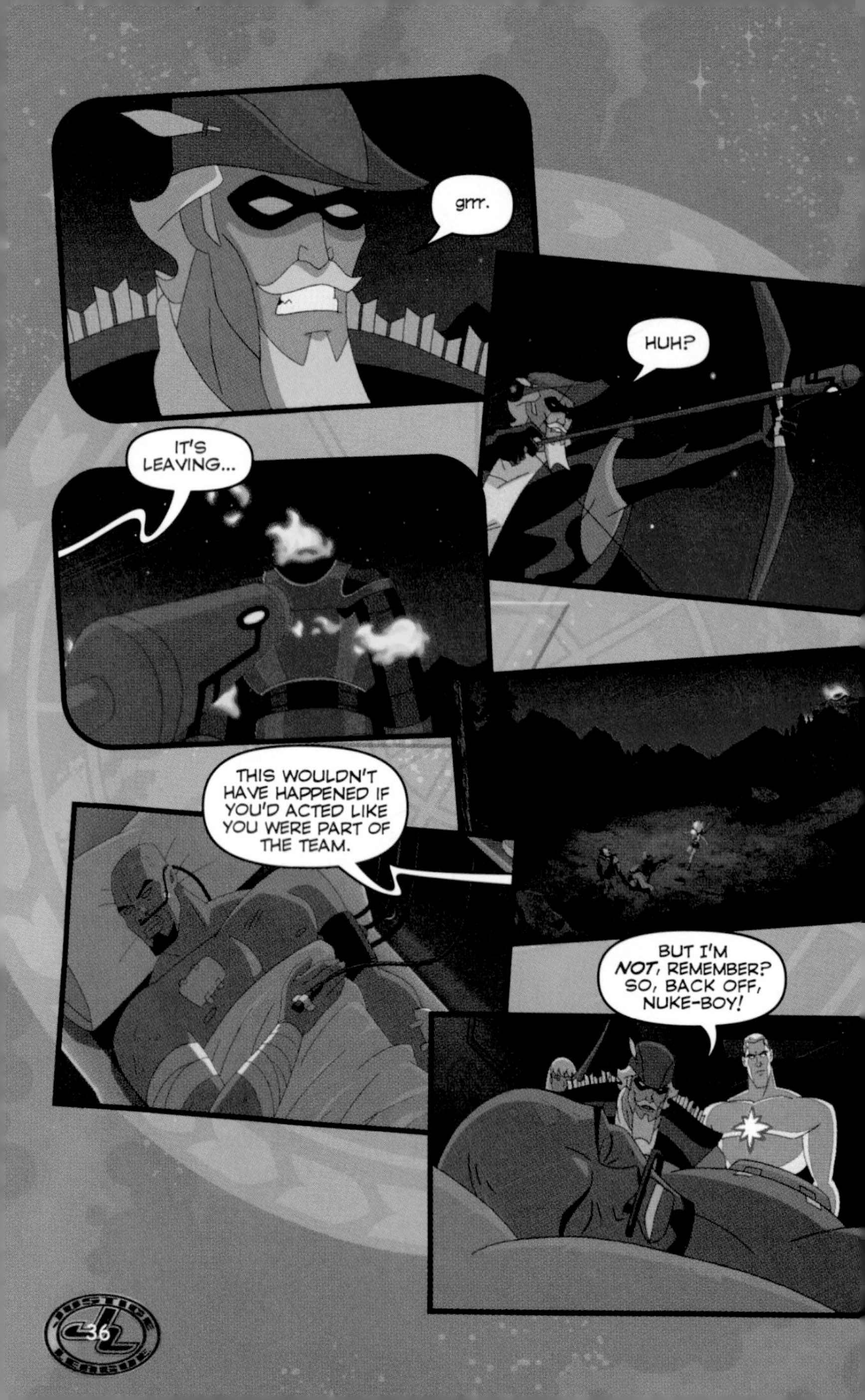
grrr.
HUH?
IT'S LEAVING...
THIS WOULDN'T HAVE HAPPENED IF YOU'D ACTED LIKE YOU WERE PART OF THE TEAM.
BUT I'M *NOT*, REMEMBER? SO, BACK OFF, NUKE-BOY!
JUSTICE LEAGUE

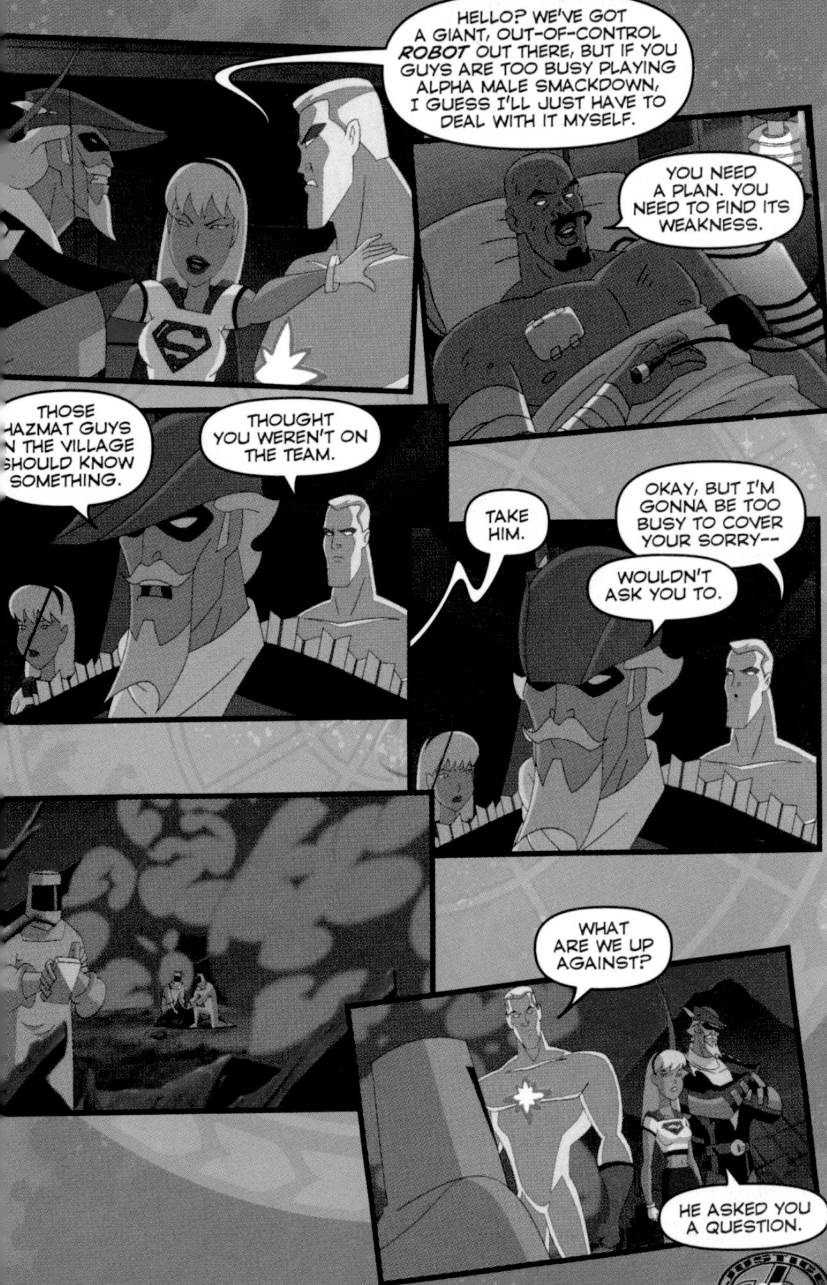
HELLO? WE'VE GOT A GIANT, OUT-OF-CONTROL ROBOT OUT THERE, BUT IF YOU GUYS ARE TOO BUSY PLAYING ALPHA MALE SMACKDOWN, I GUESS I'LL JUST HAVE TO DEAL WITH IT MYSELF.
YOU NEED A PLAN. YOU NEED TO FIND ITS WEAKNESS.
THOSE AZMAT GUYS N THE VILLAGE HOULD KNOW SOMETHING.
THOUGHT YOU WEREN'T ON THE TEAM.
TAKE HIM.
OKAY, BUT I'M GONNA BE TOO BUSY TO COVER YOUR SORRY--
WOULDN'T ASK YOU TO.
WHAT ARE WE UP AGAINST?
HE ASKED YOU A QUESTION.

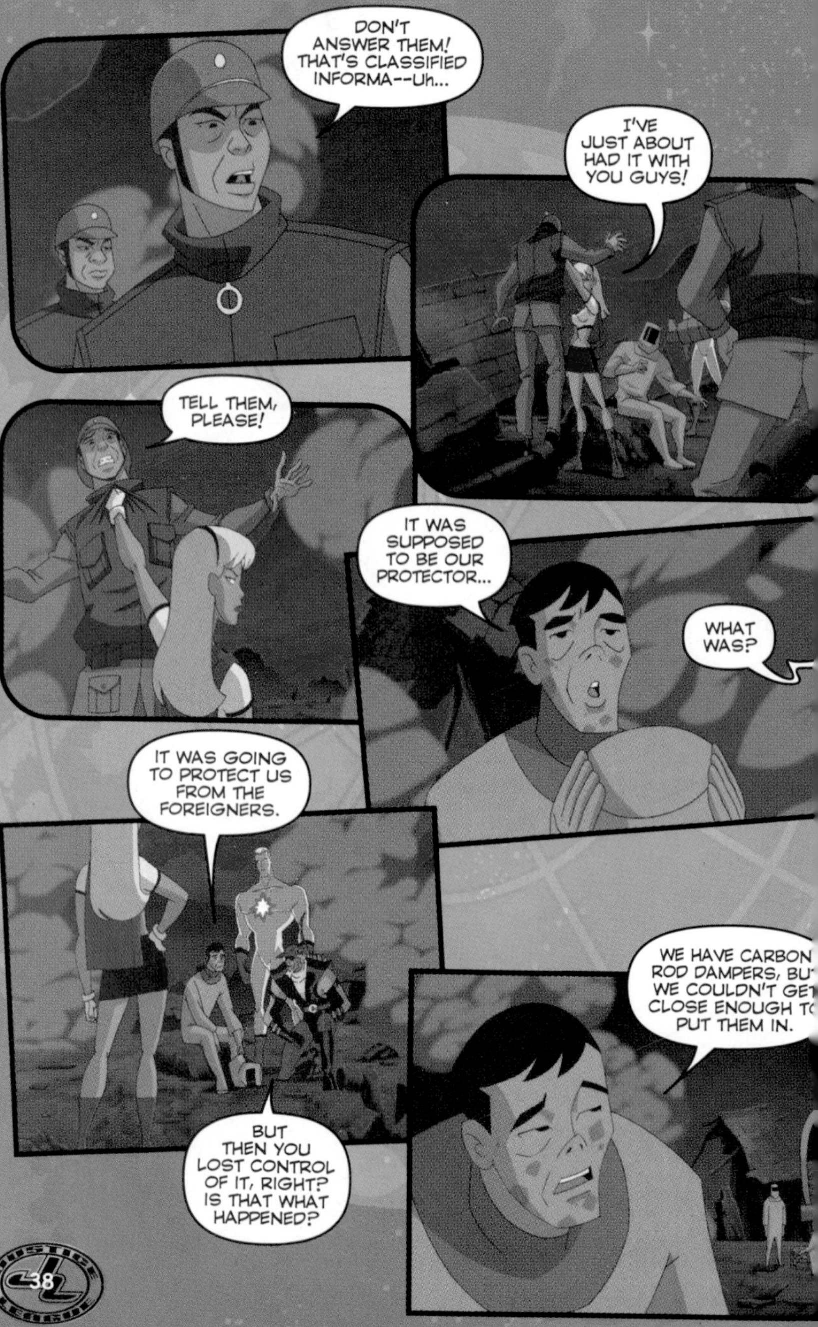

DON'T ANSWER THEM! THAT'S CLASSIFIED INFORMA--Uh...
I'VE JUST ABOUT HAD IT WITH YOU GUYS!
TELL THEM, PLEASE!
IT WAS SUPPOSED TO BE OUR PROTECTOR...
WHAT WAS?
IT WAS GOING TO PROTECT US FROM THE FOREIGNERS.
BUT THEN YOU LOST CONTROL OF IT, RIGHT? IS THAT WHAT HAPPENED?
WE HAVE CARBON ROD DAMPERS, BU WE COULDN'T GE CLOSE ENOUGH T PUT THEM IN.

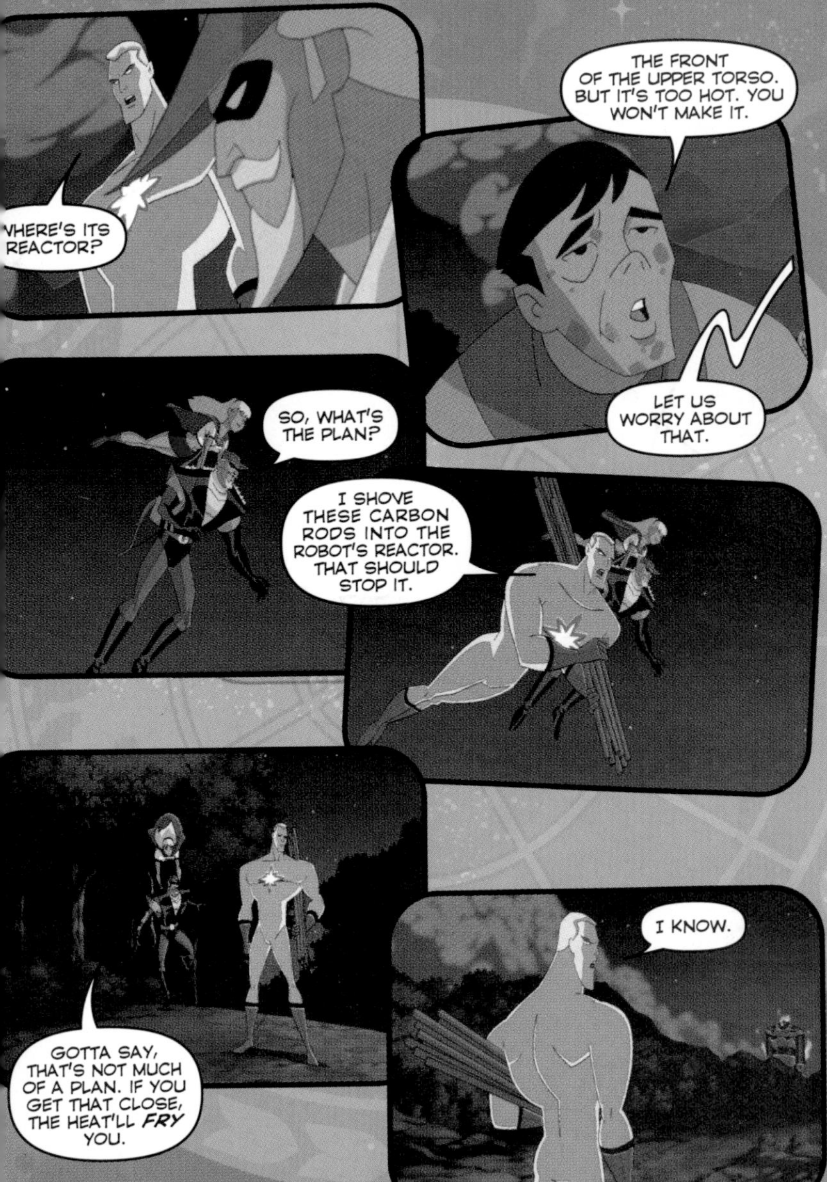

WHERE'S ITS REACTOR?
THE FRONT OF THE UPPER TORSO. BUT IT'S TOO HOT. YOU WON'T MAKE IT.
LET US WORRY ABOUT THAT.
SO, WHAT'S THE PLAN?
I SHOVE THESE CARBON RODS INTO THE ROBOT'S REACTOR. THAT SHOULD STOP IT.
GOTTA SAY, THAT'S NOT MUCH OF A PLAN. IF YOU GET THAT CLOSE, THE HEAT'LL FRY YOU.
I KNOW.

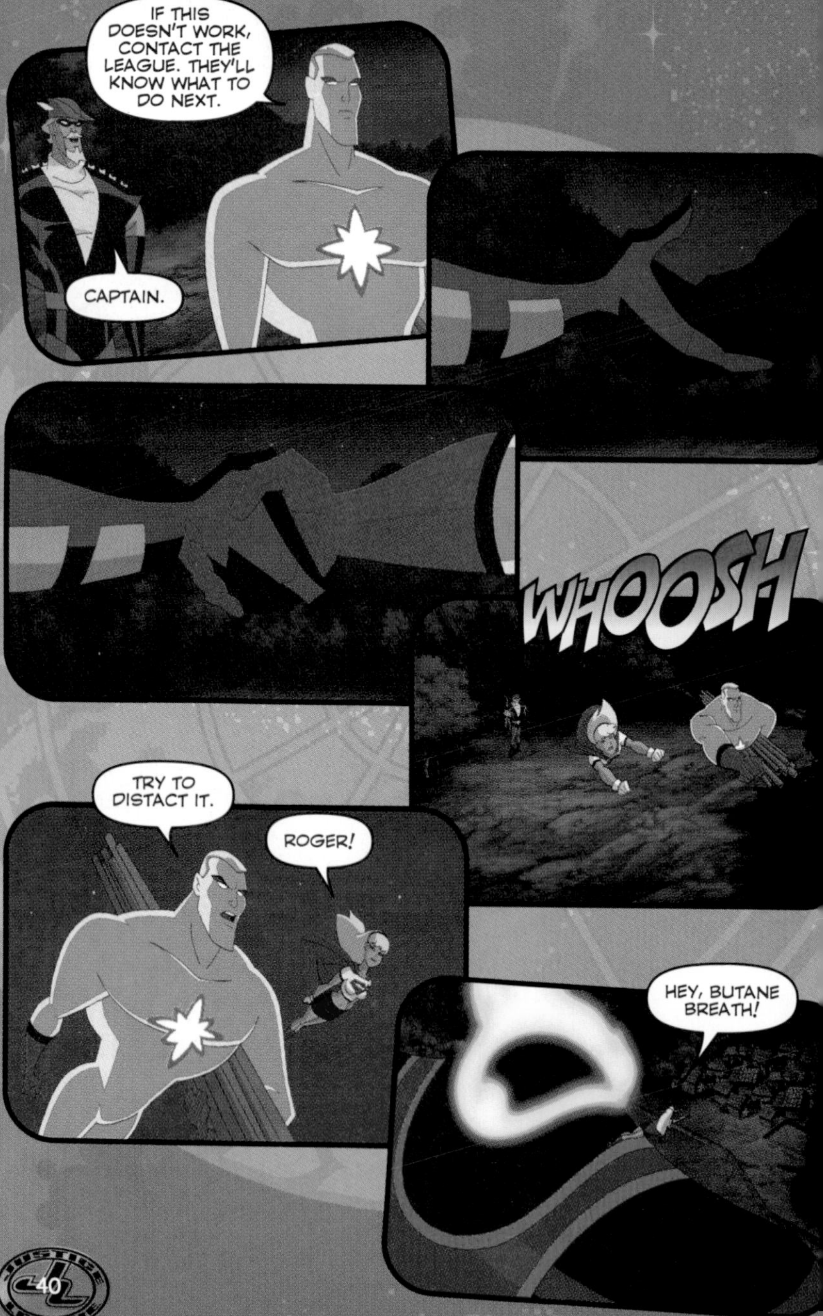
IF THIS DOESN'T WORK, CONTACT THE LEAGUE. THEY'LL KNOW WHAT TO DO NEXT.
CAPTAIN.
WHOOSH
TRY TO DISTACT IT.
ROGER!
HEY, BUTANE BREATH!

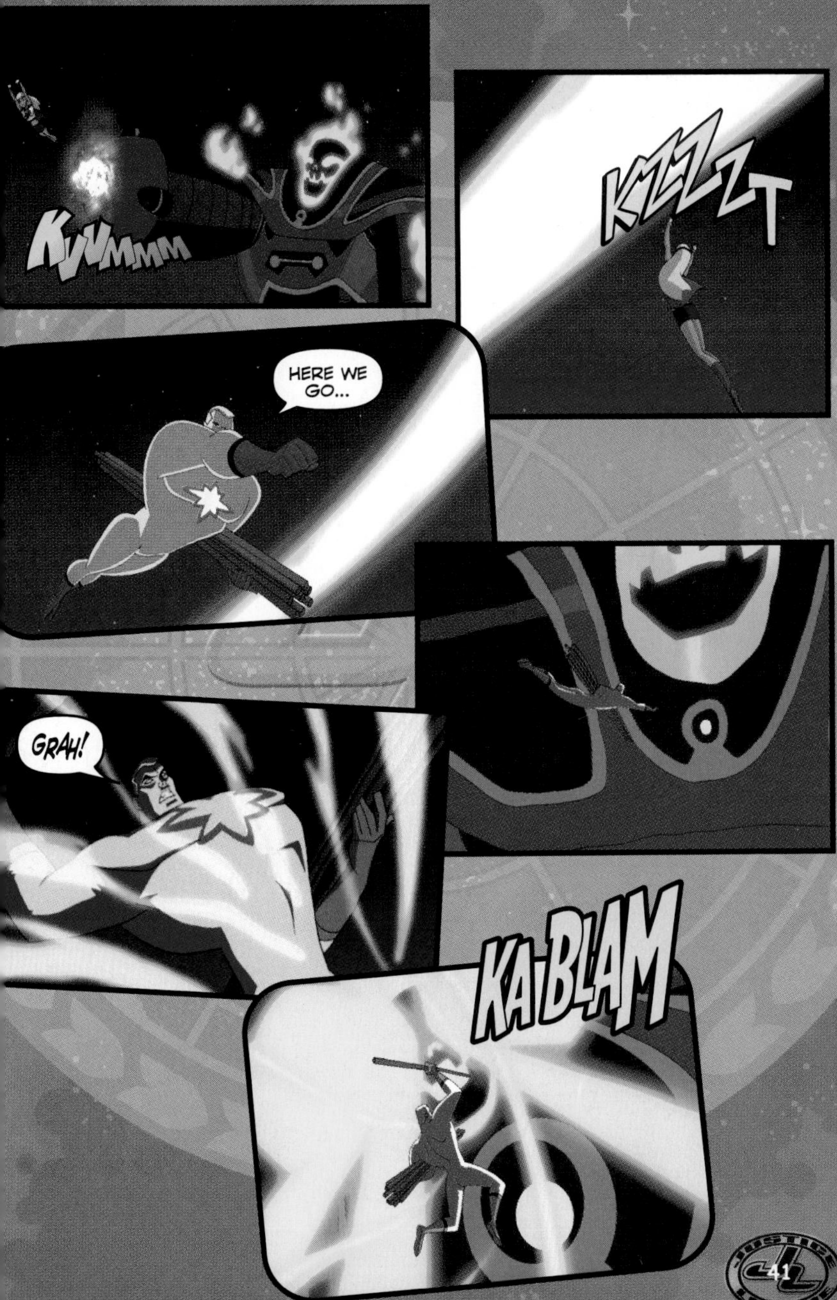
KVUMMM
KZZZZT
HERE WE GO...
GRAH!
KA-BLAM

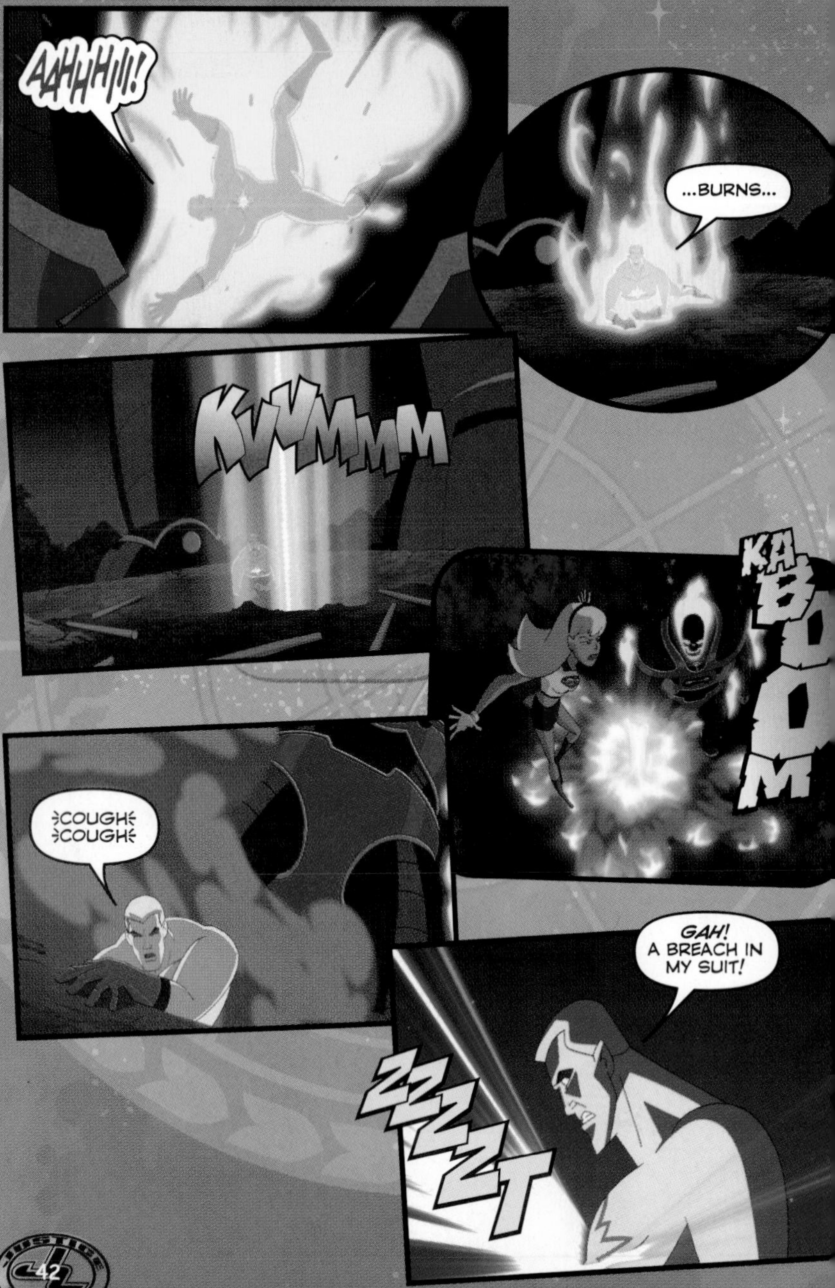
AAHHH!!!
...BURNS...
KVUMMMM
KABOOM
COUGH *COUGH*
GAH! A BREACH IN MY SUIT!
ZZZZT

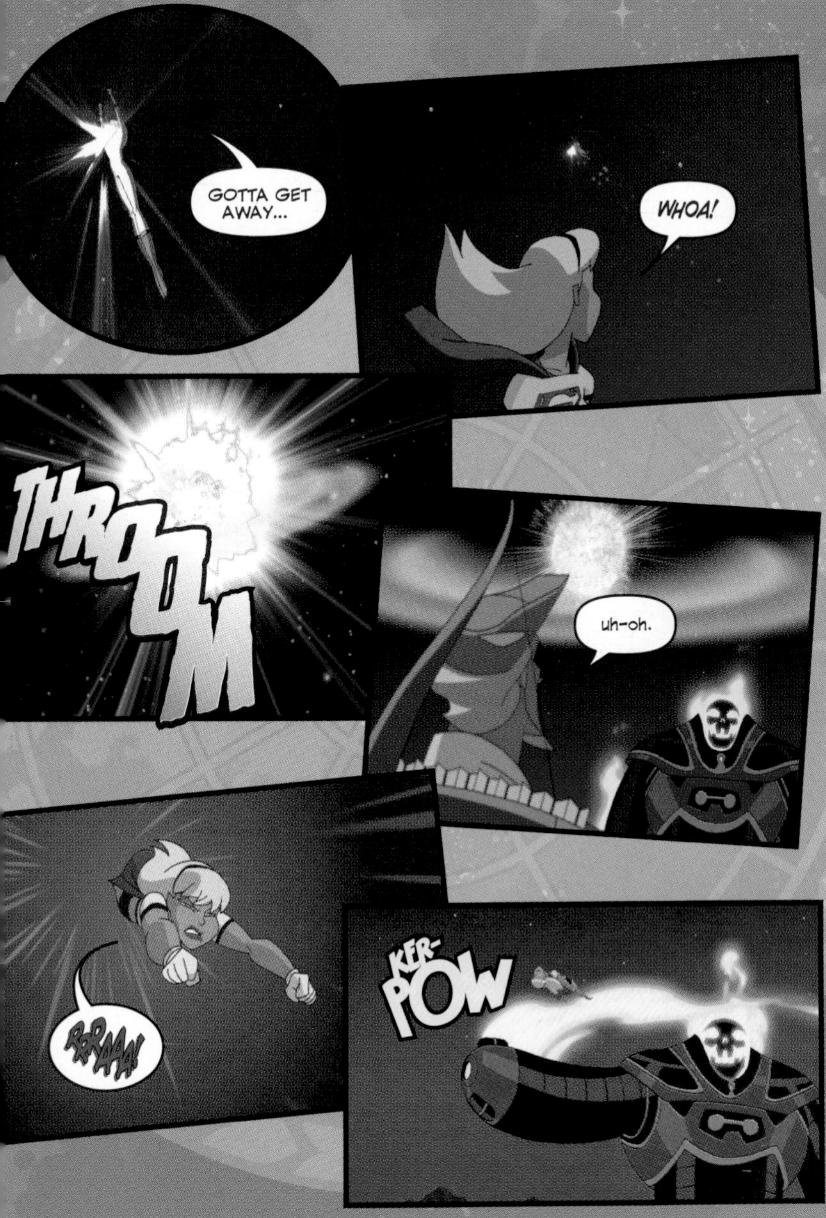
GOTTA GET AWAY...
WHOA!
THROOOM
uh-oh.
RRRAAA!
KER-POW

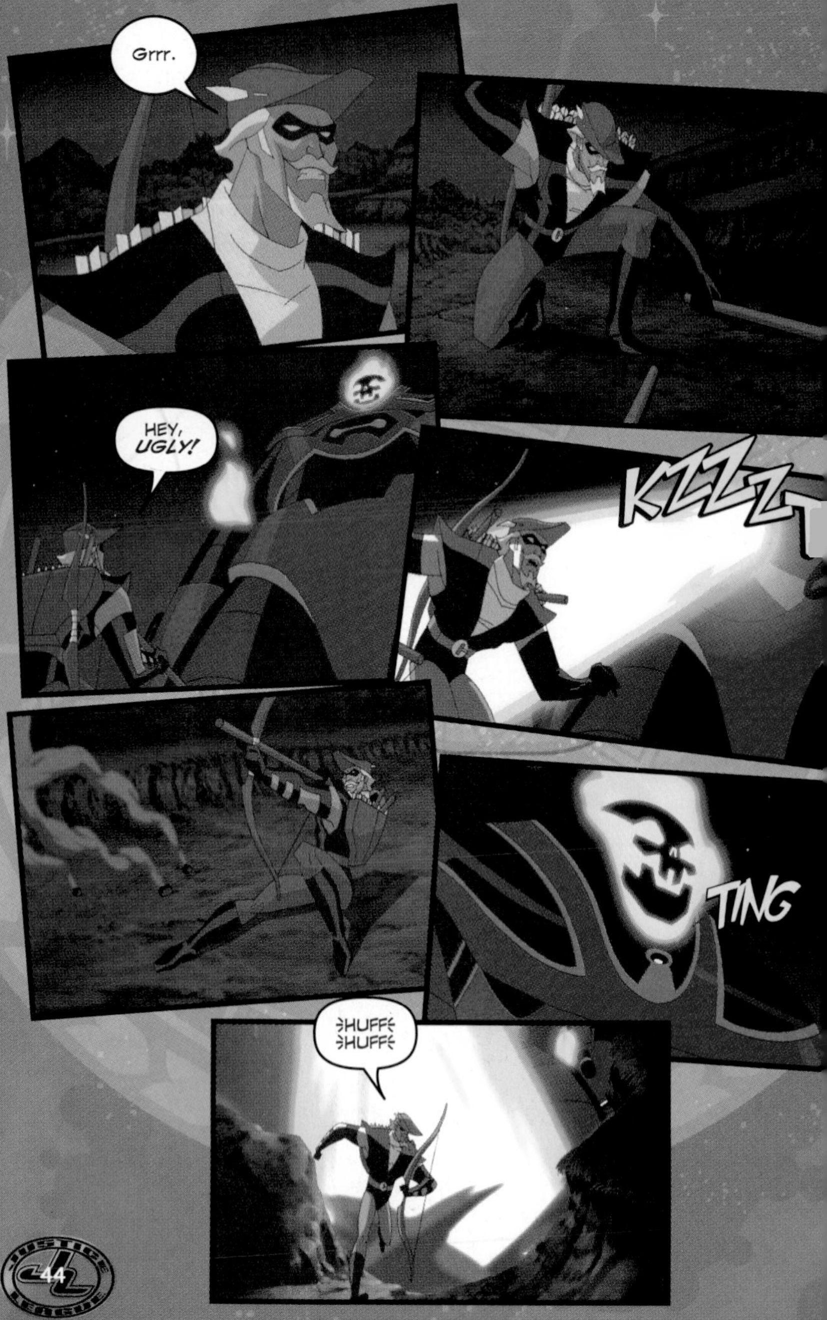

Grrr.
HEY, UGLY!
KZZZT
TING
HUFF HUFF

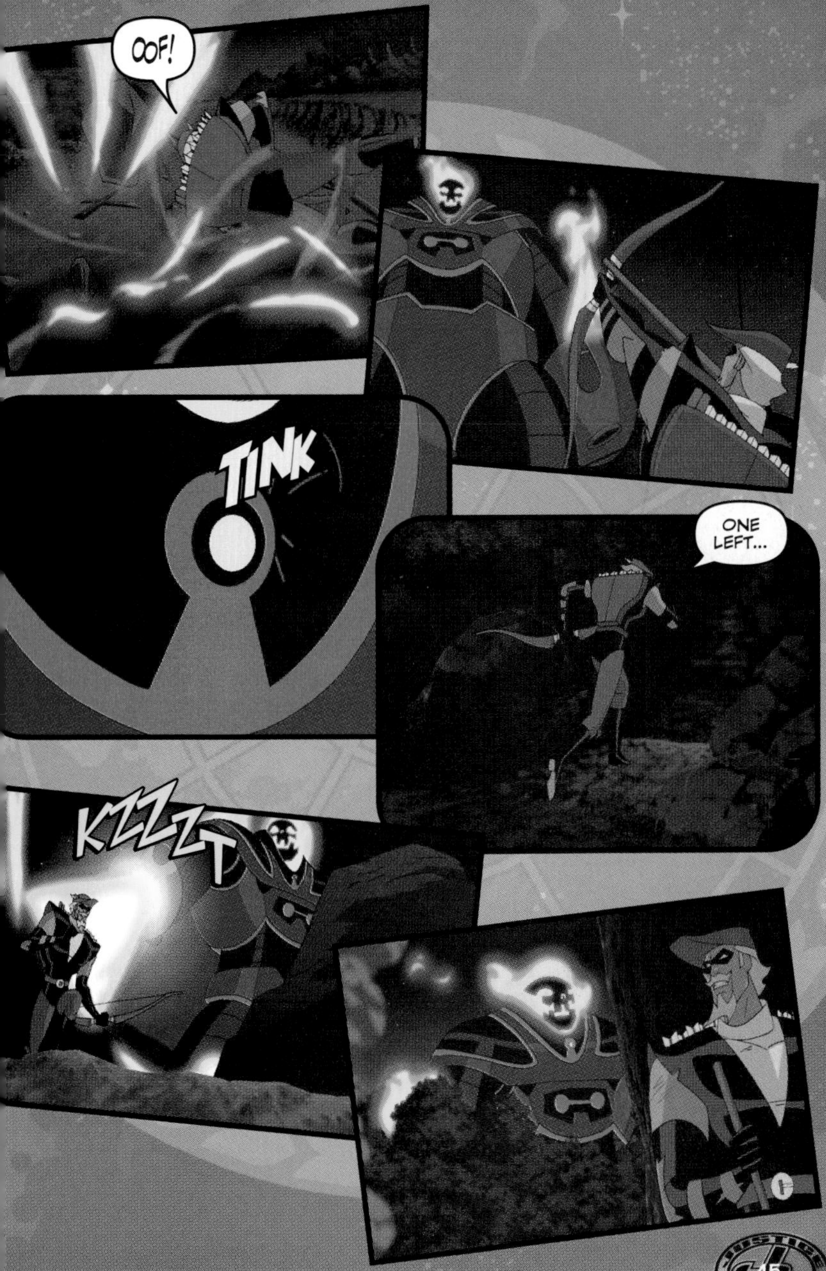

OOF!
TINK
ONE LEFT...
KZZZT

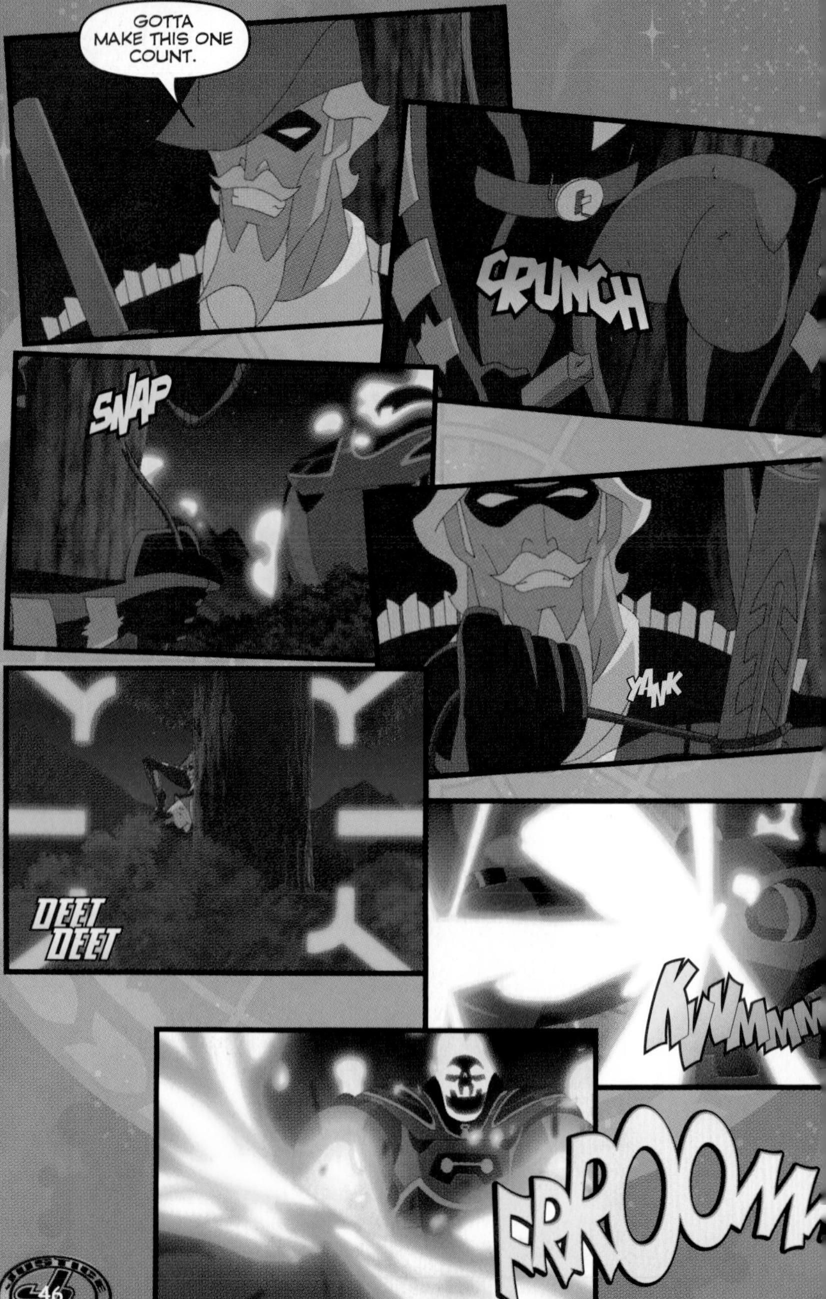

GOTTA MAKE THIS ONE COUNT.
CRUNCH
SNAP
YANK
DEET DEET
KUMMM
FRROOM

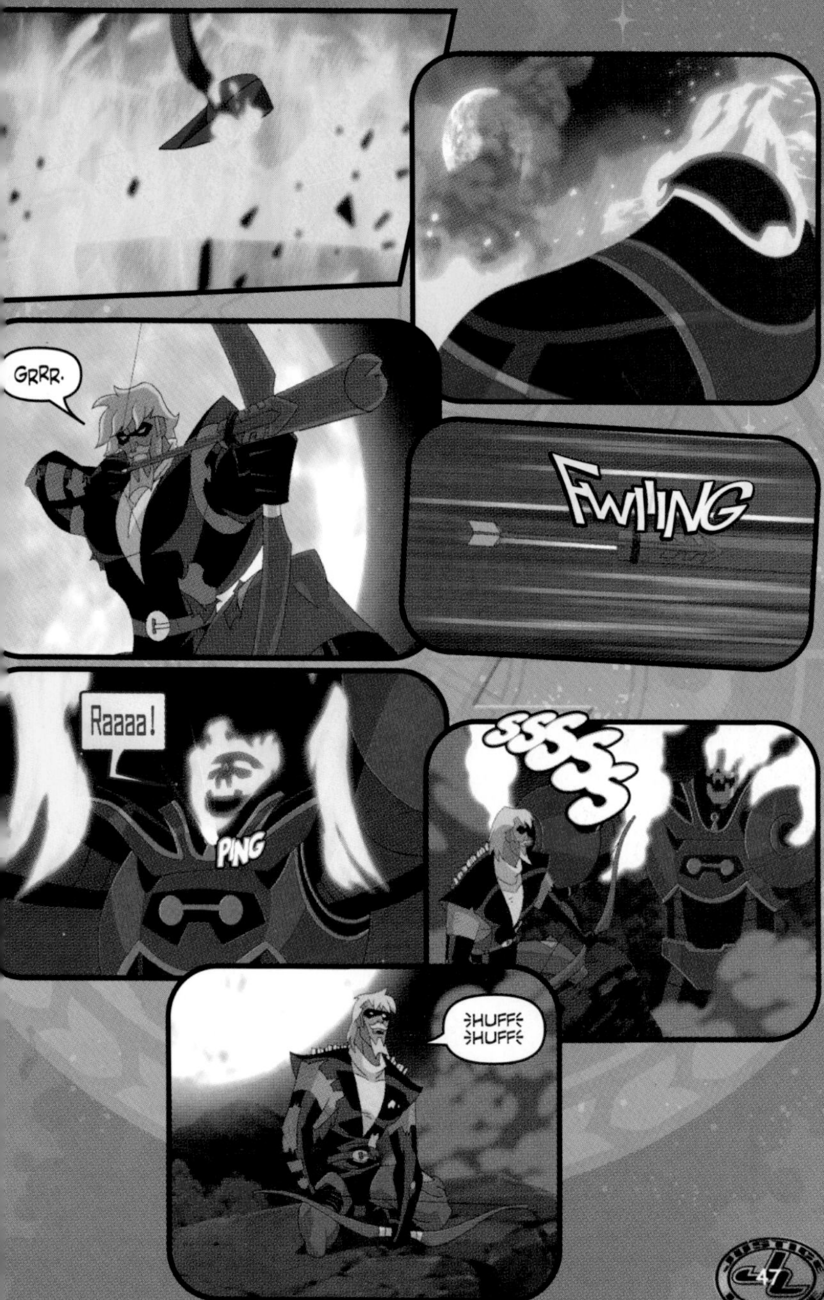

GRRR.
FWIIING
Raaaa!
PING
SSSSS
HUFF
HUFF

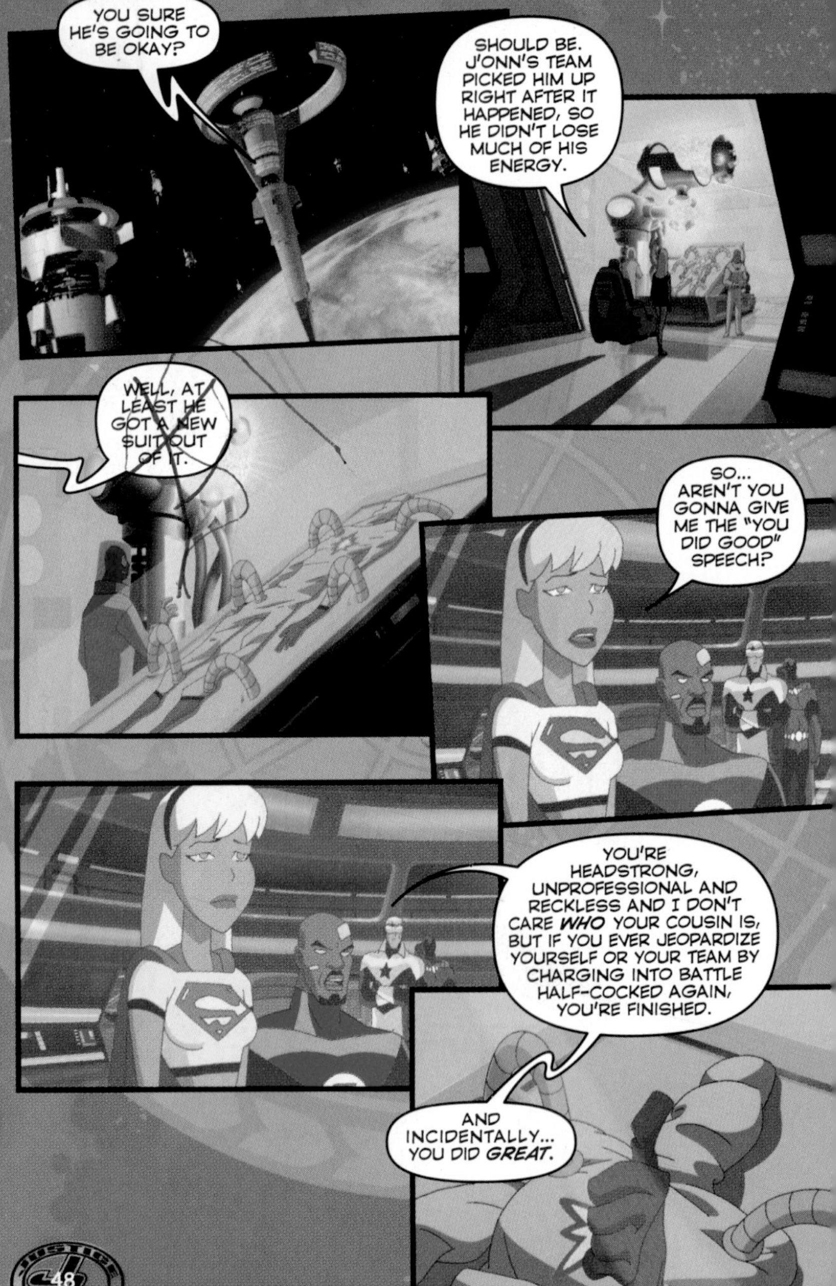
YOU SURE HE'S GOING TO BE OKAY?
SHOULD BE. J'ONN'S TEAM PICKED HIM UP RIGHT AFTER IT HAPPENED, SO HE DIDN'T LOSE MUCH OF HIS ENERGY.
WELL, AT LEAST HE GOT A NEW SUIT OUT OF IT.
SO... AREN'T YOU GONNA GIVE ME THE "YOU DID GOOD" SPEECH?
YOU'RE HEADSTRONG, UNPROFESSIONAL AND RECKLESS AND I DON'T CARE *WHO* YOUR COUSIN IS, BUT IF YOU EVER JEOPARDIZE YOURSELF OR YOUR TEAM BY CHARGING INTO BATTLE HALF-COCKED AGAIN, YOU'RE FINISHED.
AND INCIDENTALLY... YOU DID *GREAT*.

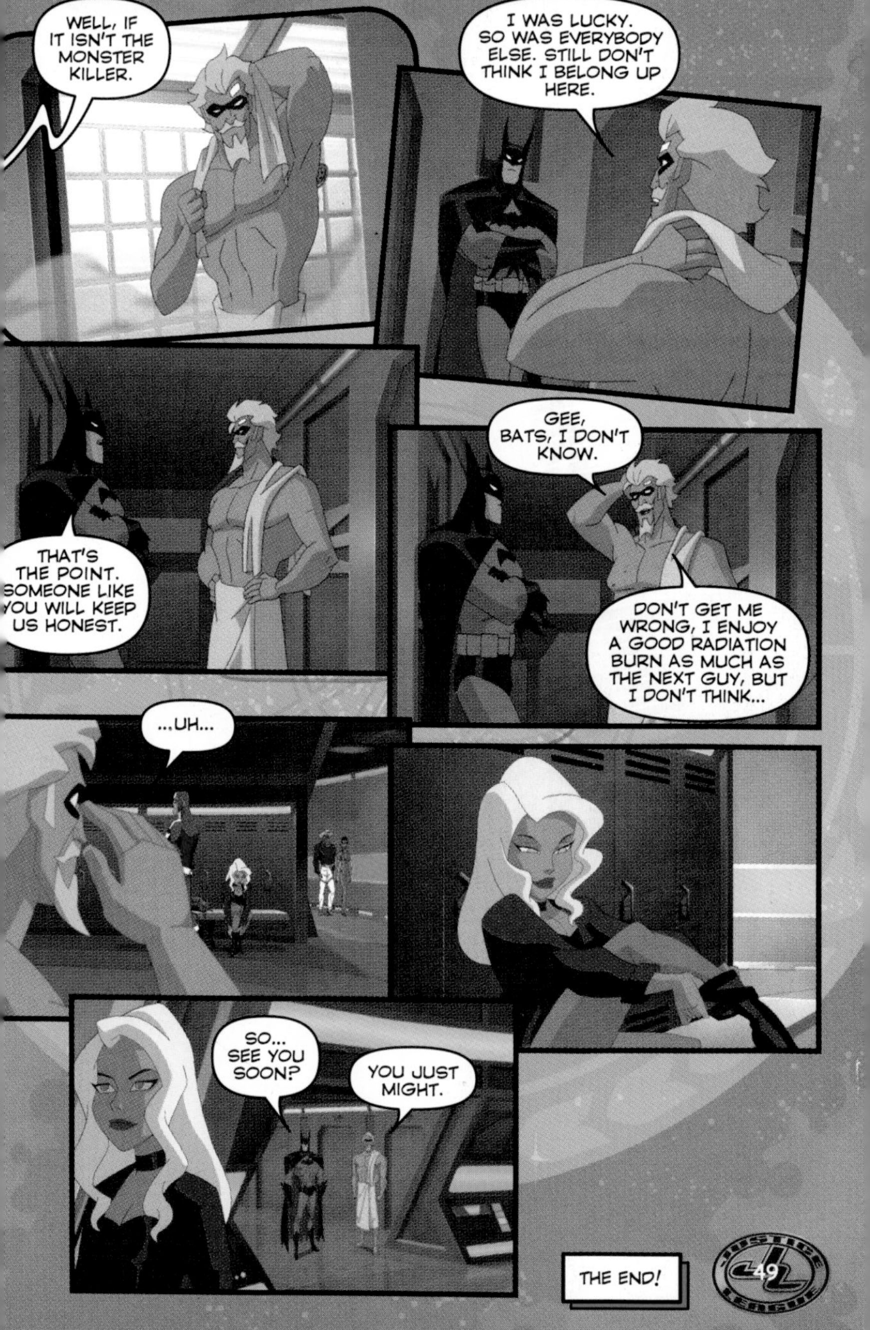
WELL, IF IT ISN'T THE MONSTER KILLER.
I WAS LUCKY. SO WAS EVERYBODY ELSE. STILL DON'T THINK I BELONG UP HERE.
THAT'S THE POINT. SOMEONE LIKE YOU WILL KEEP US HONEST.
GEE, BATS, I DON'T KNOW.
DON'T GET ME WRONG, I ENJOY A GOOD RADIATION BURN AS MUCH AS THE NEXT GUY, BUT I DON'T THINK...
...UH...
SO... SEE YOU SOON?
YOU JUST MIGHT.
THE END!

JAM PACKED ACTION!

JUSTICE LEAGUE UNLIMITED™

"FOR THE MAN WHO HAS EVERYTHING"

ORIGINAL TELEVISION SCRIPT
WRITTEN BY J. M. DeMATTEIS
ADAPTED FROM A STORY BY
ALAN MOORE

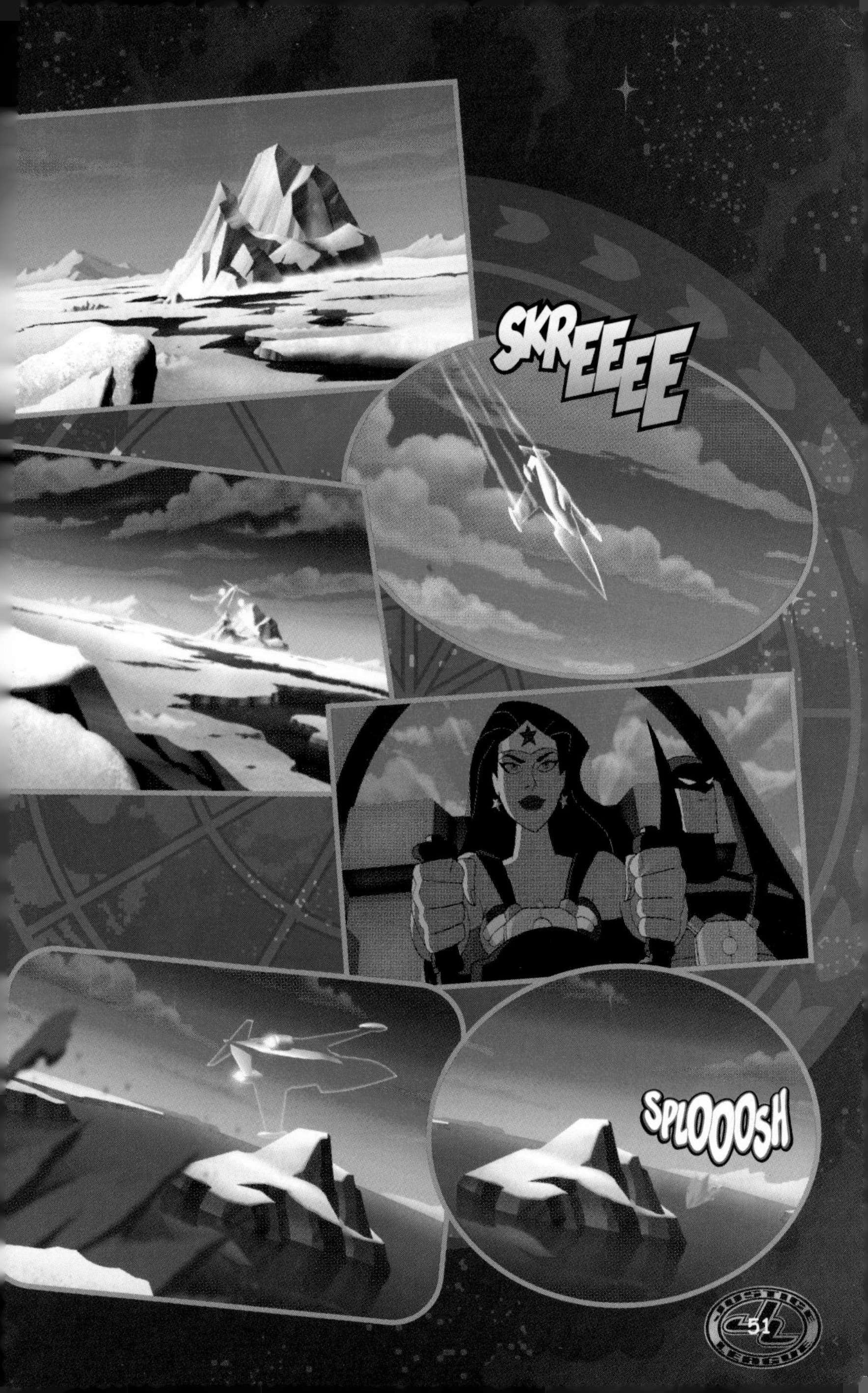
SKREEEE
SPLOOOSH

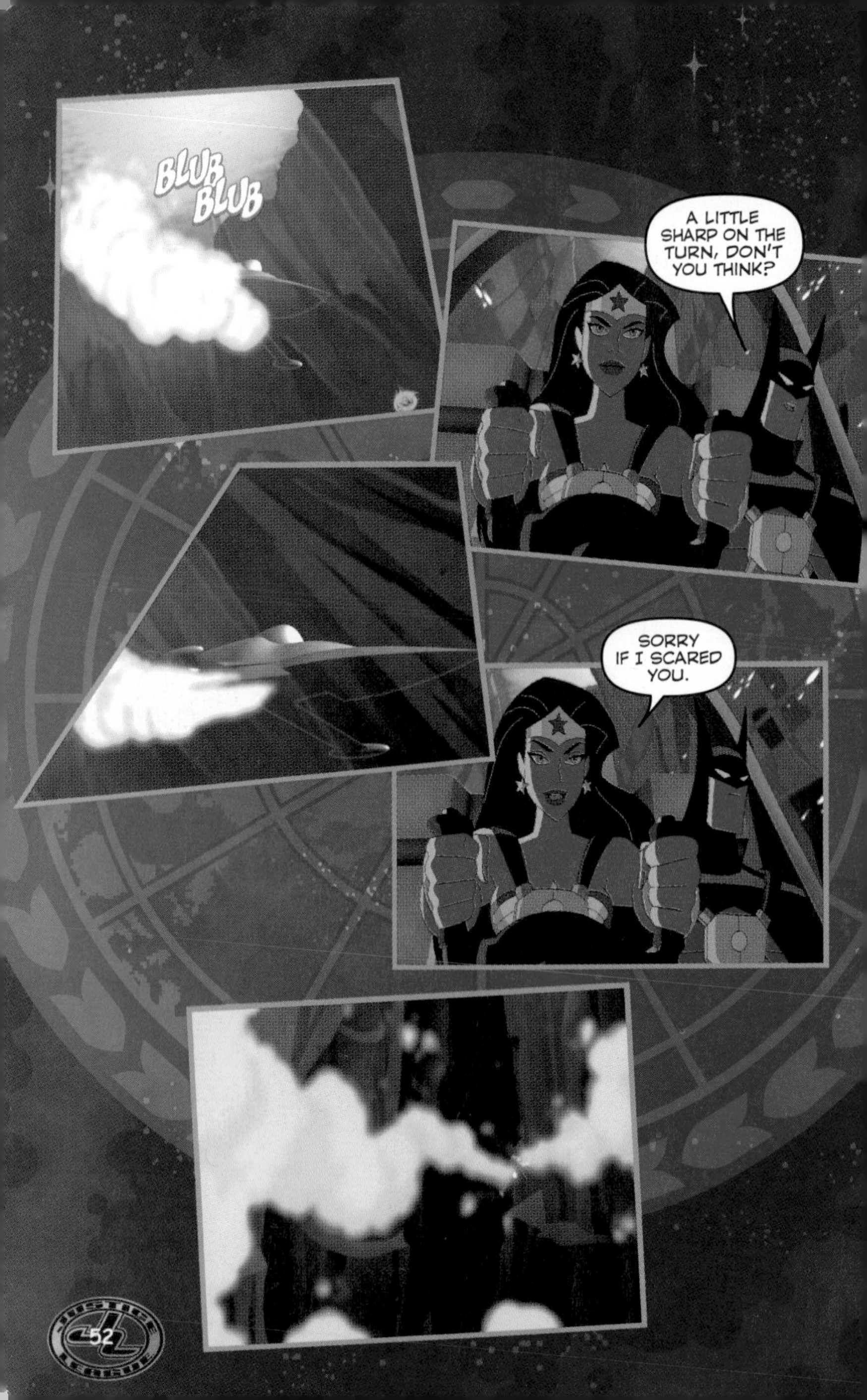
BLUB BLUB
A LITTLE SHARP ON THE TURN, DON'T YOU THINK?
SORRY IF I SCARED YOU.

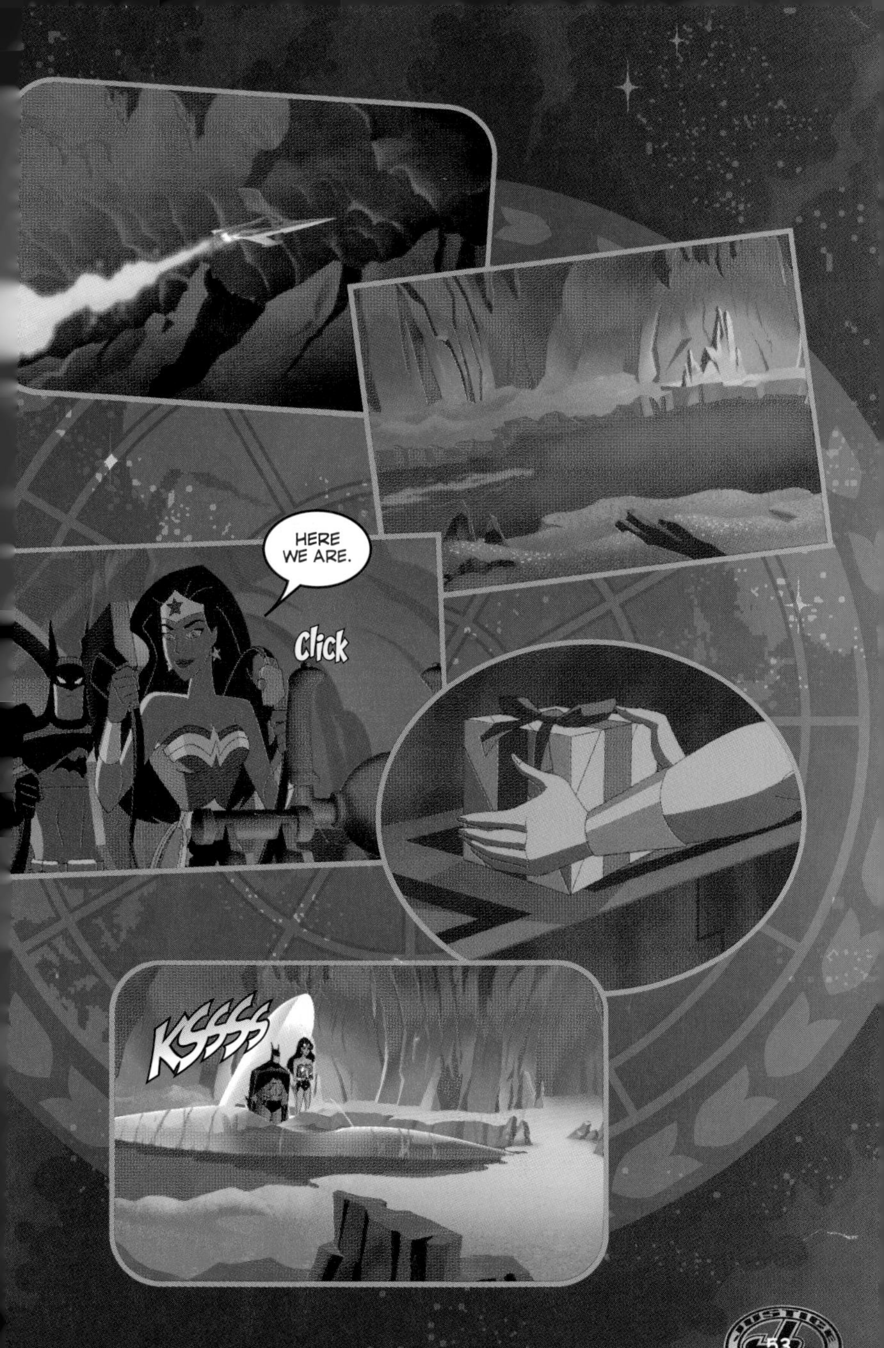
HERE WE ARE.
Click
KSSSS

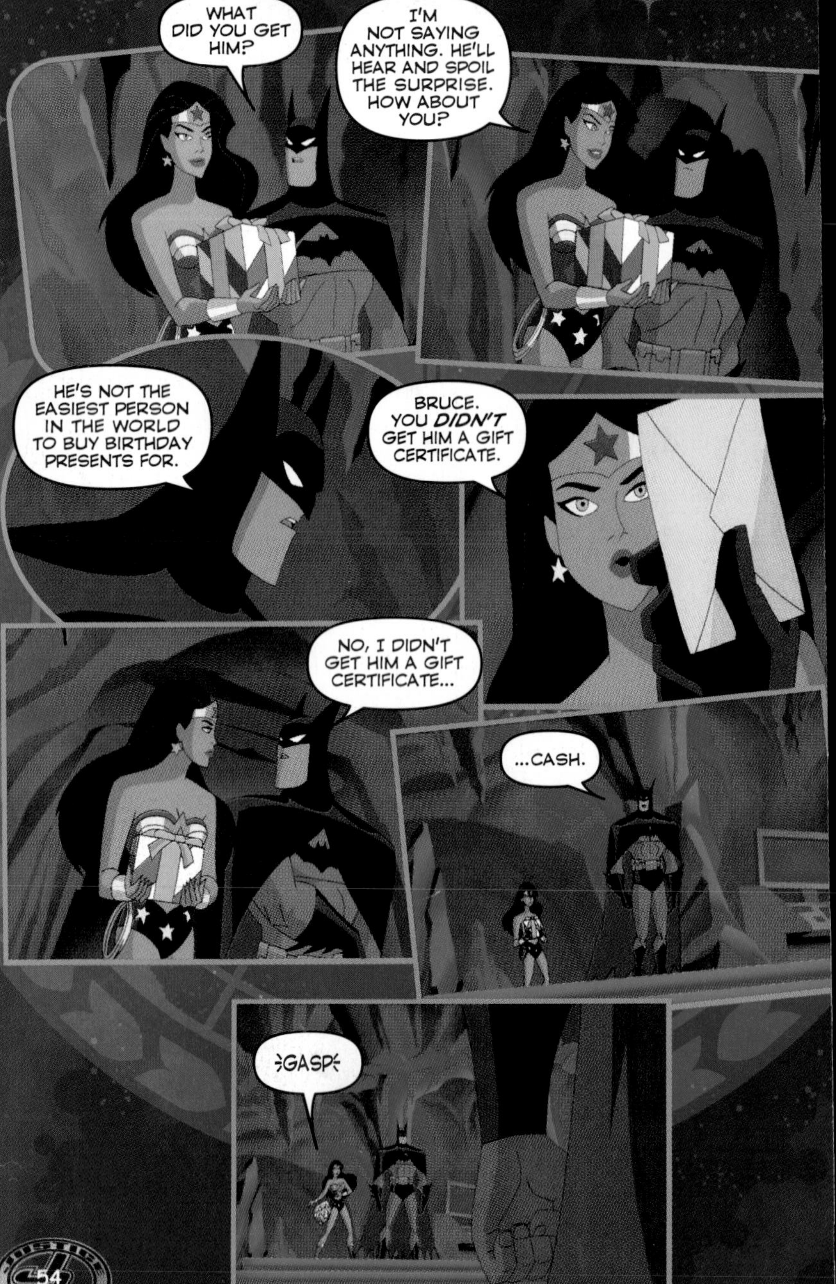
WHAT DID YOU GET HIM?
I'M NOT SAYING ANYTHING. HE'LL HEAR AND SPOIL THE SURPRISE. HOW ABOUT YOU?
HE'S NOT THE EASIEST PERSON IN THE WORLD TO BUY BIRTHDAY PRESENTS FOR.
BRUCE. YOU *DIDN'T* GET HIM A GIFT CERTIFICATE.
NO, I DIDN'T GET HIM A GIFT CERTIFICATE...
...CASH.
GASP

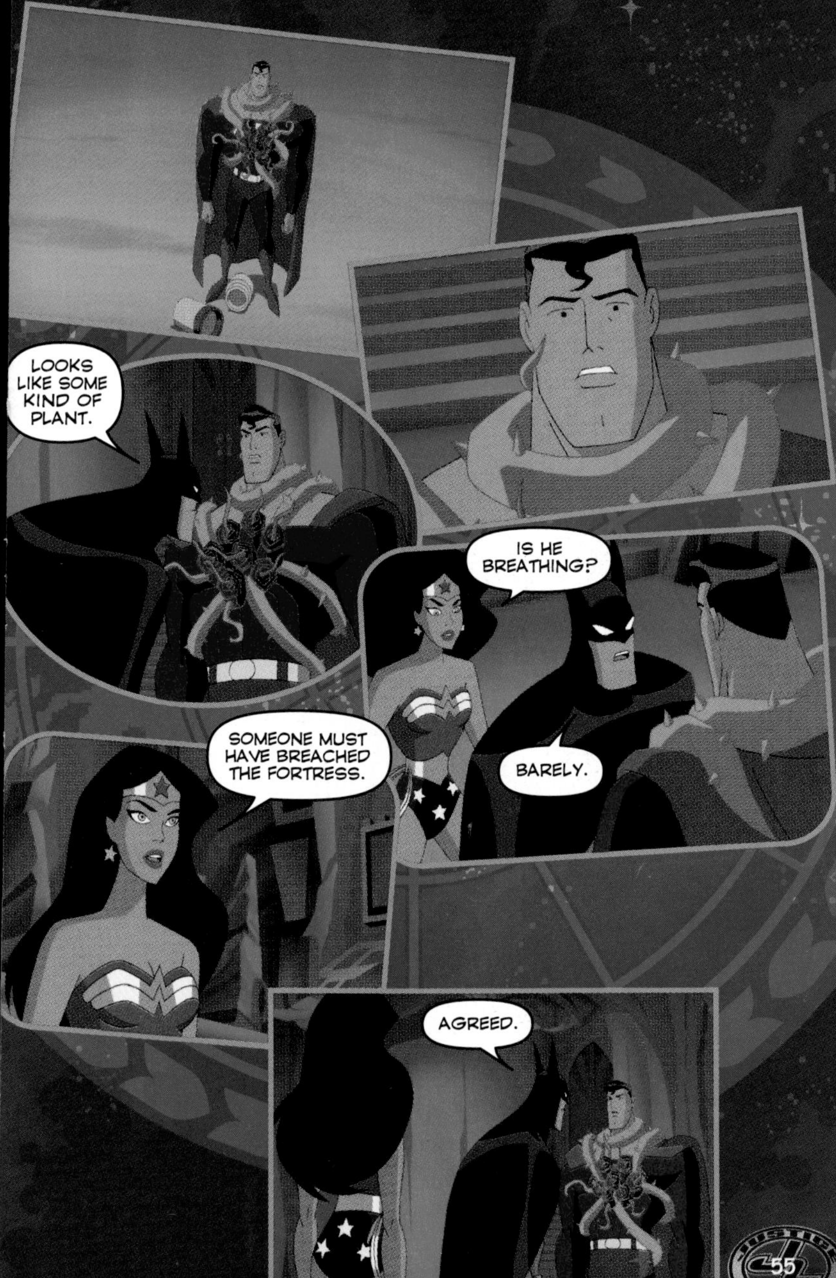
LOOKS LIKE SOME KIND OF PLANT.
IS HE BREATHING?
BARELY.
SOMEONE MUST HAVE BREACHED THE FORTRESS.
AGREED.

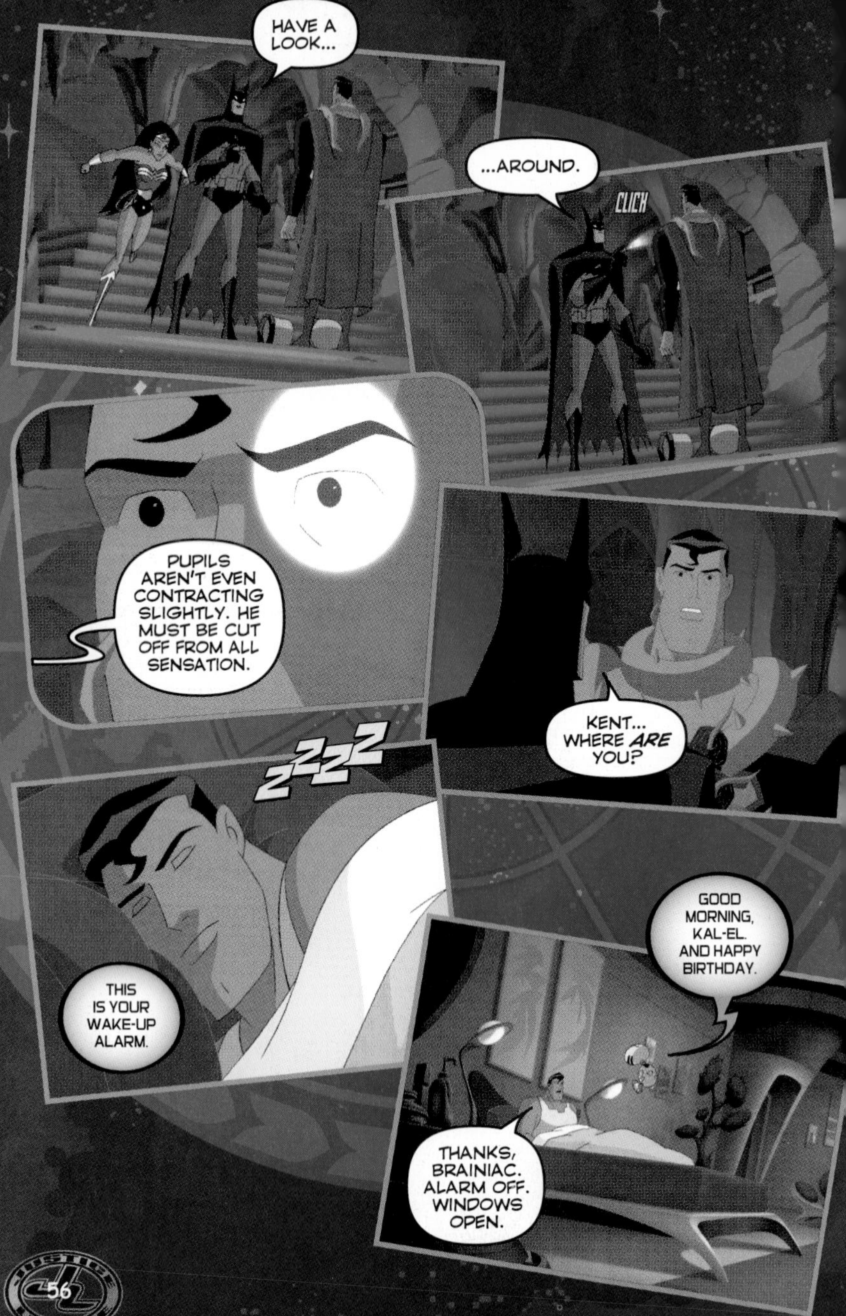
HAVE A LOOK...
...AROUND.
CLICK
PUPILS AREN'T EVEN CONTRACTING SLIGHTLY. HE MUST BE CUT OFF FROM ALL SENSATION.
KENT... WHERE ARE YOU?
ZZZZ
THIS IS YOUR WAKE-UP ALARM.
GOOD MORNING, KAL-EL. AND HAPPY BIRTHDAY.
THANKS, BRAINIAC. ALARM OFF. WINDOWS OPEN.

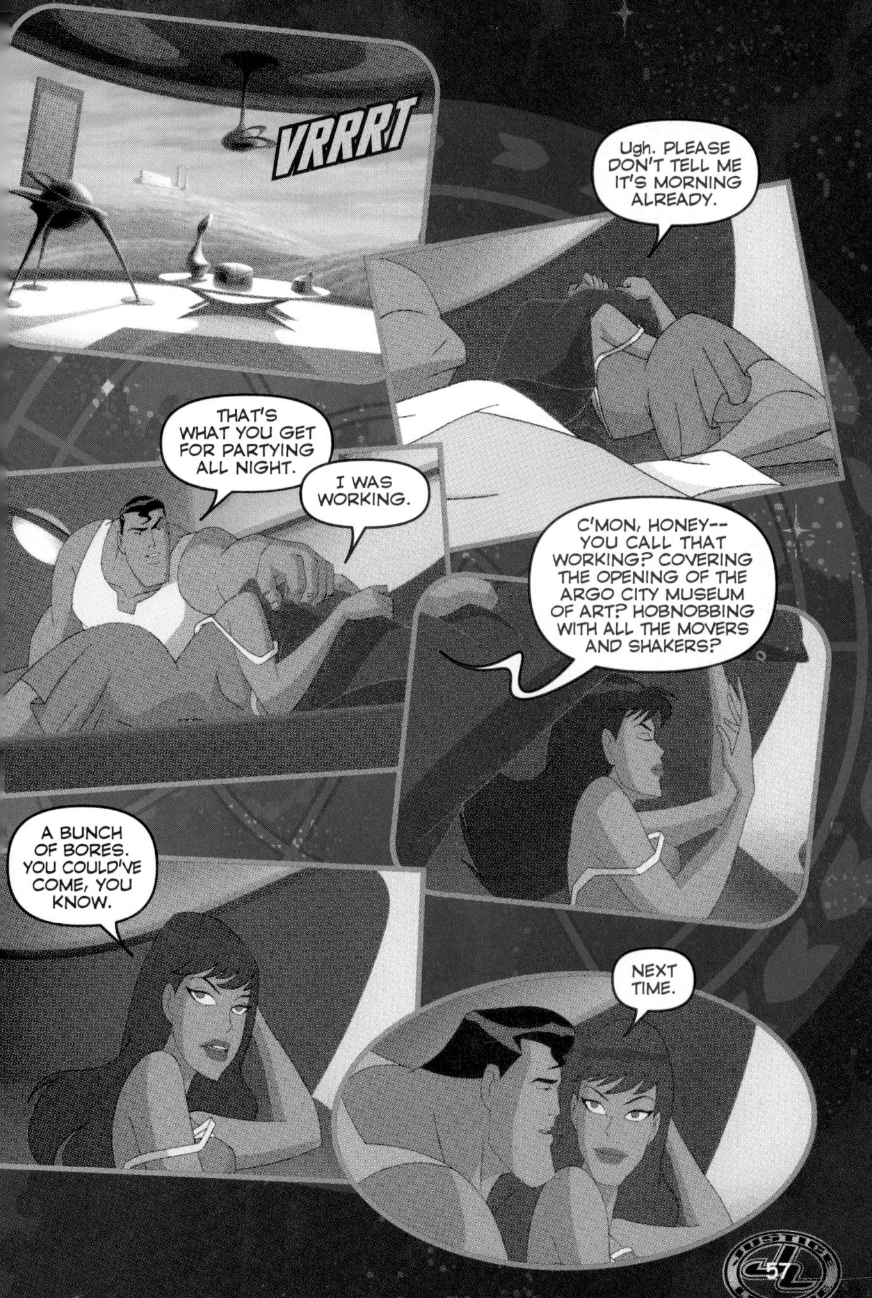
VRRRT
Ugh. PLEASE DON'T TELL ME IT'S MORNING ALREADY.
THAT'S WHAT YOU GET FOR PARTYING ALL NIGHT.
I WAS WORKING.
C'MON, HONEY-- YOU CALL THAT WORKING? COVERING THE OPENING OF THE ARGO CITY MUSEUM OF ART? HOBNOBBING WITH ALL THE MOVERS AND SHAKERS?
A BUNCH OF BORES. YOU COULD'VE COME, YOU KNOW.
NEXT TIME.

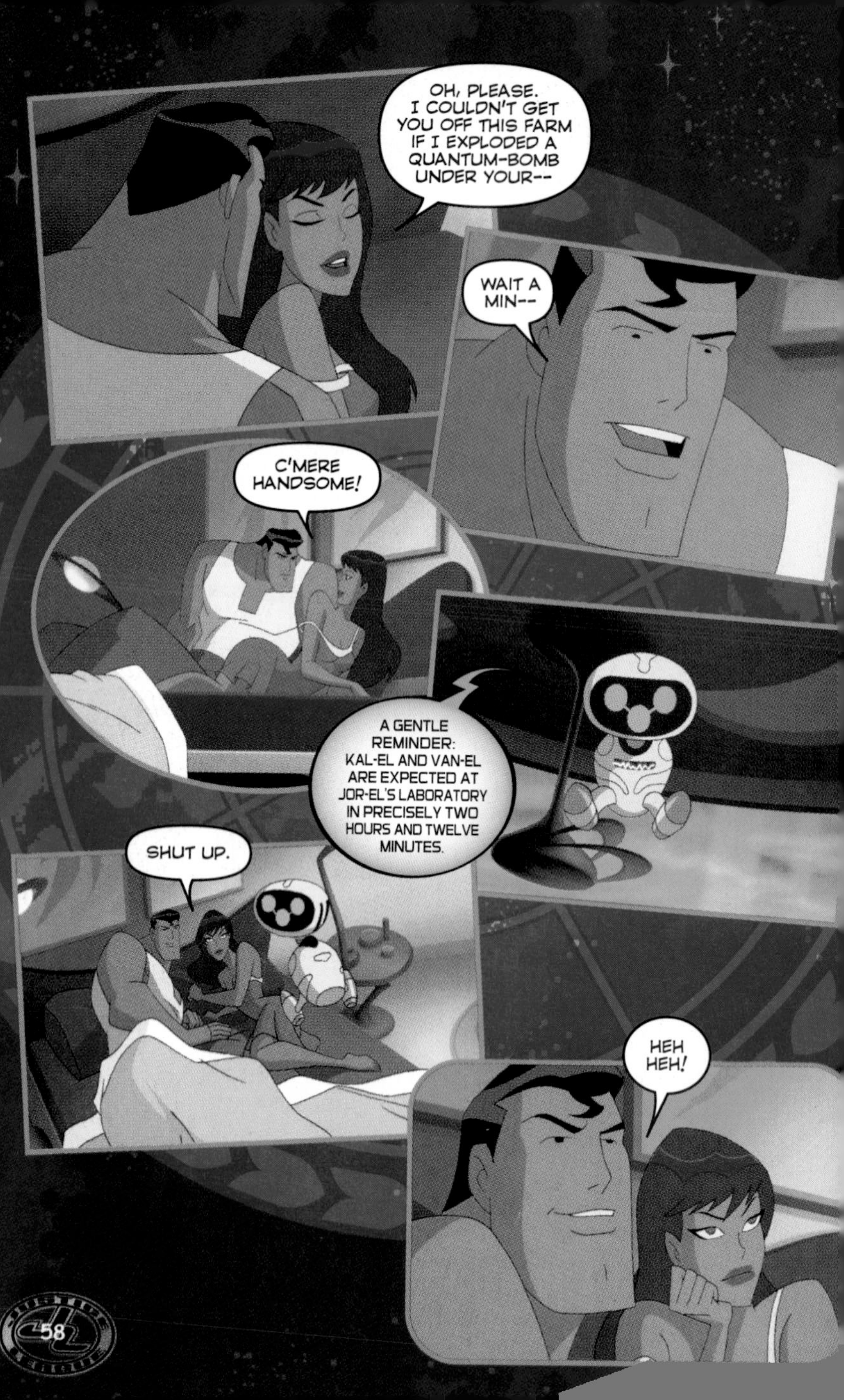
OH, PLEASE. I COULDN'T GET YOU OFF THIS FARM IF I EXPLODED A QUANTUM-BOMB UNDER YOUR--
WAIT A MIN--
C'MERE HANDSOME!
A GENTLE REMINDER: KAL-EL AND VAN-EL ARE EXPECTED AT JOR-EL'S LABORATORY IN PRECISELY TWO HOURS AND TWELVE MINUTES.
SHUT UP.
HEH HEH!

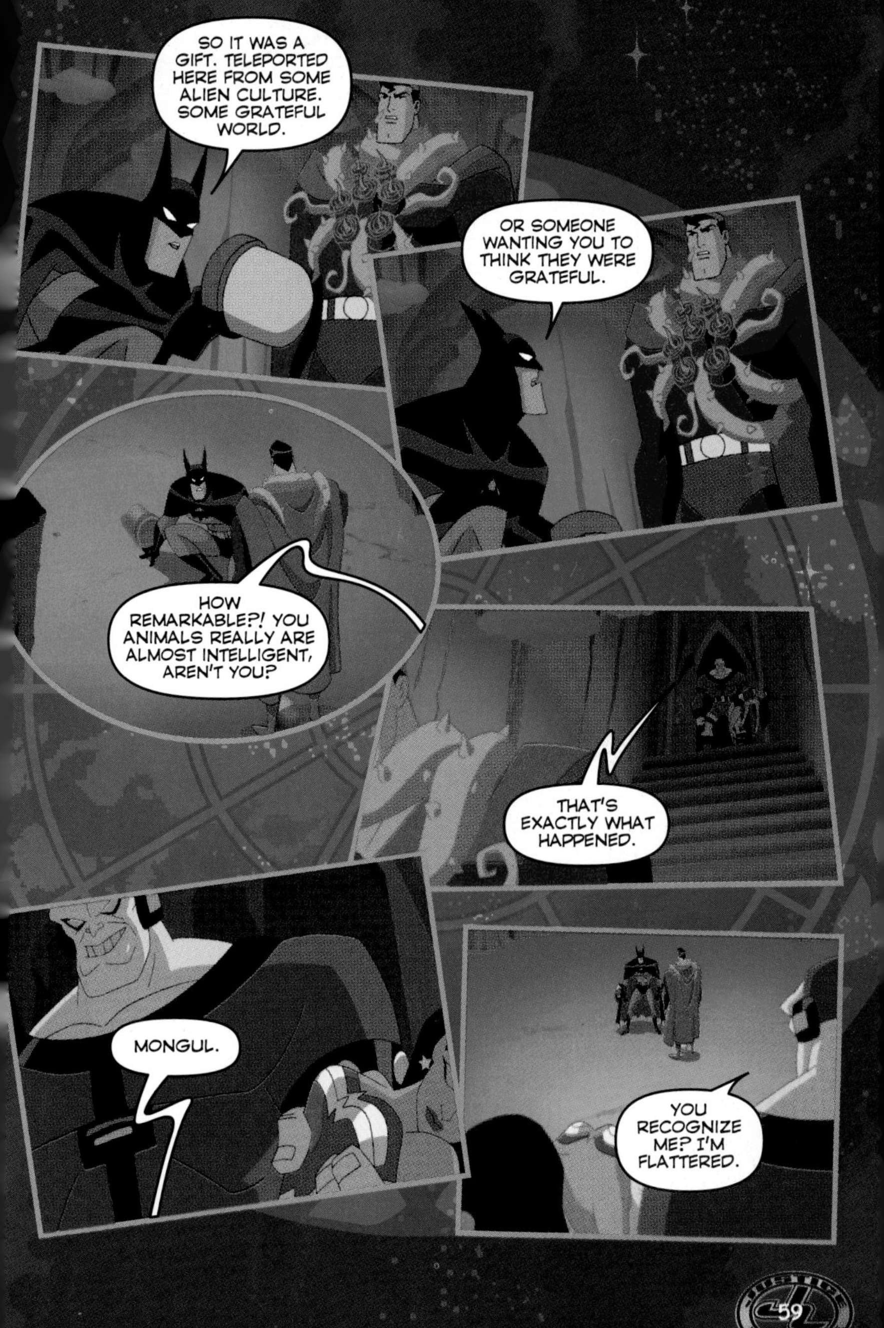
SO IT WAS A GIFT. TELEPORTED HERE FROM SOME ALIEN CULTURE. SOME GRATEFUL WORLD.
OR SOMEONE WANTING YOU TO THINK THEY WERE GRATEFUL.
HOW REMARKABLE?! YOU ANIMALS REALLY ARE ALMOST INTELLIGENT, AREN'T YOU?
THAT'S EXACTLY WHAT HAPPENED.
MONGUL.
YOU RECOGNIZE ME? I'M FLATTERED.

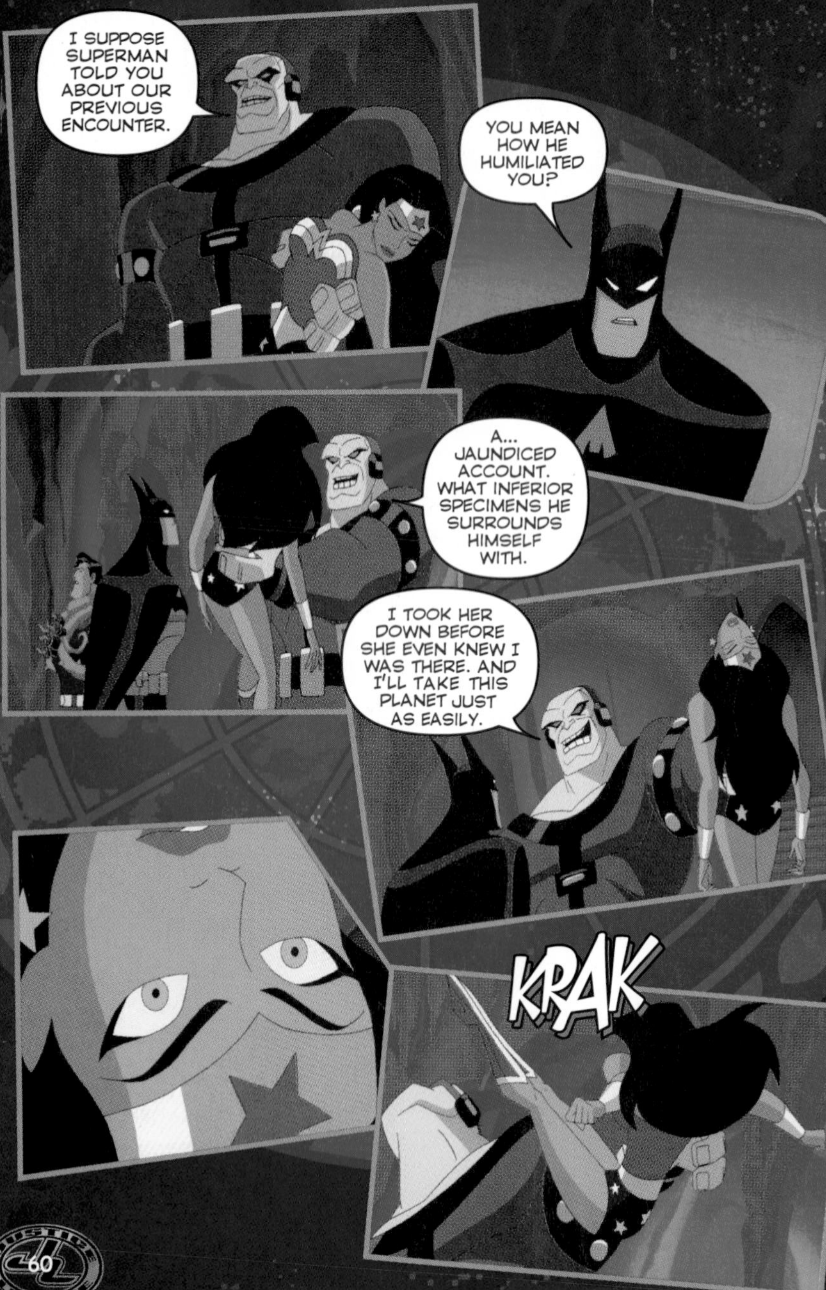
I SUPPOSE SUPERMAN TOLD YOU ABOUT OUR PREVIOUS ENCOUNTER.
YOU MEAN HOW HE HUMILIATED YOU?
A... JAUNDICED ACCOUNT. WHAT INFERIOR SPECIMENS HE SURROUNDS HIMSELF WITH.
I TOOK HER DOWN BEFORE SHE EVEN KNEW I WAS THERE. AND I'LL TAKE THIS PLANET JUST AS EASILY.
KRAK

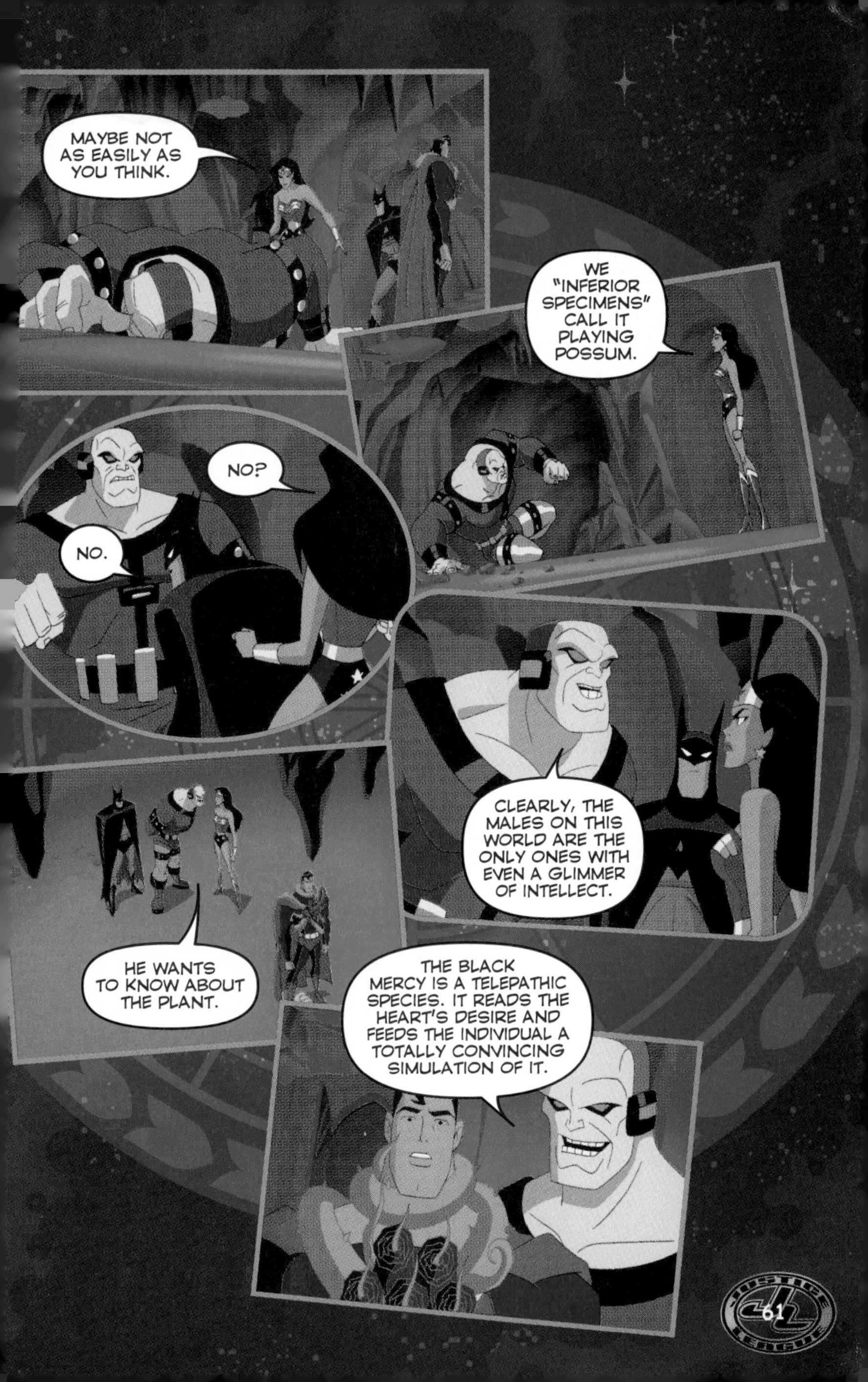
MAYBE NOT AS EASILY AS YOU THINK.
WE "INFERIOR SPECIMENS" CALL IT PLAYING POSSUM.
NO?
NO.
CLEARLY, THE MALES ON THIS WORLD ARE THE ONLY ONES WITH EVEN A GLIMMER OF INTELLECT.
HE WANTS TO KNOW ABOUT THE PLANT.
THE BLACK MERCY IS A TELEPATHIC SPECIES. IT READS THE HEART'S DESIRE AND FEEDS THE INDIVIDUAL A TOTALLY CONVINCING SIMULATION OF IT.
JUSTICE LEAGUE

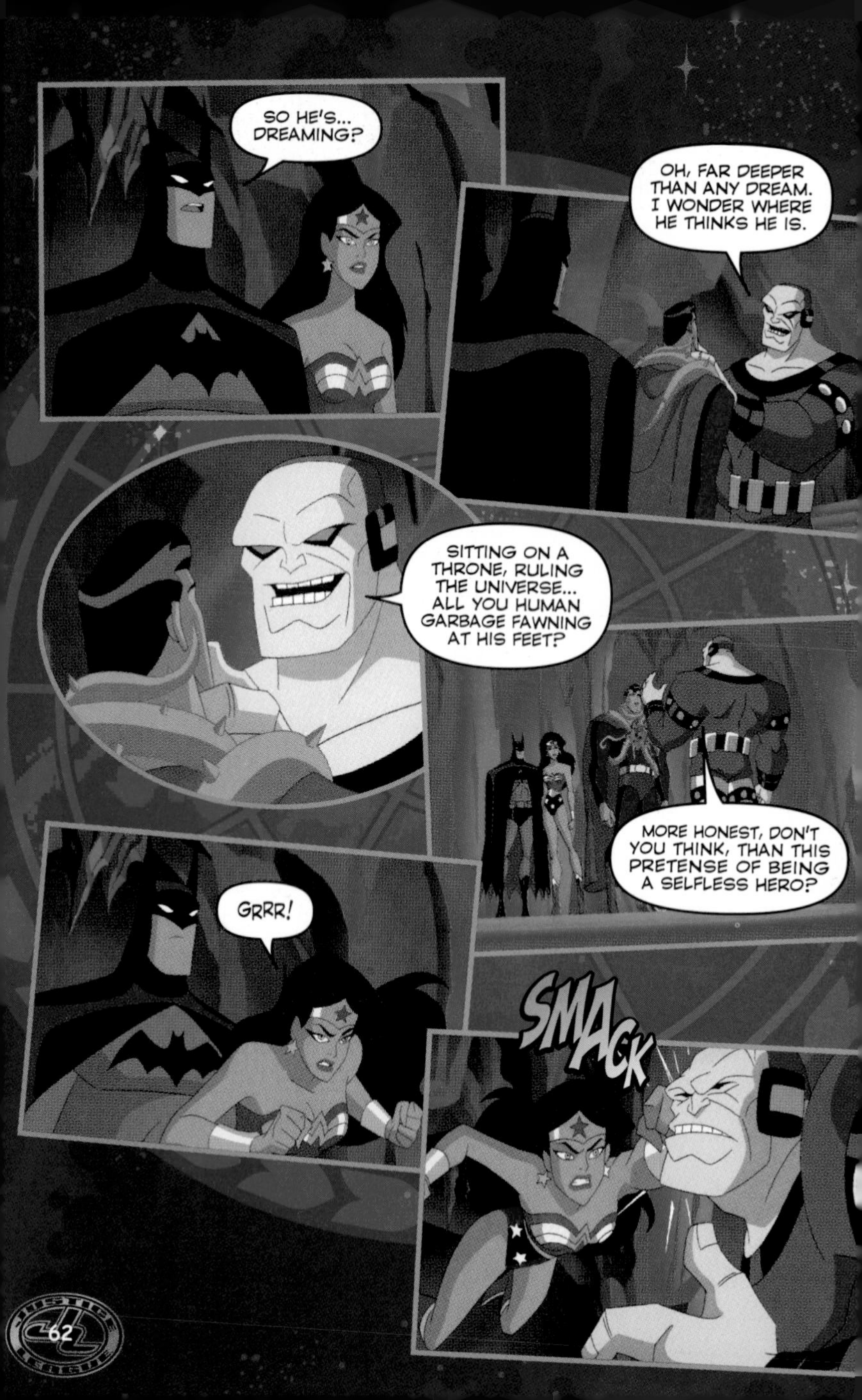
SO HE'S... DREAMING?
OH, FAR DEEPER THAN ANY DREAM. I WONDER WHERE HE THINKS HE IS.
SITTING ON A THRONE, RULING THE UNIVERSE... ALL YOU HUMAN GARBAGE FAWNING AT HIS FEET?
MORE HONEST, DON'T YOU THINK, THAN THIS PRETENSE OF BEING A SELFLESS HERO?
GRRR!
SMACK

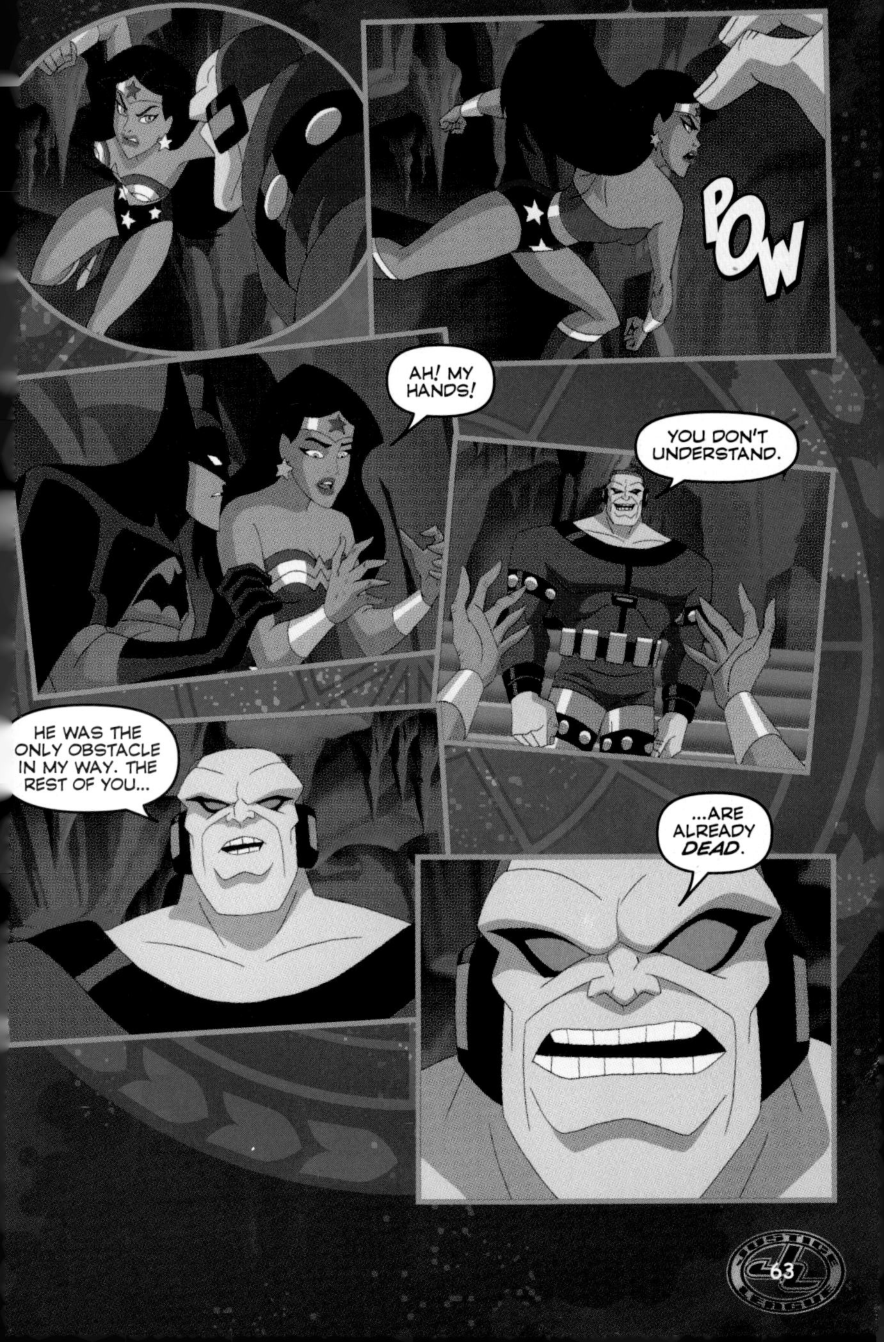
POW
AH! MY HANDS!
YOU DON'T UNDERSTAND.
HE WAS THE ONLY OBSTACLE IN MY WAY. THE REST OF YOU...
...ARE ALREADY *DEAD*.
JUSTICE LEAGUE

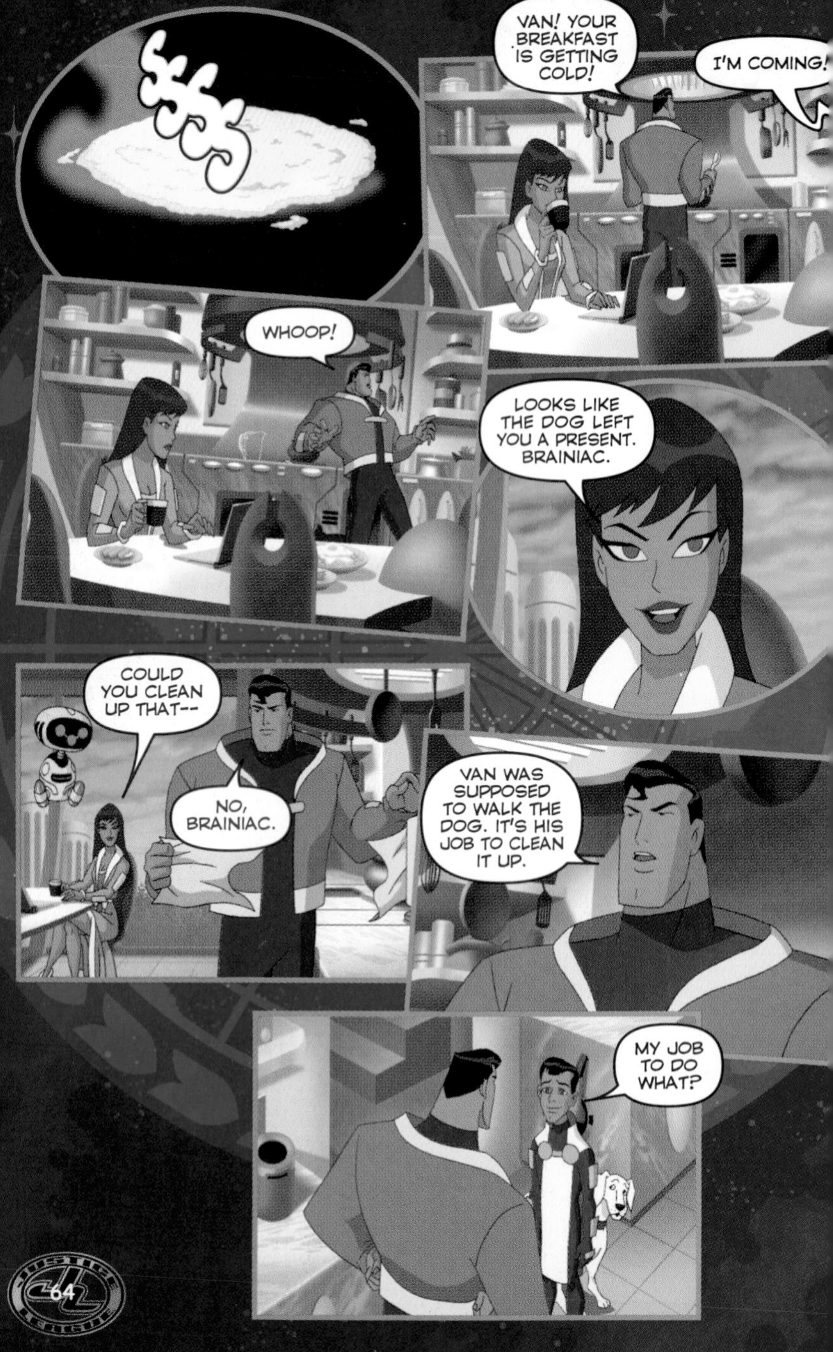

SSSS
VAN! YOUR BREAKFAST IS GETTING COLD!
I'M COMING!
WHOOP!
LOOKS LIKE THE DOG LEFT YOU A PRESENT. BRAINIAC.
COULD YOU CLEAN UP THAT--
NO, BRAINIAC.
VAN WAS SUPPOSED TO WALK THE DOG. IT'S HIS JOB TO CLEAN IT UP.
MY JOB TO DO WHAT?

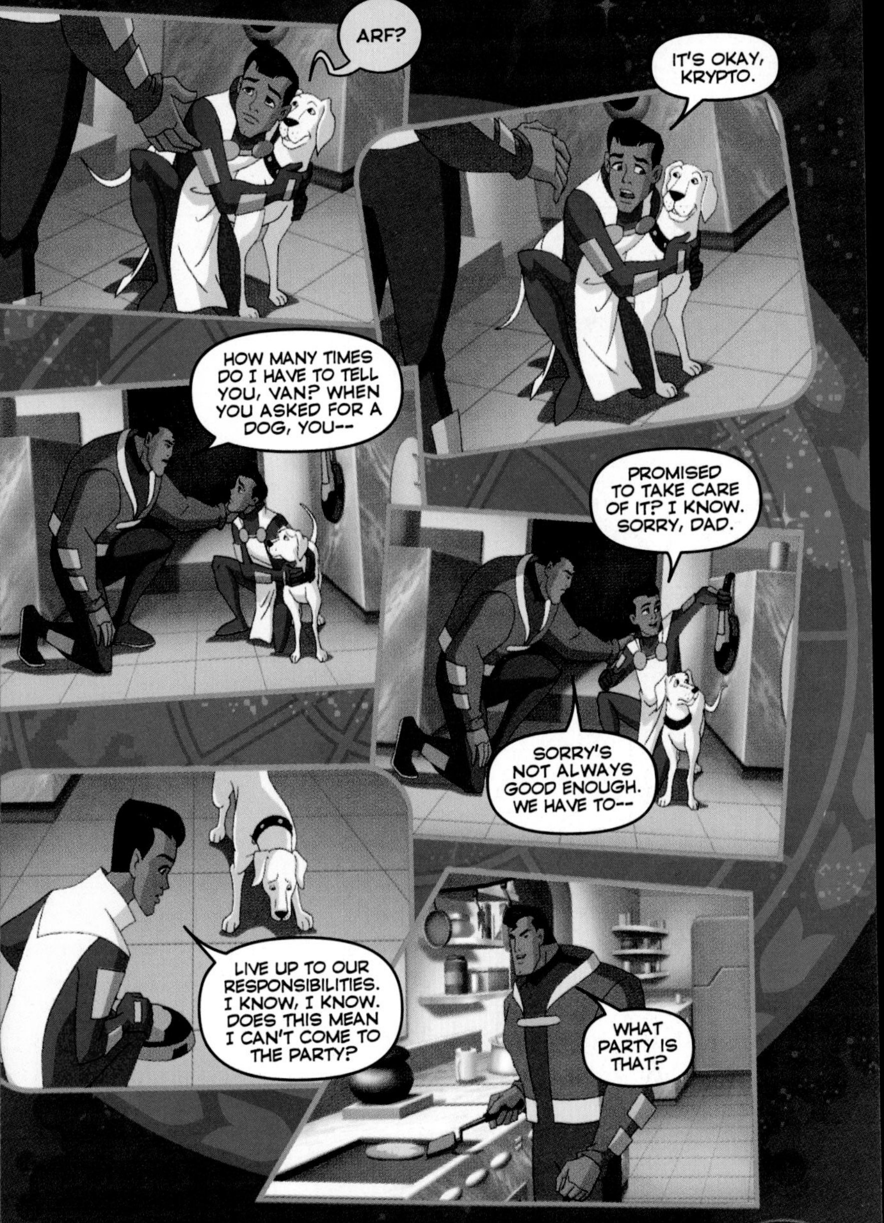
ARF?
IT'S OKAY, KRYPTO.
HOW MANY TIMES DO I HAVE TO TELL YOU, VAN? WHEN YOU ASKED FOR A DOG, YOU--
PROMISED TO TAKE CARE OF IT? I KNOW. SORRY, DAD.
SORRY'S NOT ALWAYS GOOD ENOUGH. WE HAVE TO--
LIVE UP TO OUR RESPONSIBILITIES. I KNOW, I KNOW. DOES THIS MEAN I CAN'T COME TO THE PARTY?
WHAT PARTY IS THAT?

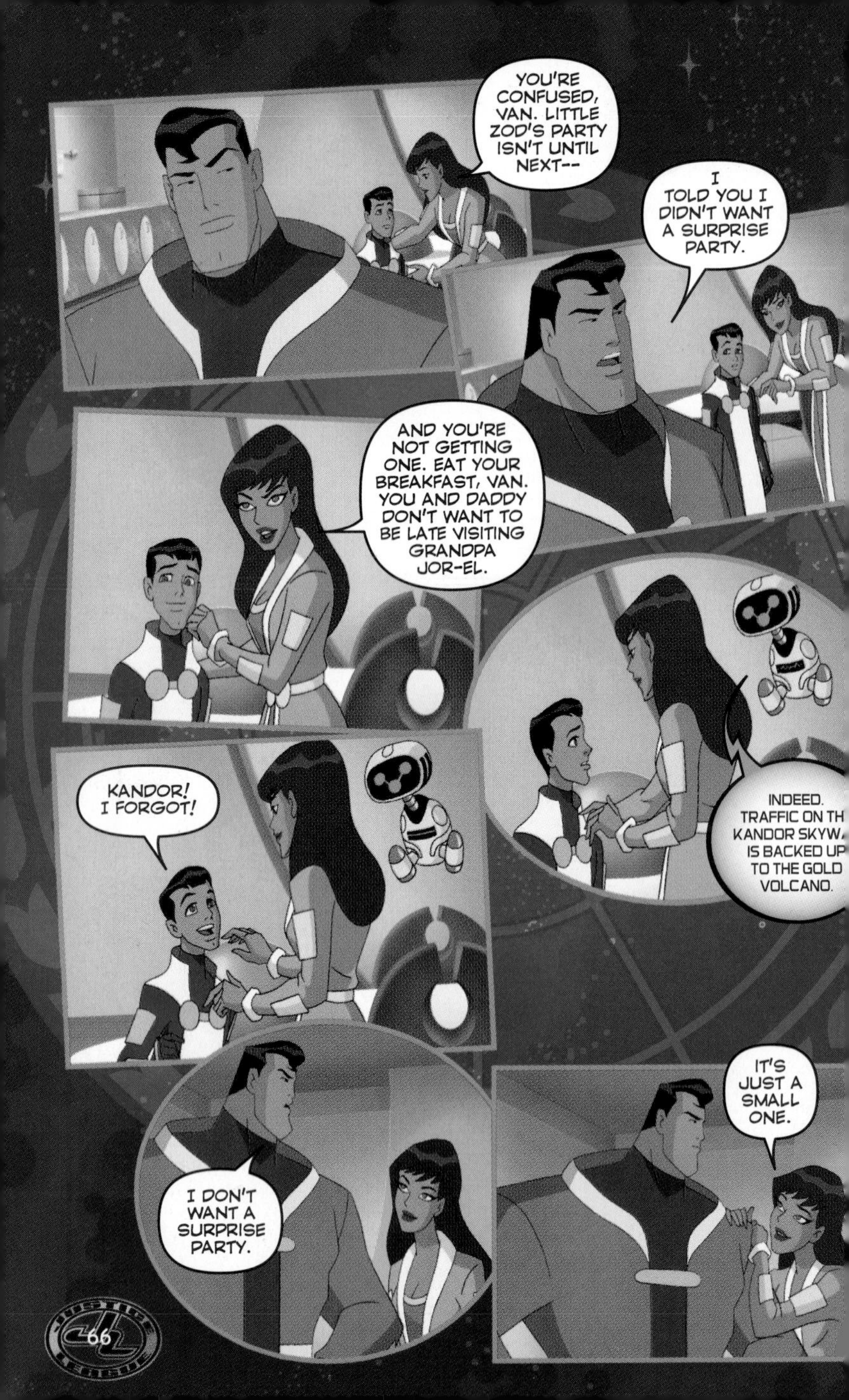
YOU'RE CONFUSED, VAN. LITTLE ZOD'S PARTY ISN'T UNTIL NEXT--
I TOLD YOU I DIDN'T WANT A SURPRISE PARTY.
AND YOU'RE NOT GETTING ONE. EAT YOUR BREAKFAST, VAN. YOU AND DADDY DON'T WANT TO BE LATE VISITING GRANDPA JOR-EL.
KANDOR! I FORGOT!
INDEED. TRAFFIC ON TH KANDOR SKYW. IS BACKED UP TO THE GOLD VOLCANO.
I DON'T WANT A SURPRISE PARTY.
IT'S JUST A SMALL ONE.

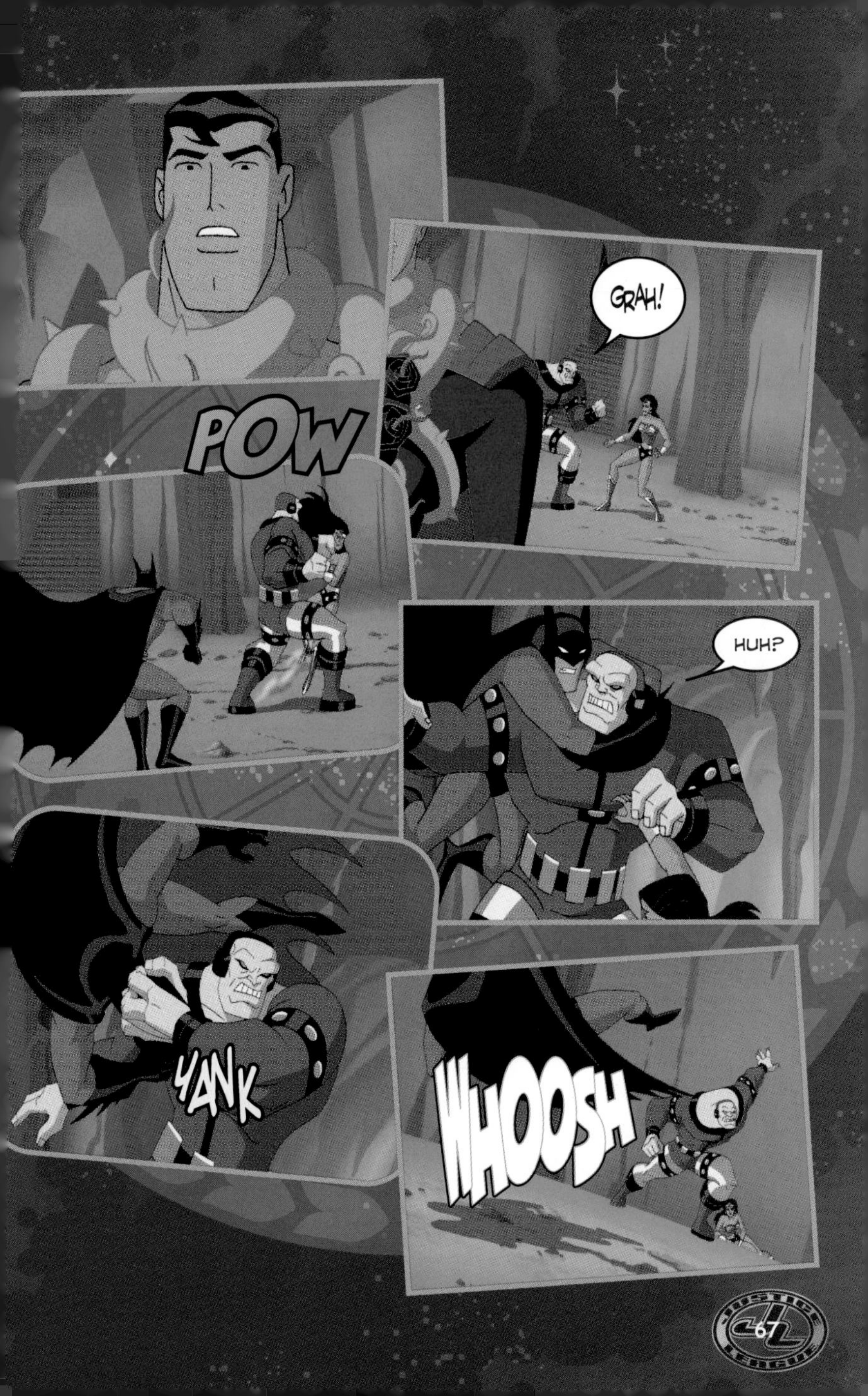
GRAH!
POW
HUH?
YANK
WHOOSH

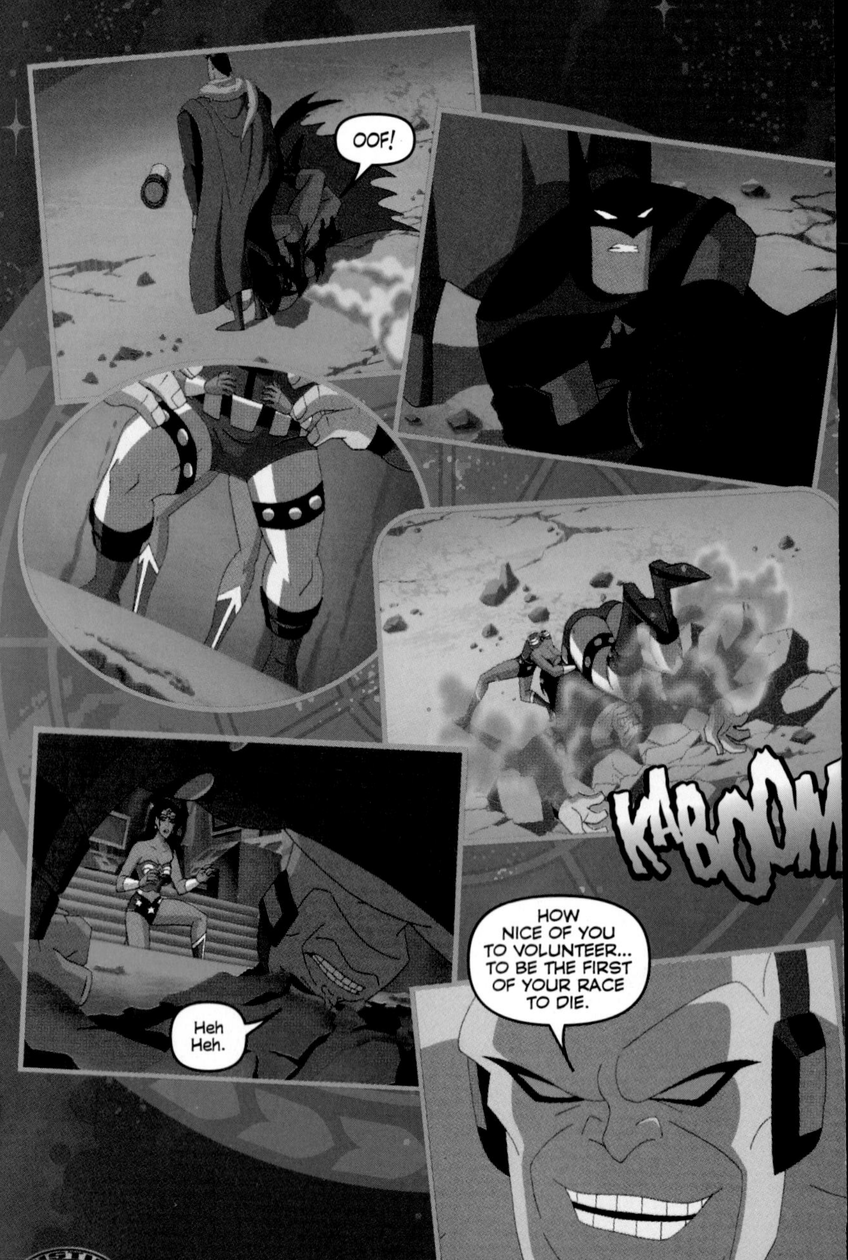
OOF!
KABOOM
Heh Heh.
HOW NICE OF YOU TO VOLUNTEER... TO BE THE FIRST OF YOUR RACE TO DIE.

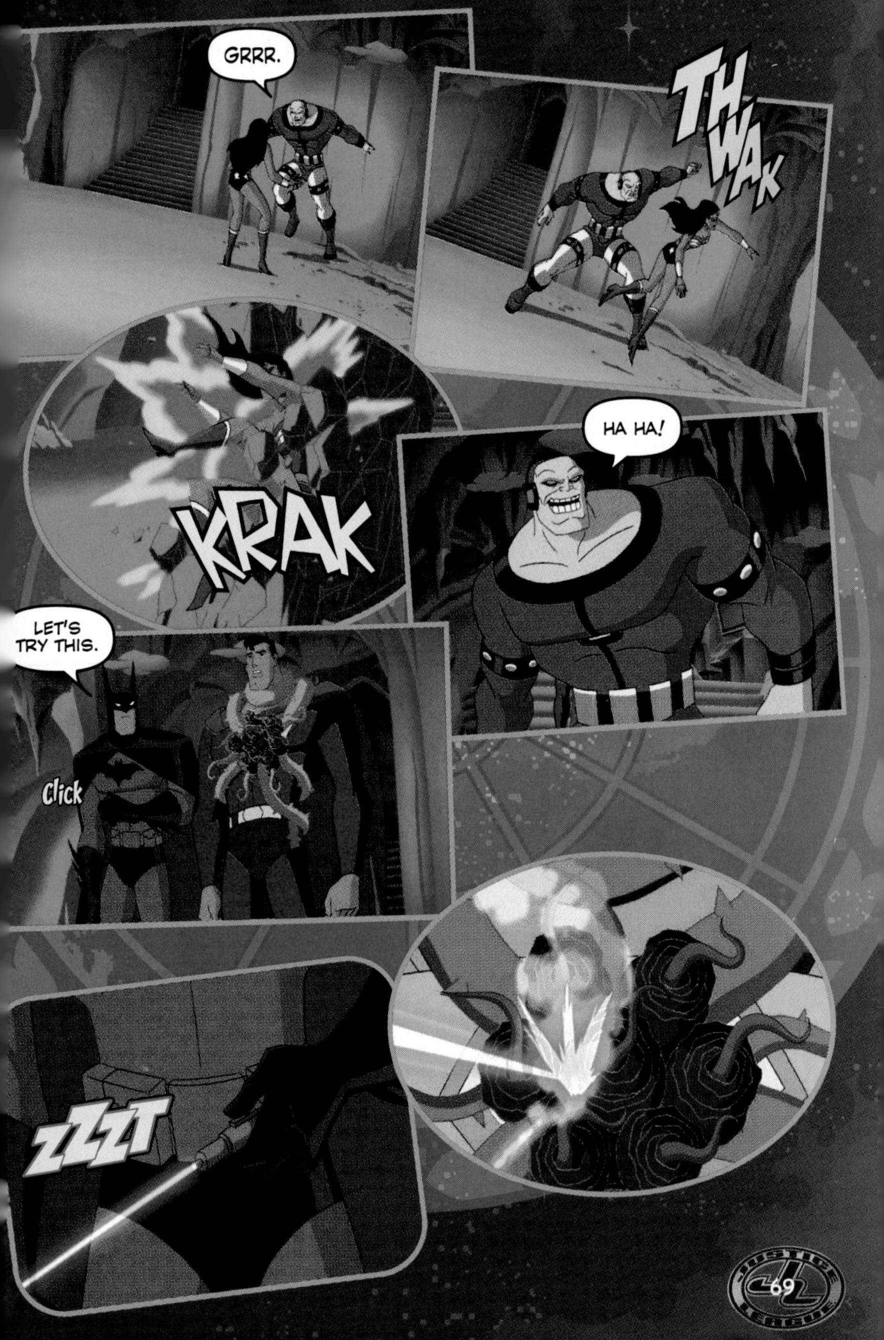
GRRR.
THWAK
KRAK
HA HA!
LET'S TRY THIS.
Click
ZZZT

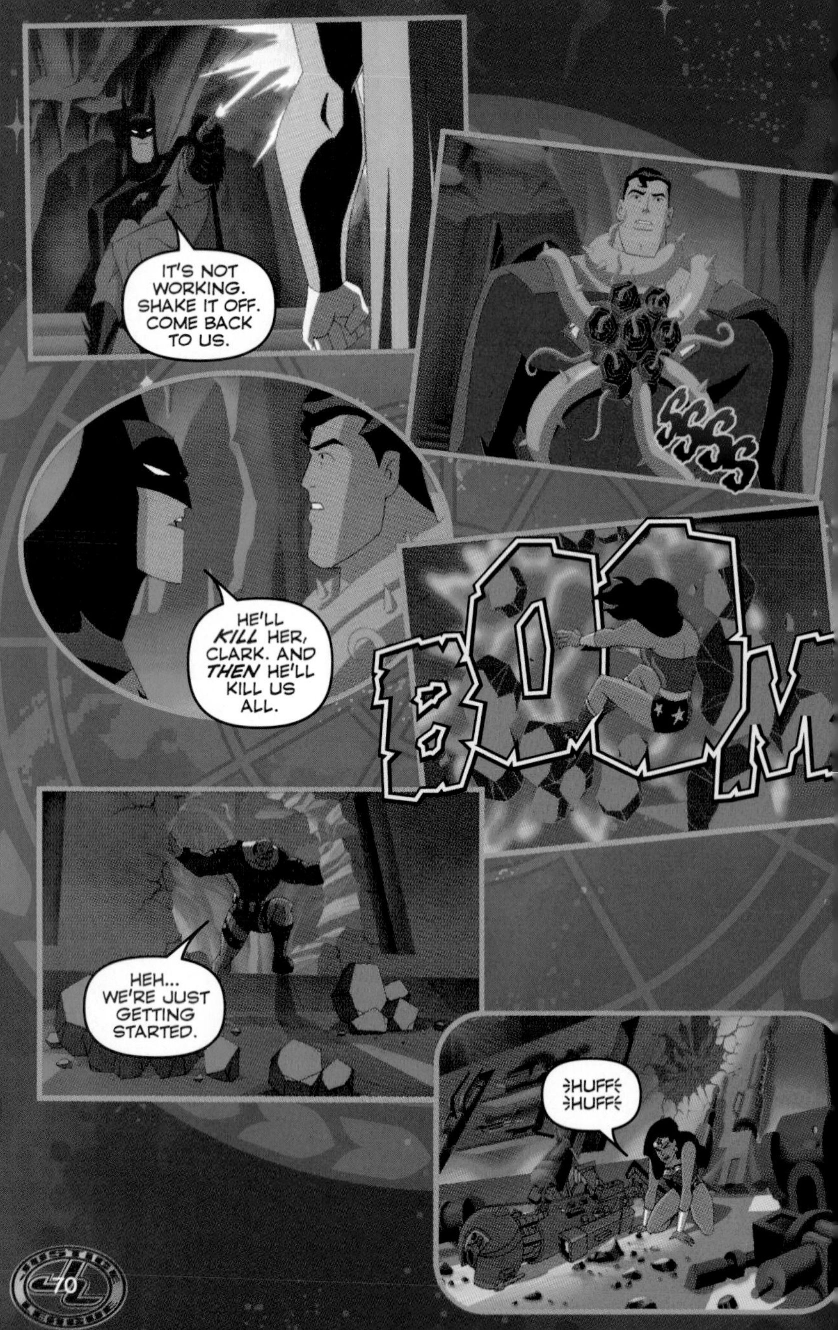
IT'S NOT WORKING. SHAKE IT OFF. COME BACK TO US.
SSSS
HE'LL *KILL* HER, CLARK. AND *THEN* HE'LL KILL US ALL.
BOOM
HEH... WE'RE JUST GETTING STARTED.
HUFF HUFF

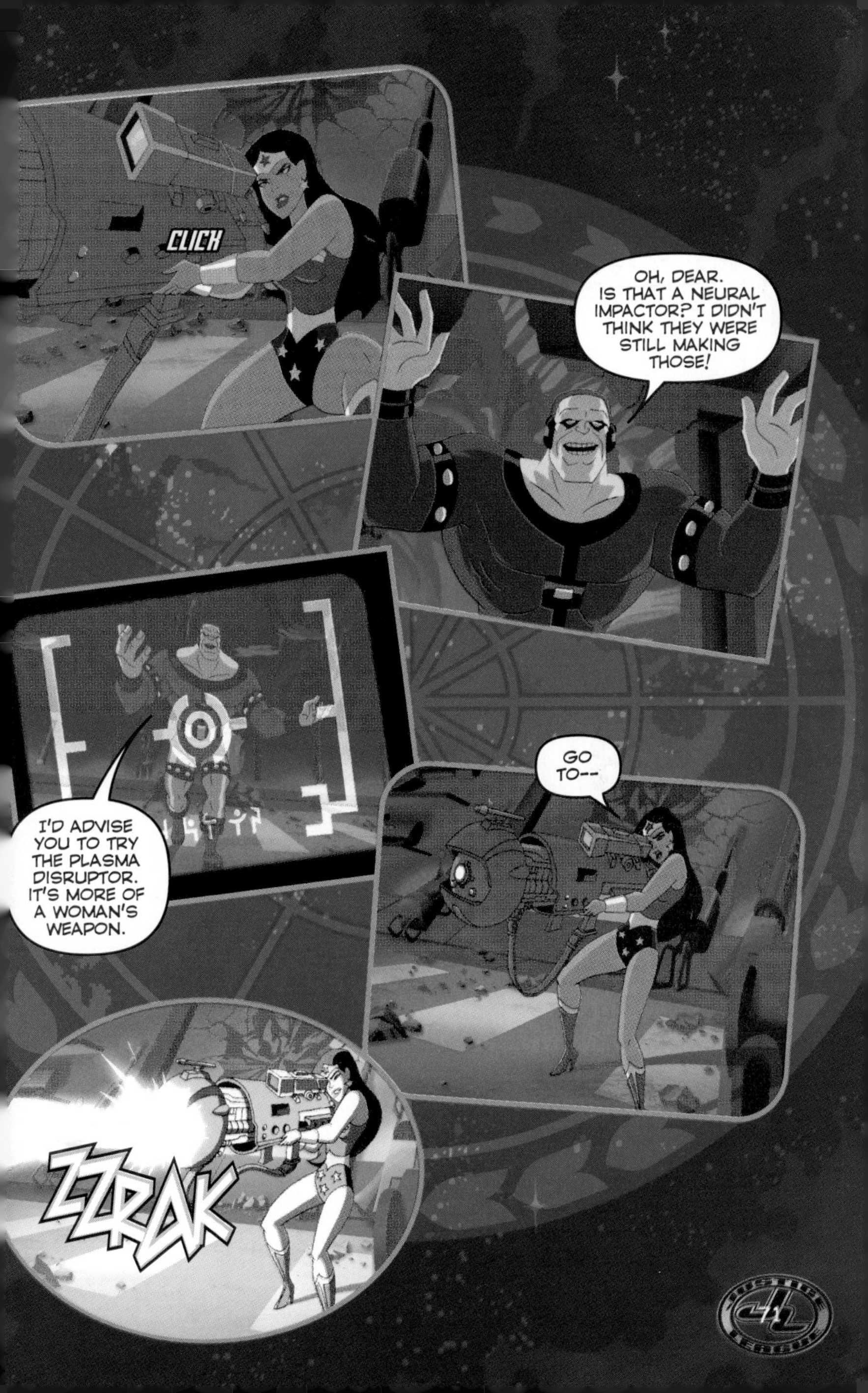
CLICK
OH, DEAR. IS THAT A NEURAL IMPACTOR? I DIDN'T THINK THEY WERE STILL MAKING THOSE!
I'D ADVISE YOU TO TRY THE PLASMA DISRUPTOR. IT'S MORE OF A WOMAN'S WEAPON.
GO TO--
ZZRAK

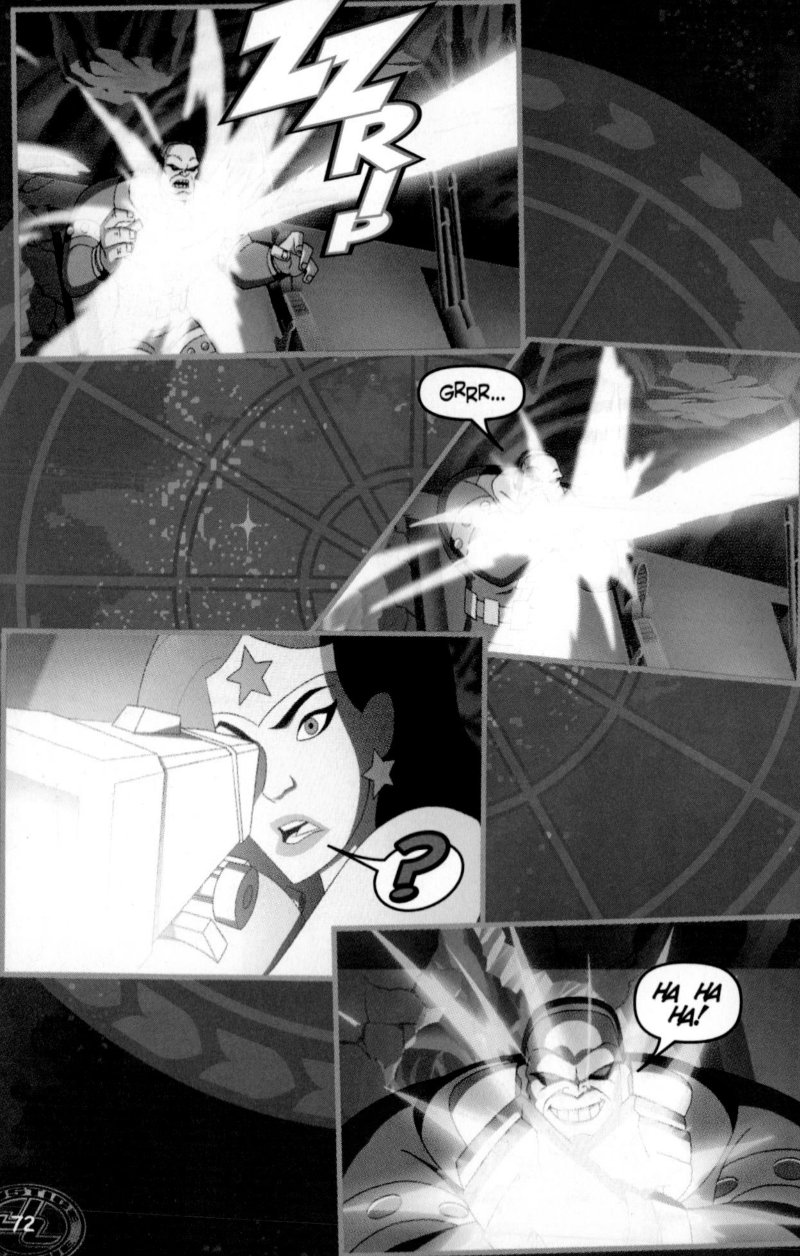
ZZRIP
GRRR...
?
HA HA HA!

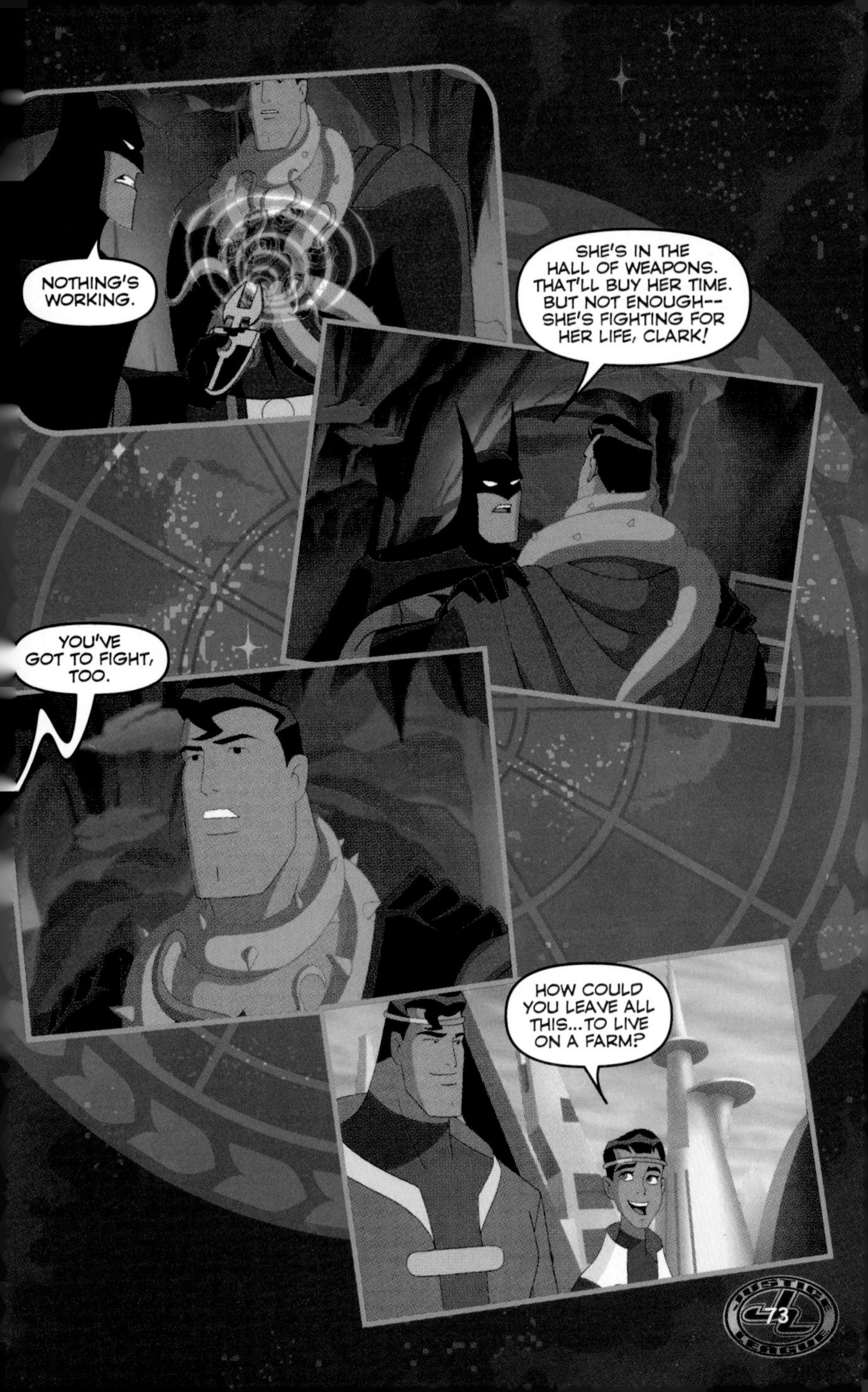
NOTHING'S WORKING.
SHE'S IN THE HALL OF WEAPONS. THAT'LL BUY HER TIME. BUT NOT ENOUGH-- SHE'S FIGHTING FOR HER LIFE, CLARK!
YOU'VE GOT TO FIGHT, TOO.
HOW COULD YOU LEAVE ALL THIS...TO LIVE ON A FARM?

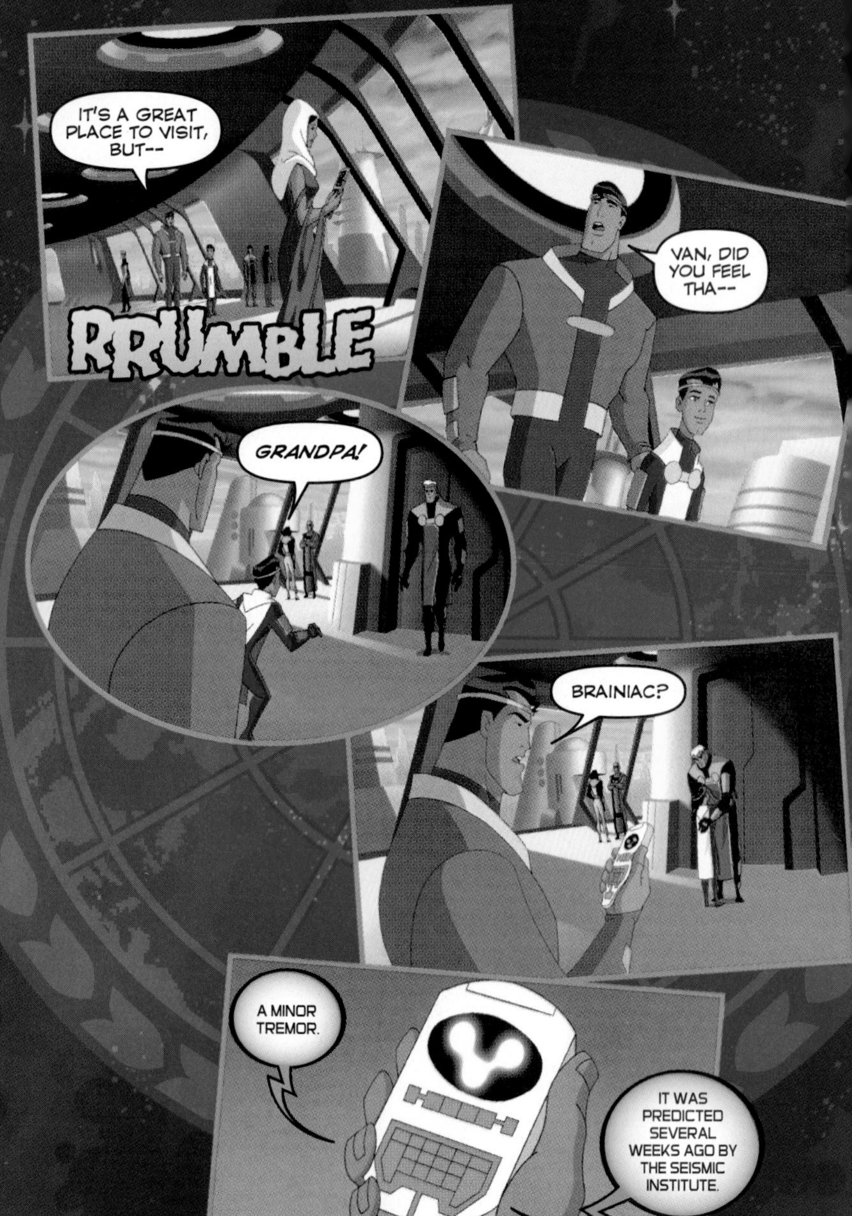
IT'S A GREAT PLACE TO VISIT, BUT--
RRUMBLE
VAN, DID YOU FEEL THA--
GRANDPA!
BRAINIAC?
A MINOR TREMOR.
IT WAS PREDICTED SEVERAL WEEKS AGO BY THE SEISMIC INSTITUTE.

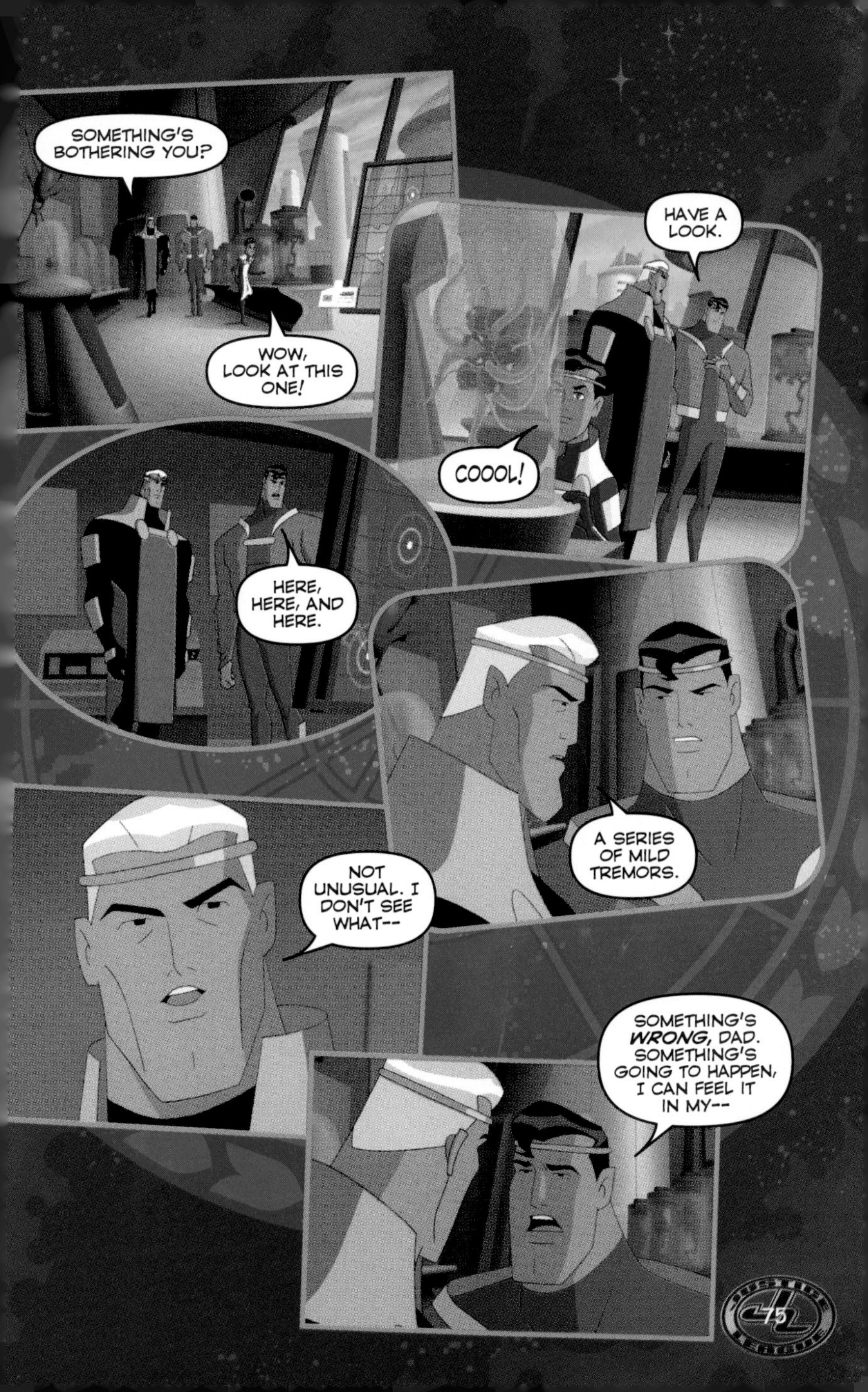
SOMETHING'S BOTHERING YOU?
WOW, LOOK AT THIS ONE!
HAVE A LOOK.
COOOL!
HERE, HERE, AND HERE.
A SERIES OF MILD TREMORS.
NOT UNUSUAL. I DON'T SEE WHAT--
SOMETHING'S ***WRONG,*** DAD. SOMETHING'S GOING TO HAPPEN, I CAN FEEL IT IN MY--

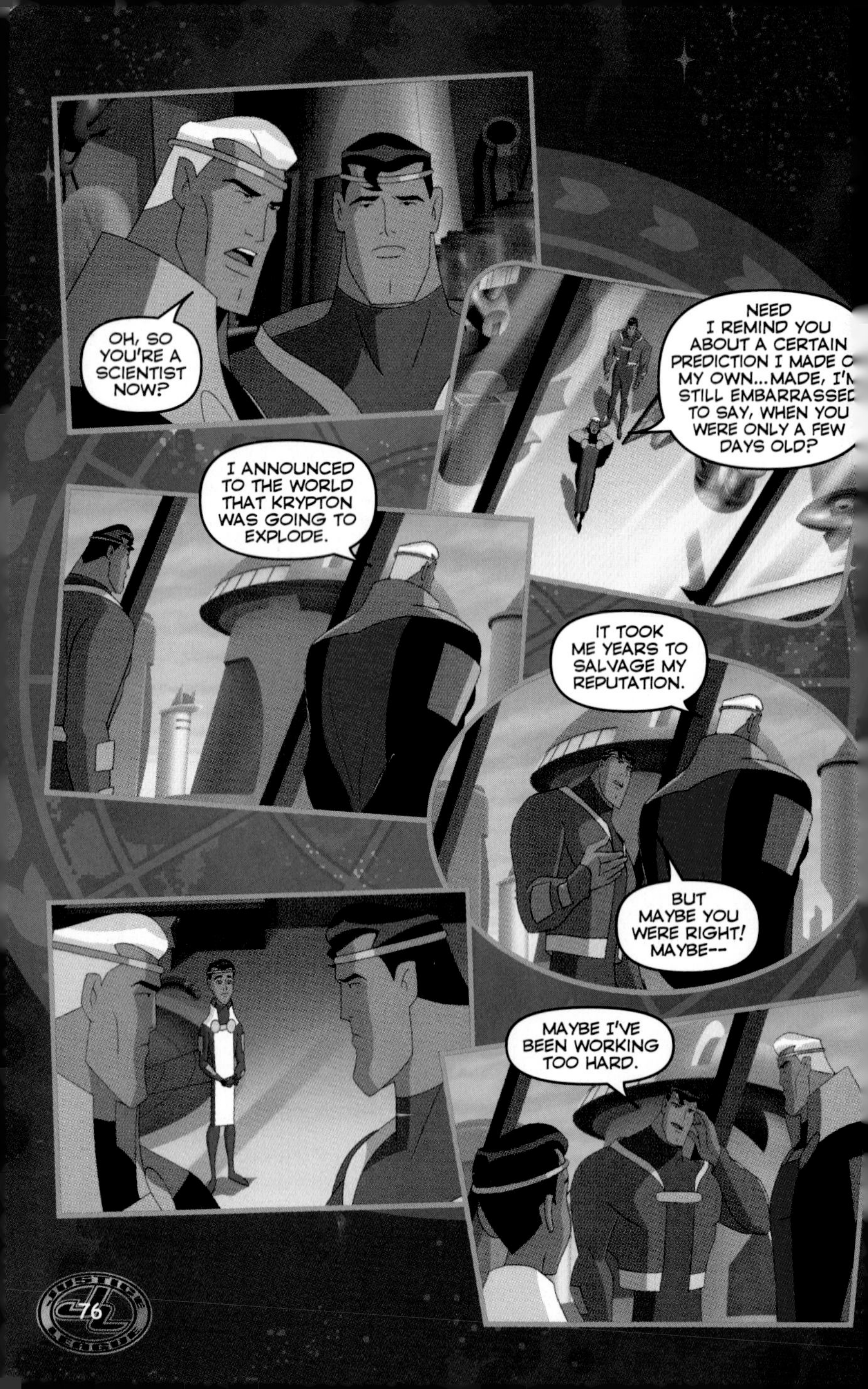
OH, SO YOU'RE A SCIENTIST NOW?
NEED I REMIND YOU ABOUT A CERTAIN PREDICTION I MADE O MY OWN...MADE, I'M STILL EMBARRASSED TO SAY, WHEN YOU WERE ONLY A FEW DAYS OLD?
I ANNOUNCED TO THE WORLD THAT KRYPTON WAS GOING TO EXPLODE.
IT TOOK ME YEARS TO SALVAGE MY REPUTATION.
BUT MAYBE YOU WERE RIGHT! MAYBE--
MAYBE I'VE BEEN WORKING TOO HARD.

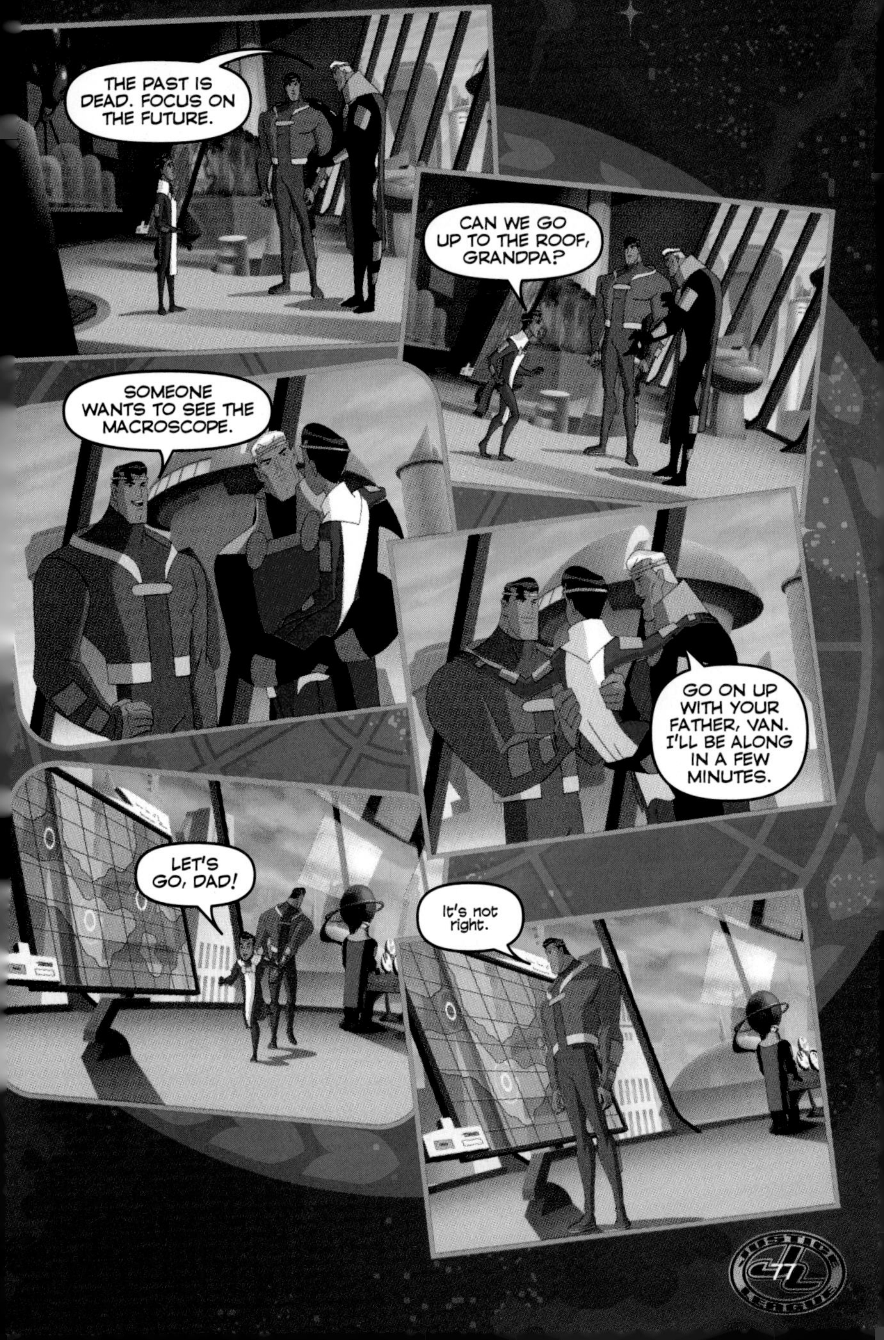
THE PAST IS DEAD. FOCUS ON THE FUTURE.
CAN WE GO UP TO THE ROOF, GRANDPA?
SOMEONE WANTS TO SEE THE MACROSCOPE.
GO ON UP WITH YOUR FATHER, VAN. I'LL BE ALONG IN A FEW MINUTES.
LET'S GO, DAD!
It's not right.

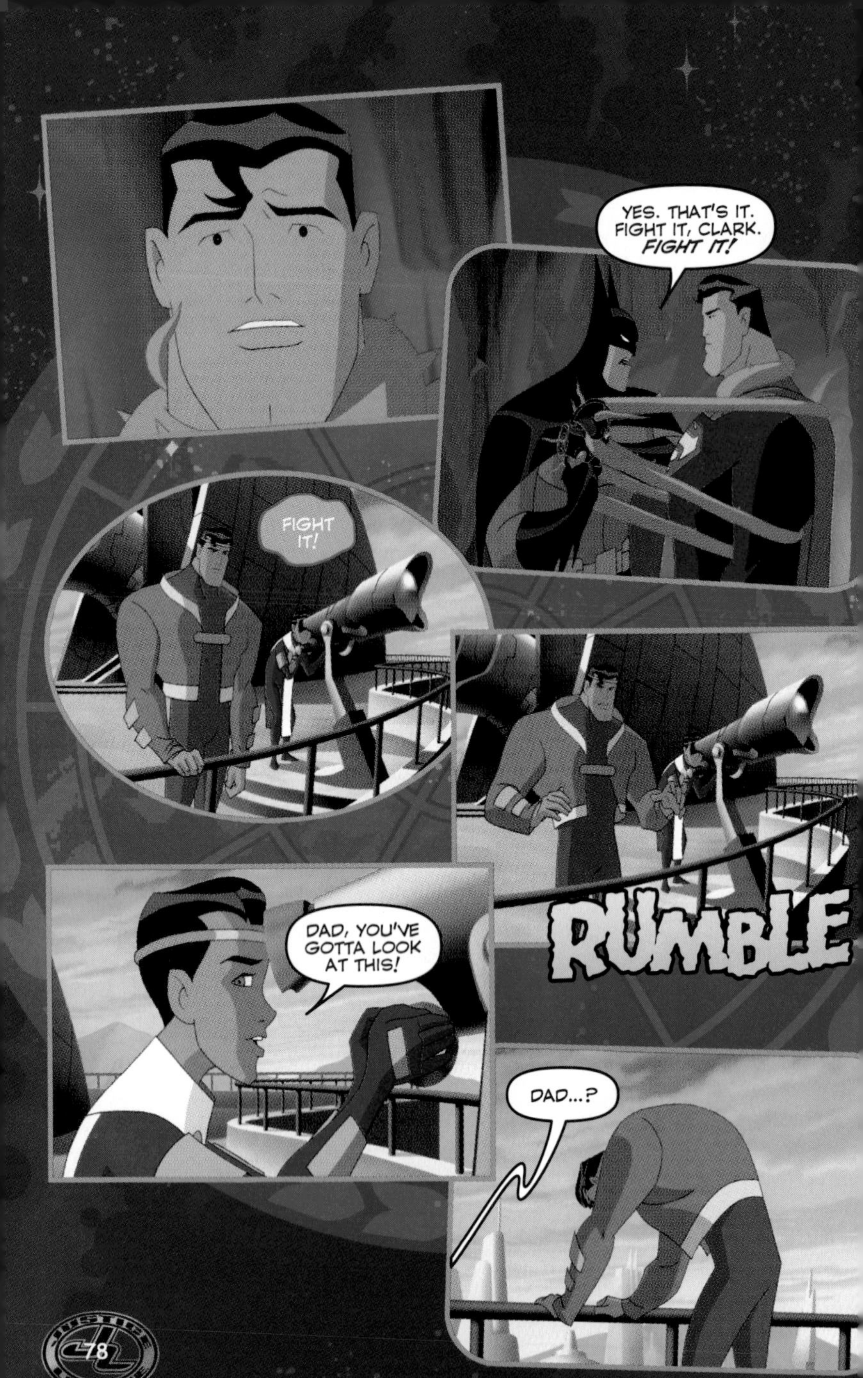
YES. THAT'S IT. FIGHT IT, CLARK. *FIGHT IT!*
FIGHT IT!
RUMBLE
DAD, YOU'VE GOTTA LOOK AT THIS!
DAD...?

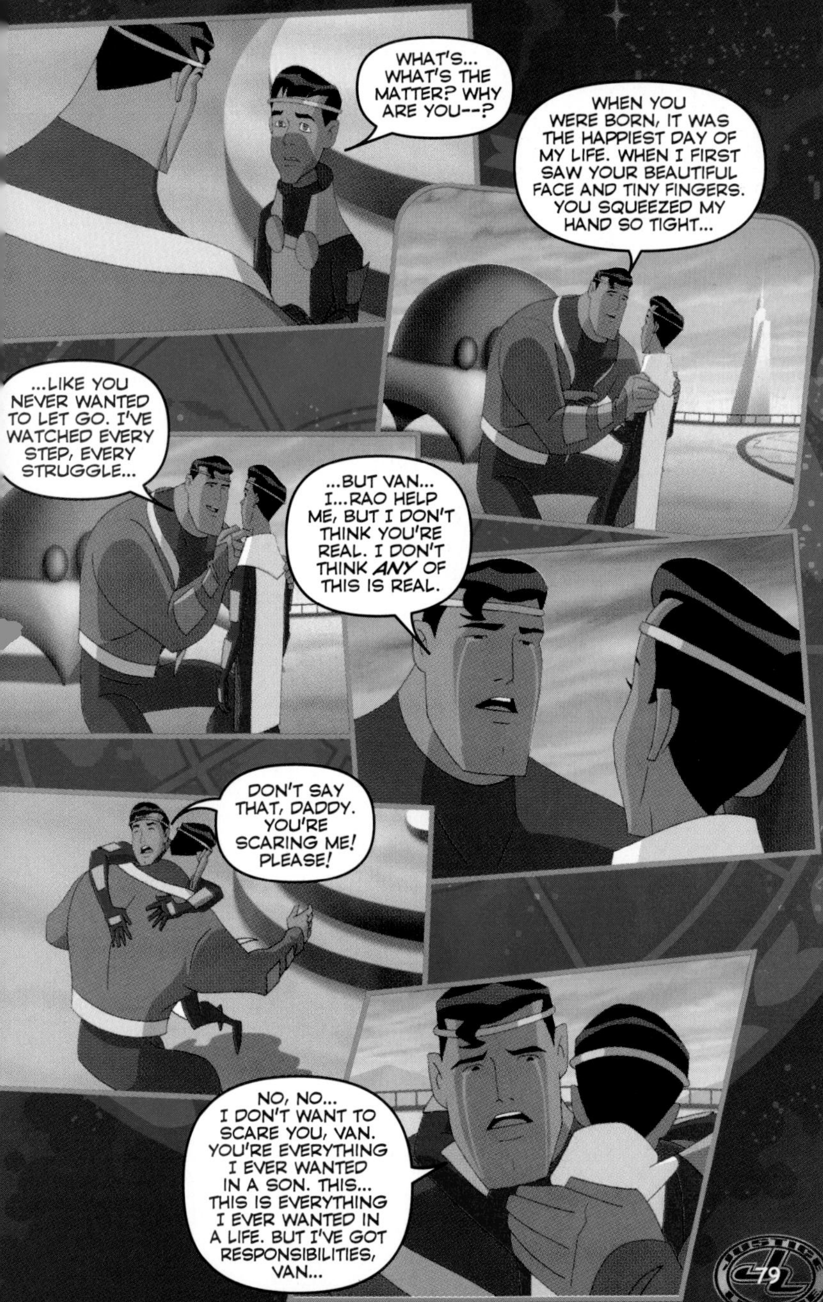

WHAT'S... WHAT'S THE MATTER? WHY ARE YOU--?
WHEN YOU WERE BORN, IT WAS THE HAPPIEST DAY OF MY LIFE. WHEN I FIRST SAW YOUR BEAUTIFUL FACE AND TINY FINGERS. YOU SQUEEZED MY HAND SO TIGHT...
...LIKE YOU NEVER WANTED TO LET GO. I'VE WATCHED EVERY STEP, EVERY STRUGGLE...
...BUT VAN... I...RAO HELP ME, BUT I DON'T THINK YOU'RE REAL. I DON'T THINK ANY OF THIS IS REAL.
DON'T SAY THAT, DADDY. YOU'RE SCARING ME! PLEASE!
NO, NO... I DON'T WANT TO SCARE YOU, VAN. YOU'RE EVERYTHING I EVER WANTED IN A SON. THIS... THIS IS EVERYTHING I EVER WANTED IN A LIFE. BUT I'VE GOT RESPONSIBILITIES, VAN...

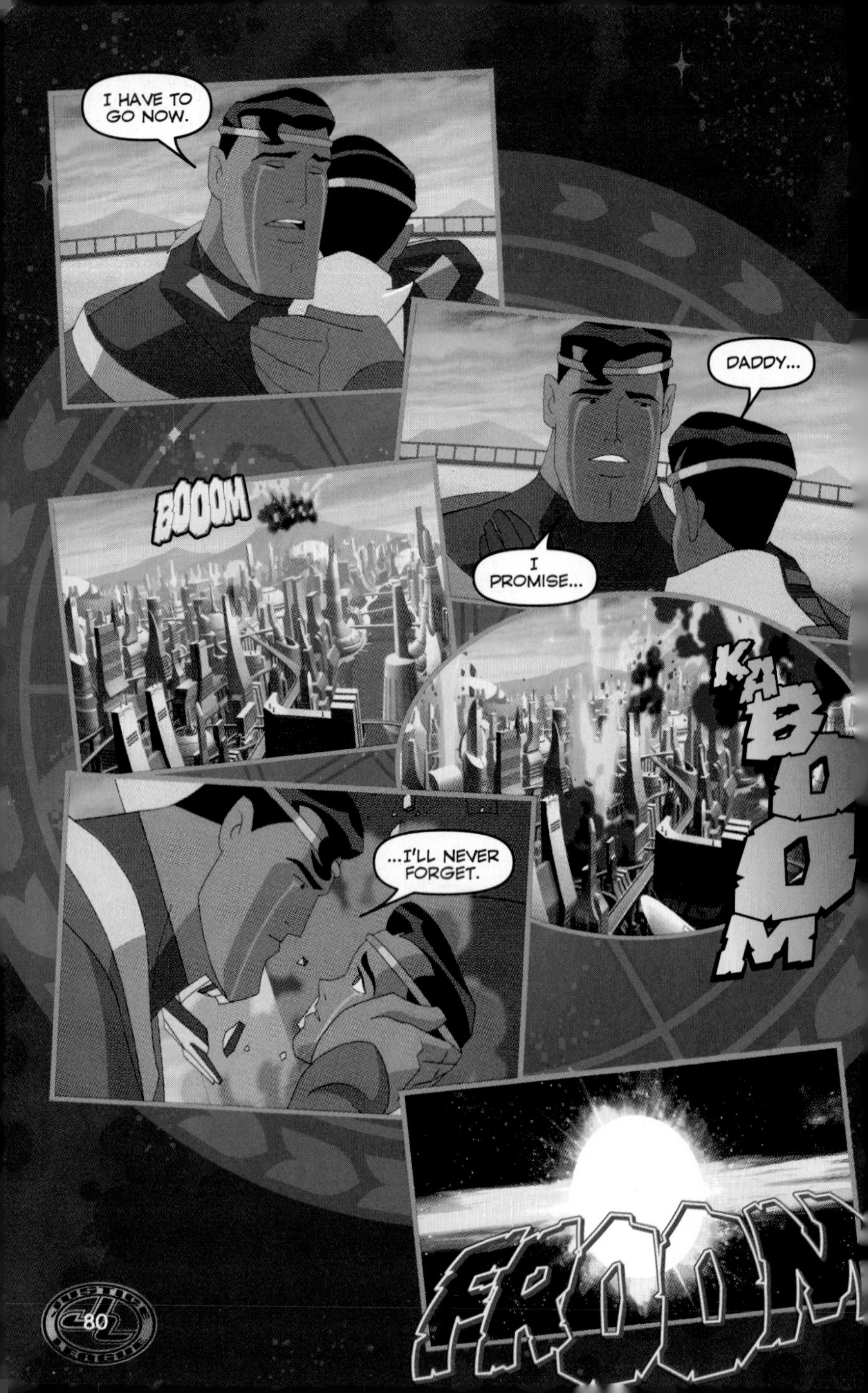

I HAVE TO GO NOW.
DADDY...
I PROMISE...
BOOOM
KABOOM
...I'LL NEVER FORGET.
FROOM

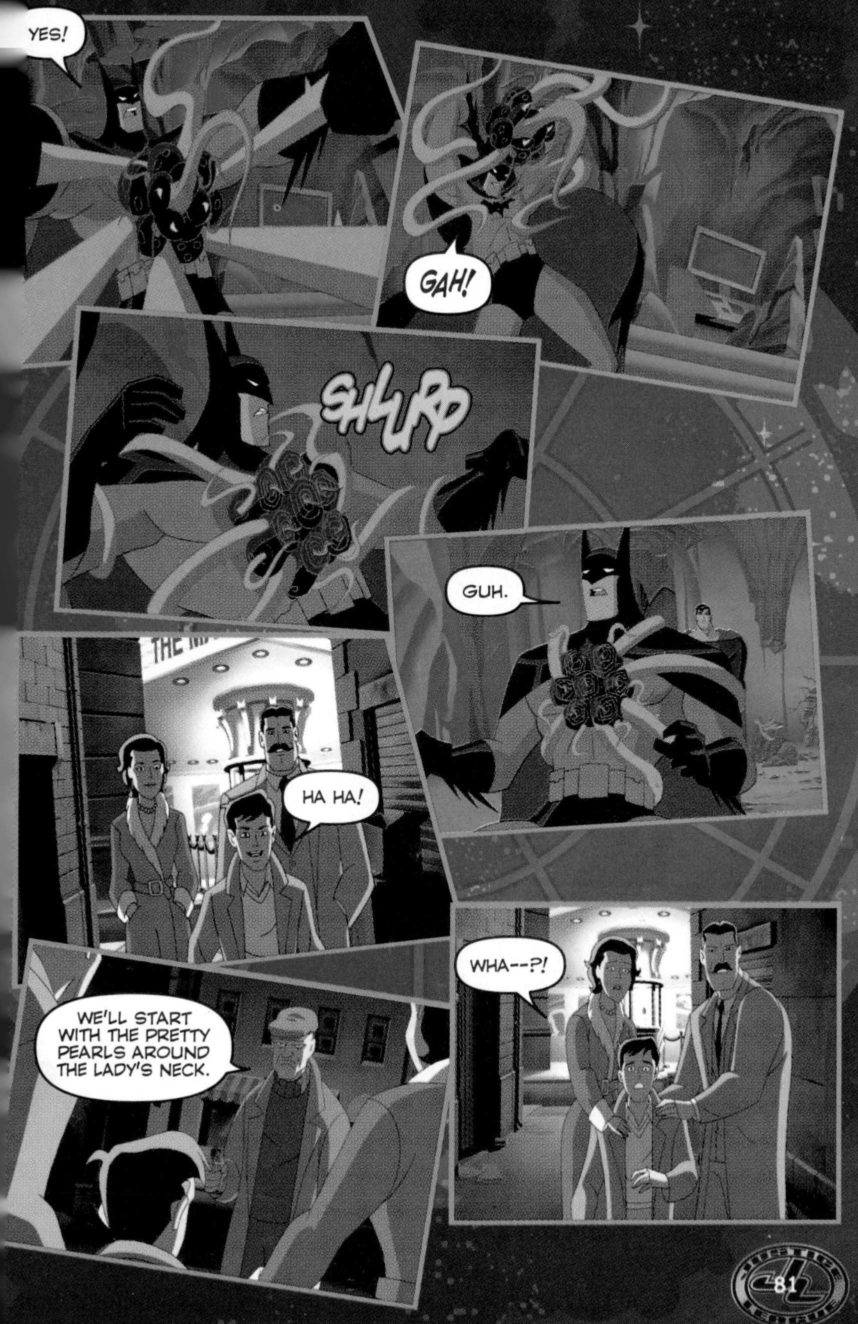
YES!
GAH!
SHLURP
GUH.
HA HA!
WE'LL START WITH THE PRETTY PEARLS AROUND THE LADY'S NECK.
WHA--?!

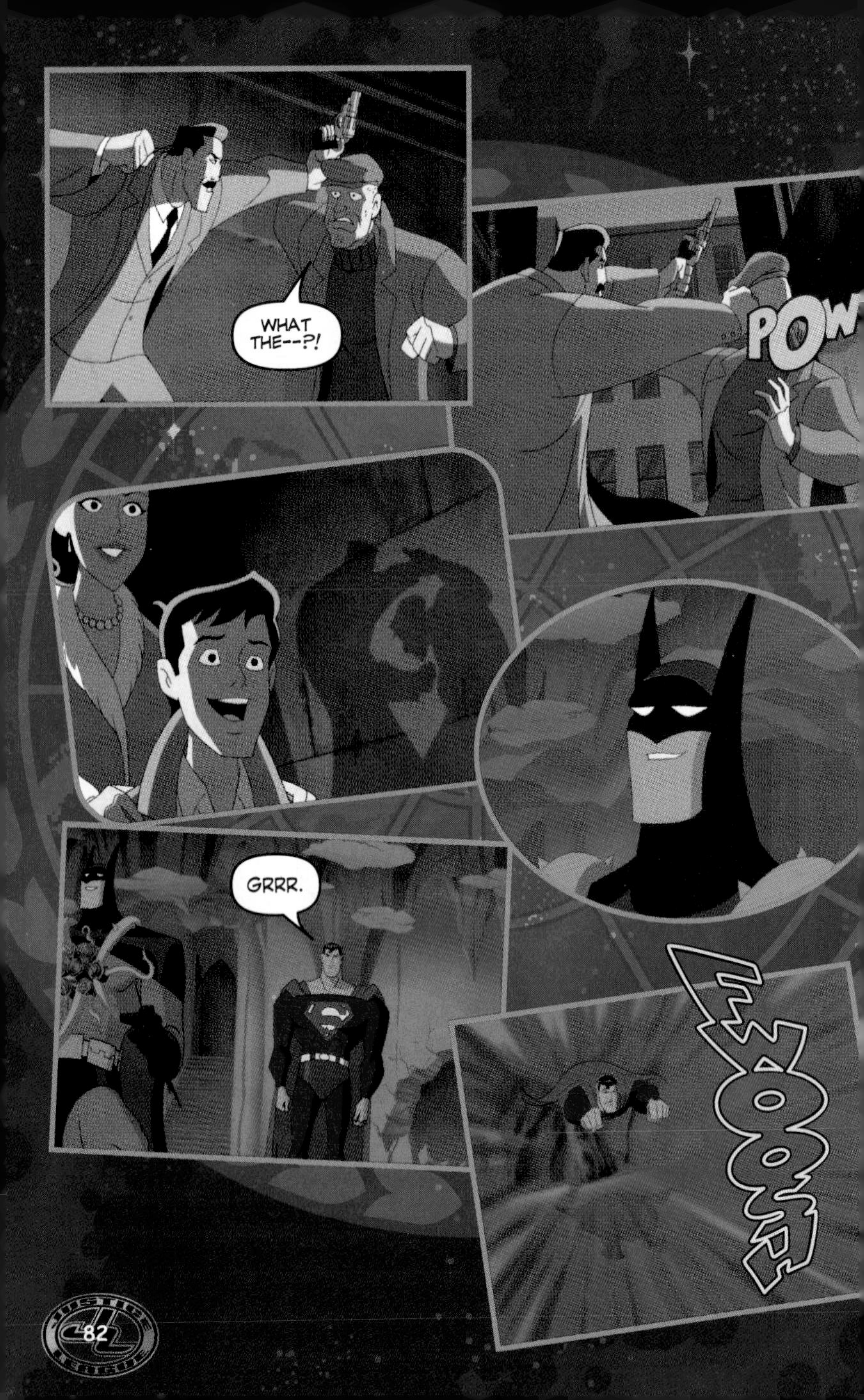
WHAT THE--?!
POW
GRRR.

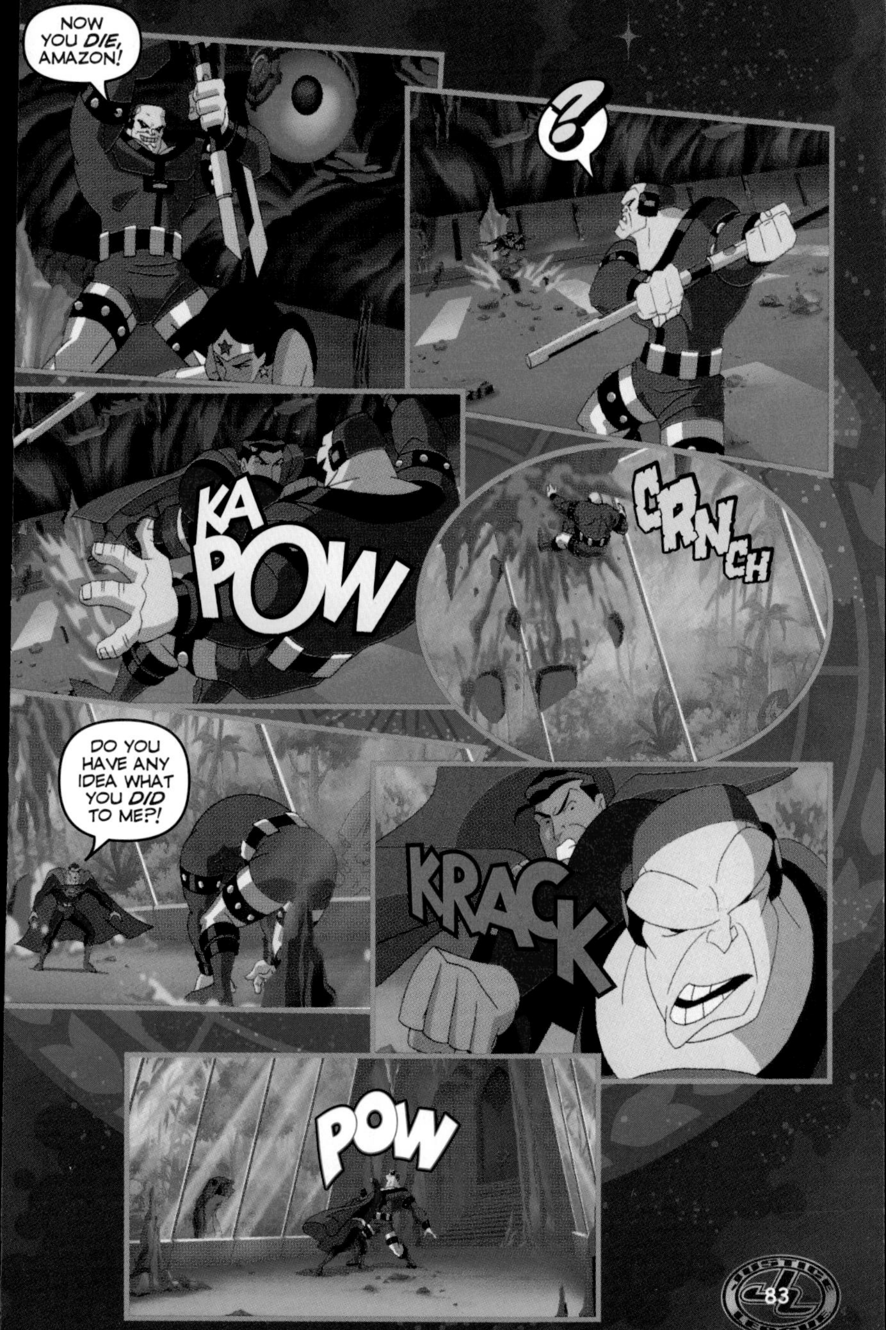
NOW YOU DIE, AMAZON!
?
KA POW
CRNCH
DO YOU HAVE ANY IDEA WHAT YOU DID TO ME?!
KRACK
POW

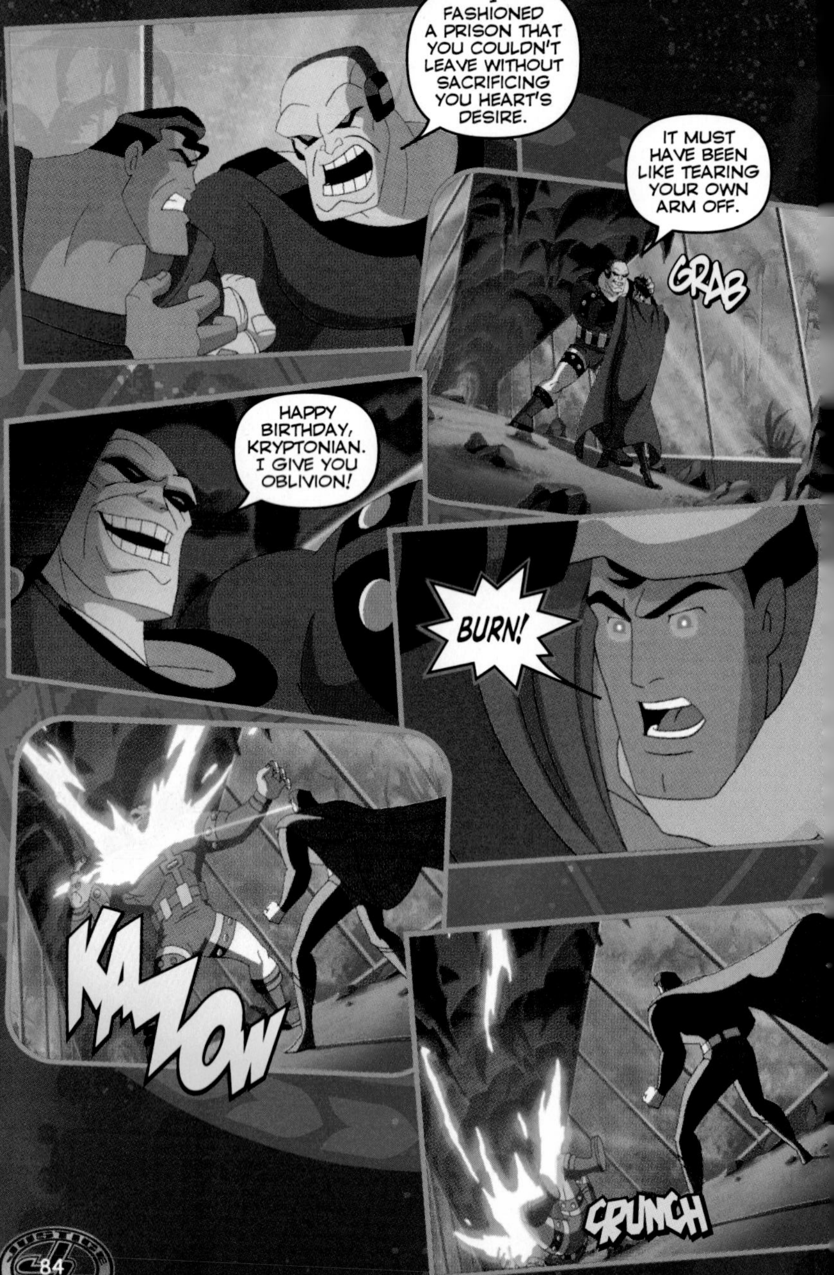
I FASHIONED A PRISON THAT YOU COULDN'T LEAVE WITHOUT SACRIFICING YOU HEART'S DESIRE.
IT MUST HAVE BEEN LIKE TEARING YOUR OWN ARM OFF.
GRAB
HAPPY BIRTHDAY, KRYPTONIAN. I GIVE YOU OBLIVION!
BURN!
KAPOW
CRUNCH

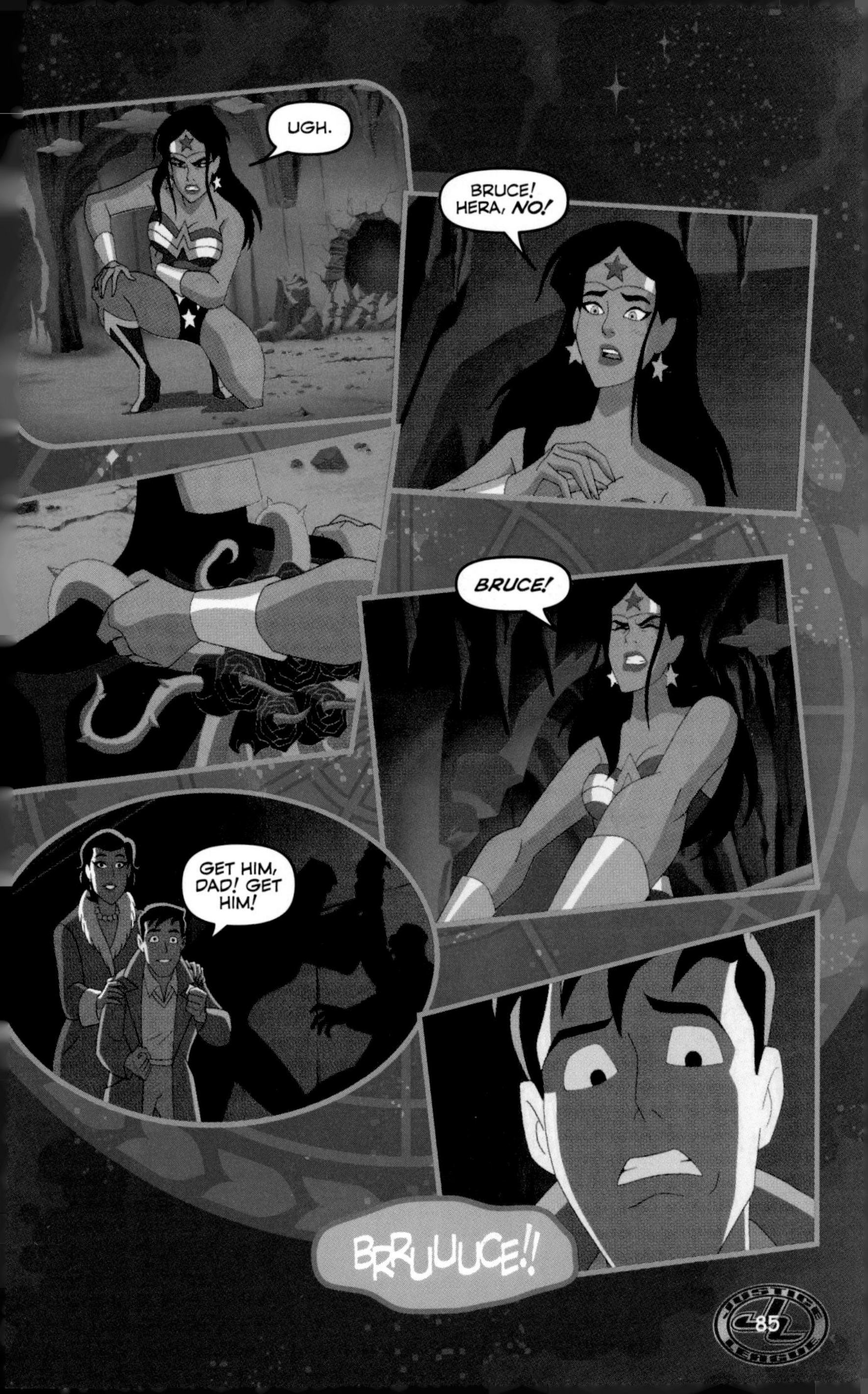

UGH.
BRUCE! HERA, NO!
BRUCE!
GET HIM, DAD! GET HIM!
BRRUUUUCE!!

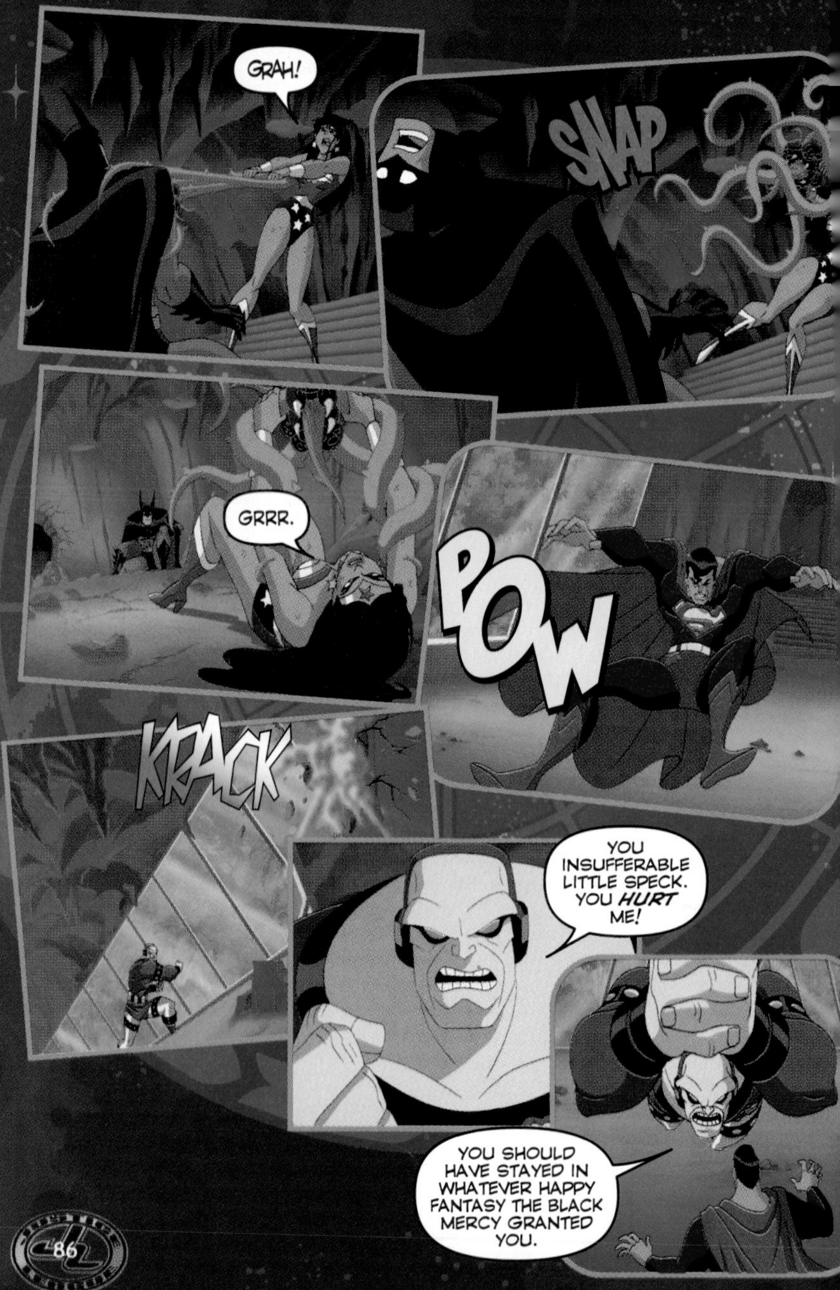
GRAH!
SNAP
GRRR.
POW
KRACK
YOU INSUFFERABLE LITTLE SPECK. YOU *HURT* ME!
YOU SHOULD HAVE STAYED IN WHATEVER HAPPY FANTASY THE BLACK MERCY GRANTED YOU.

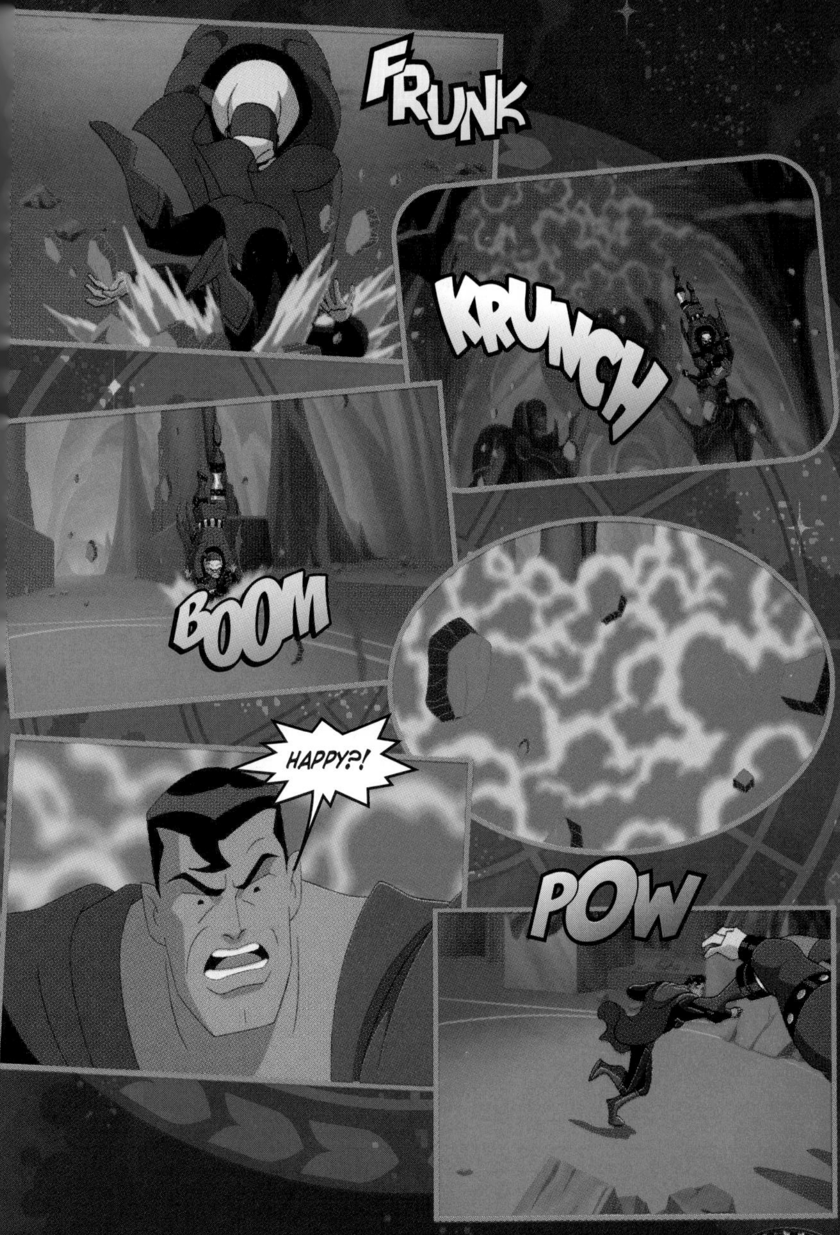
FRUNK
KRUNCH
BOOM
HAPPY?!
POW

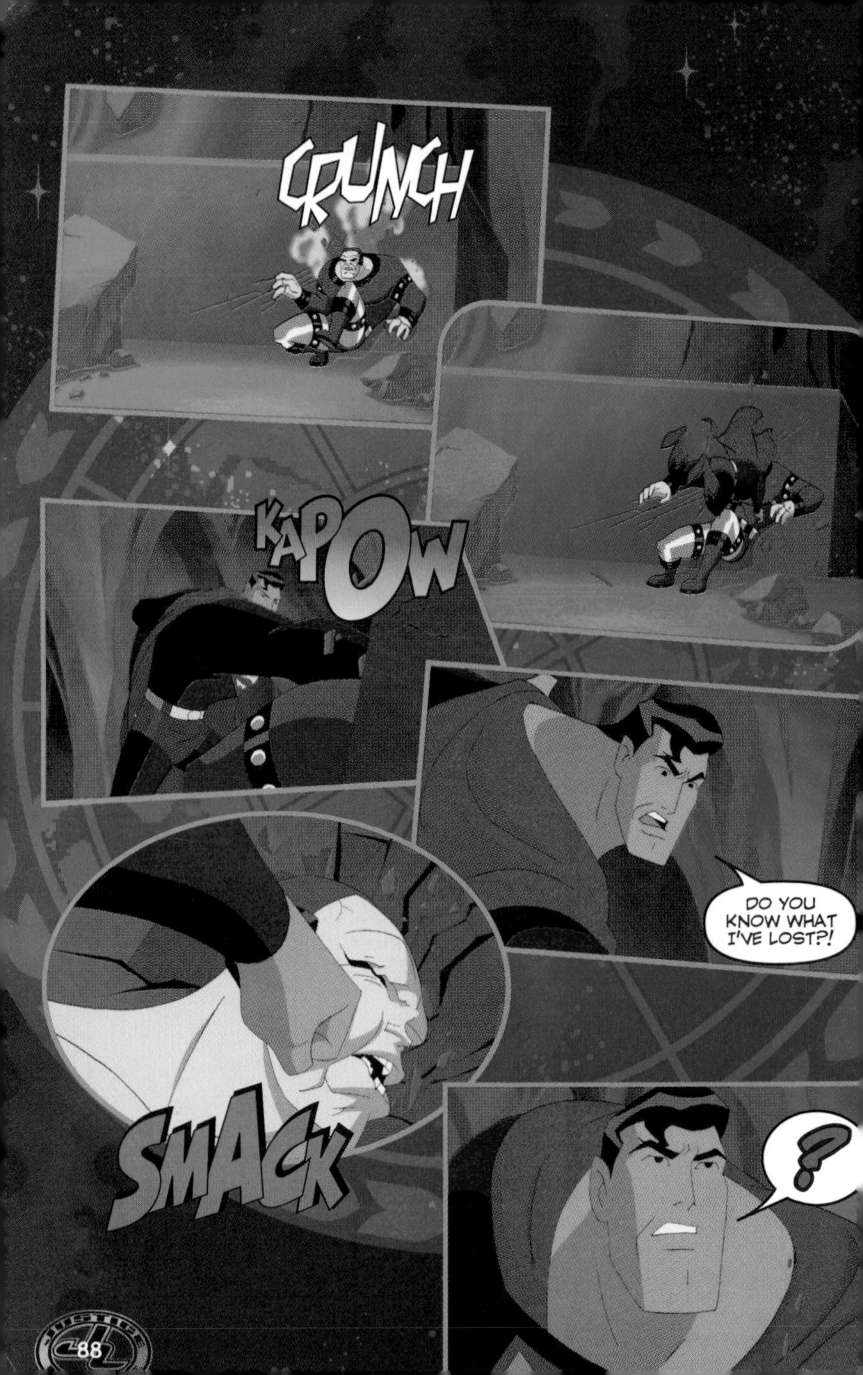
CRUNCH
KAPOW
DO YOU KNOW WHAT I'VE LOST?!
SMACK
?

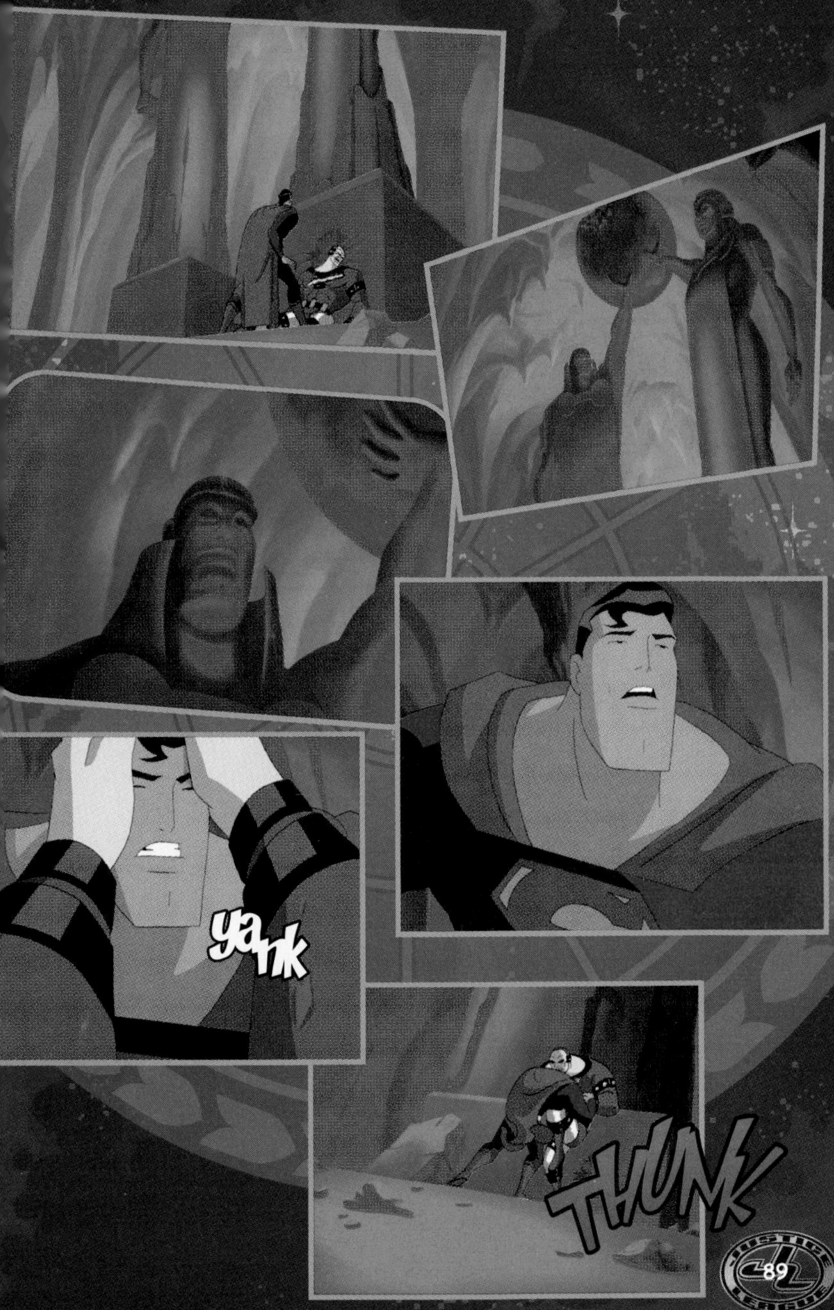
yank
THUNK
JUSTICE LEAGUE

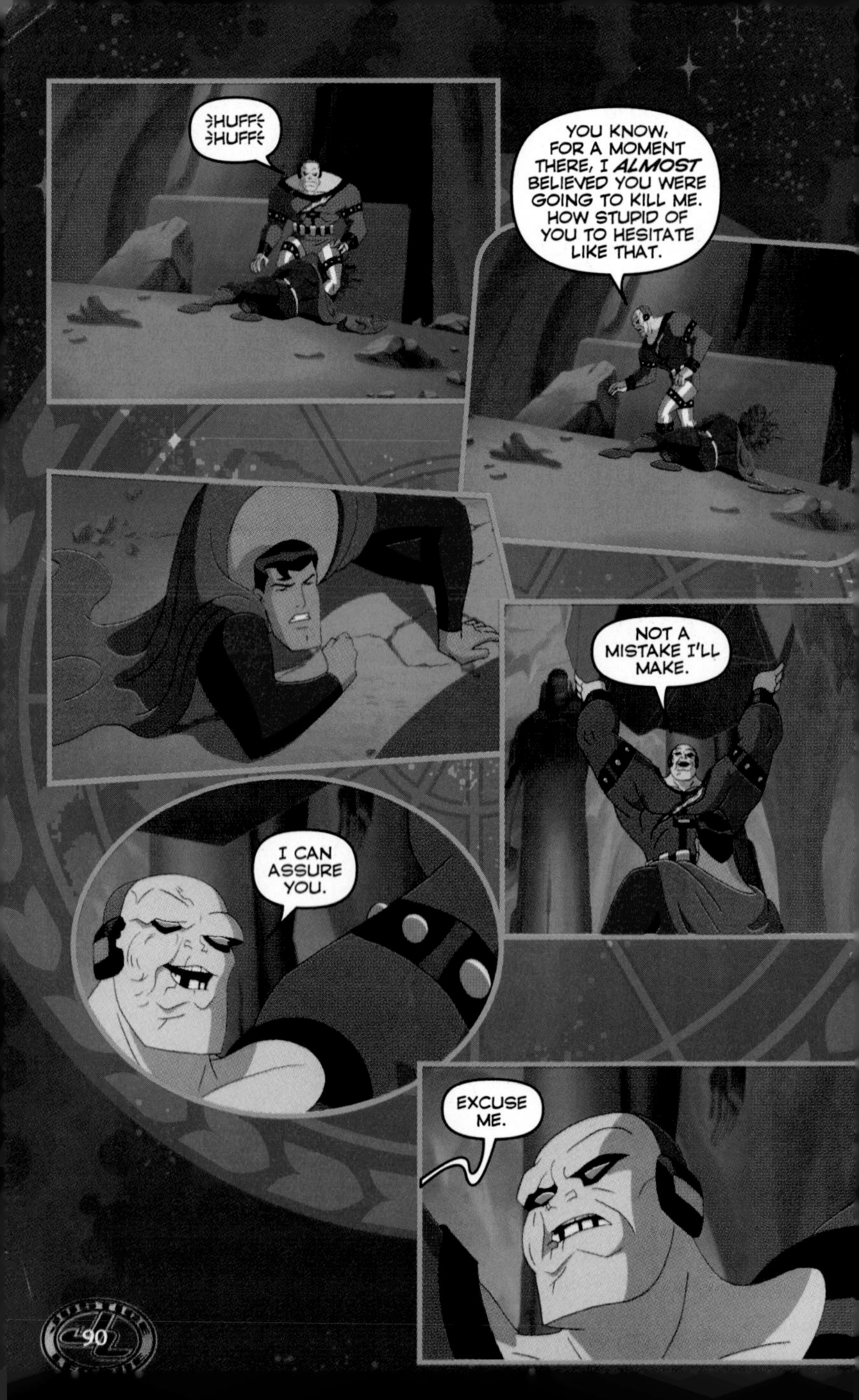
HUFF HUFF
YOU KNOW, FOR A MOMENT THERE, I ALMOST BELIEVED YOU WERE GOING TO KILL ME. HOW STUPID OF YOU TO HESITATE LIKE THAT.
NOT A MISTAKE I'LL MAKE.
I CAN ASSURE YOU.
EXCUSE ME.

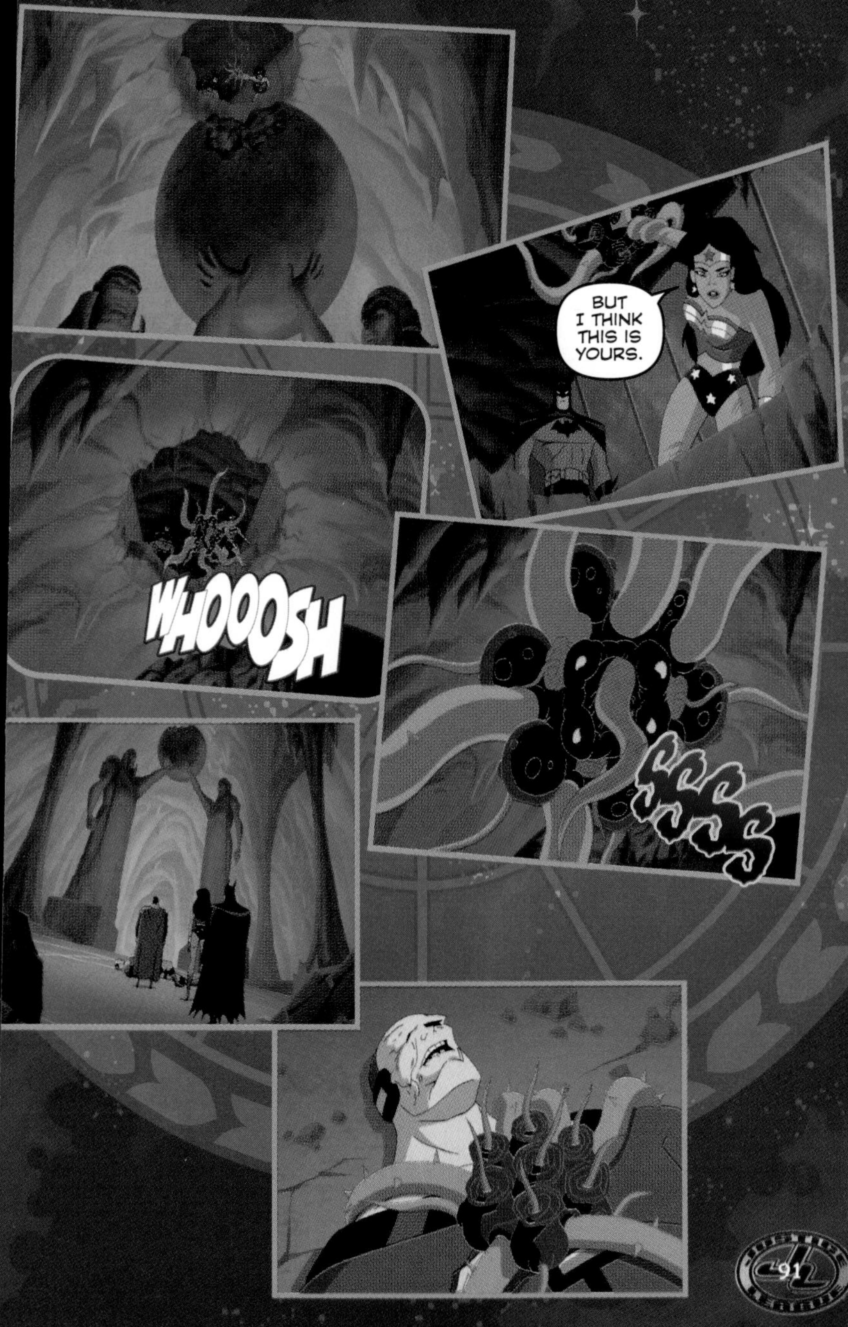
WHOOOSH
BUT I THINK THIS IS YOURS.

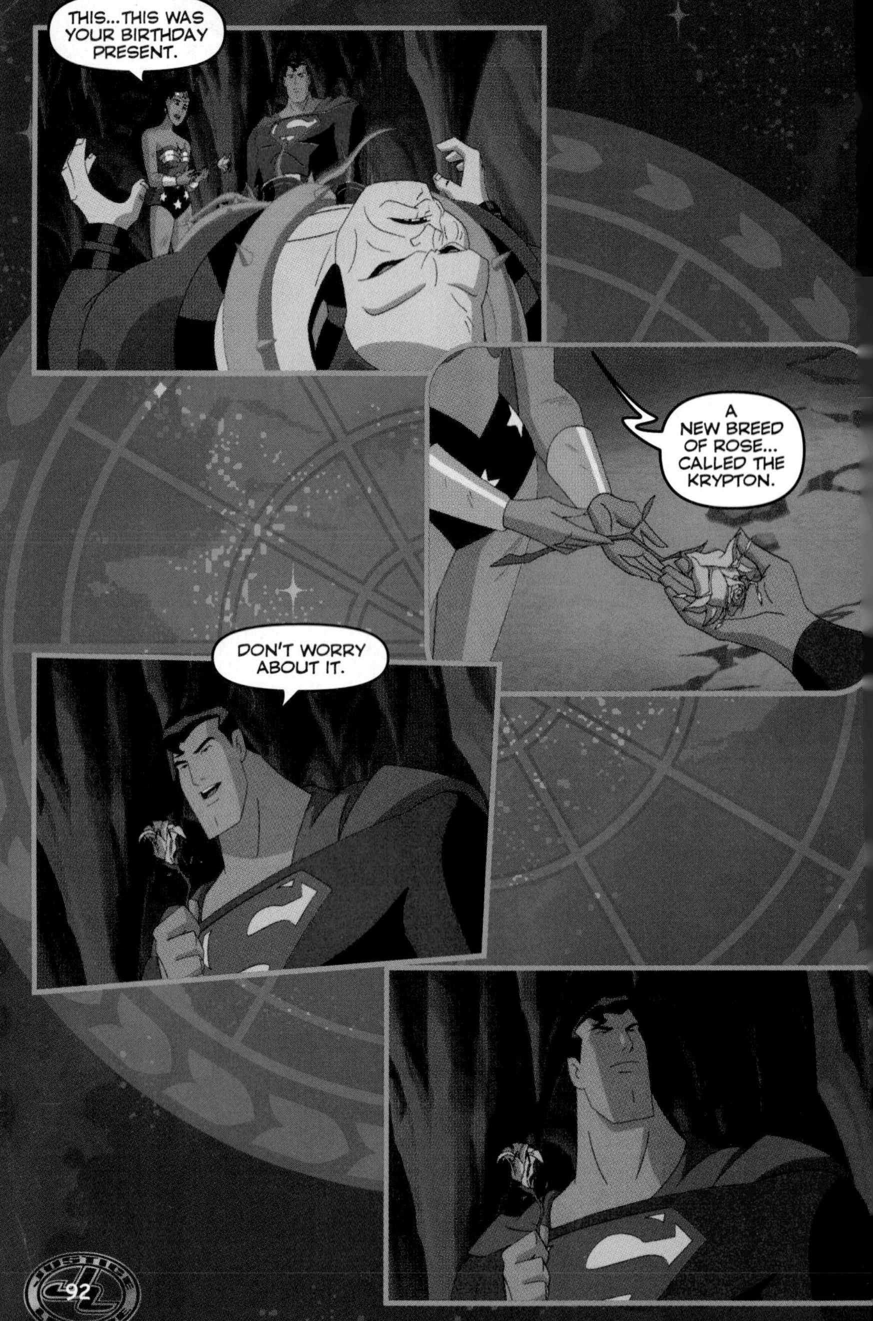
THIS...THIS WAS YOUR BIRTHDAY PRESENT.
A NEW BREED OF ROSE... CALLED THE KRYPTON.
DON'T WORRY ABOUT IT.

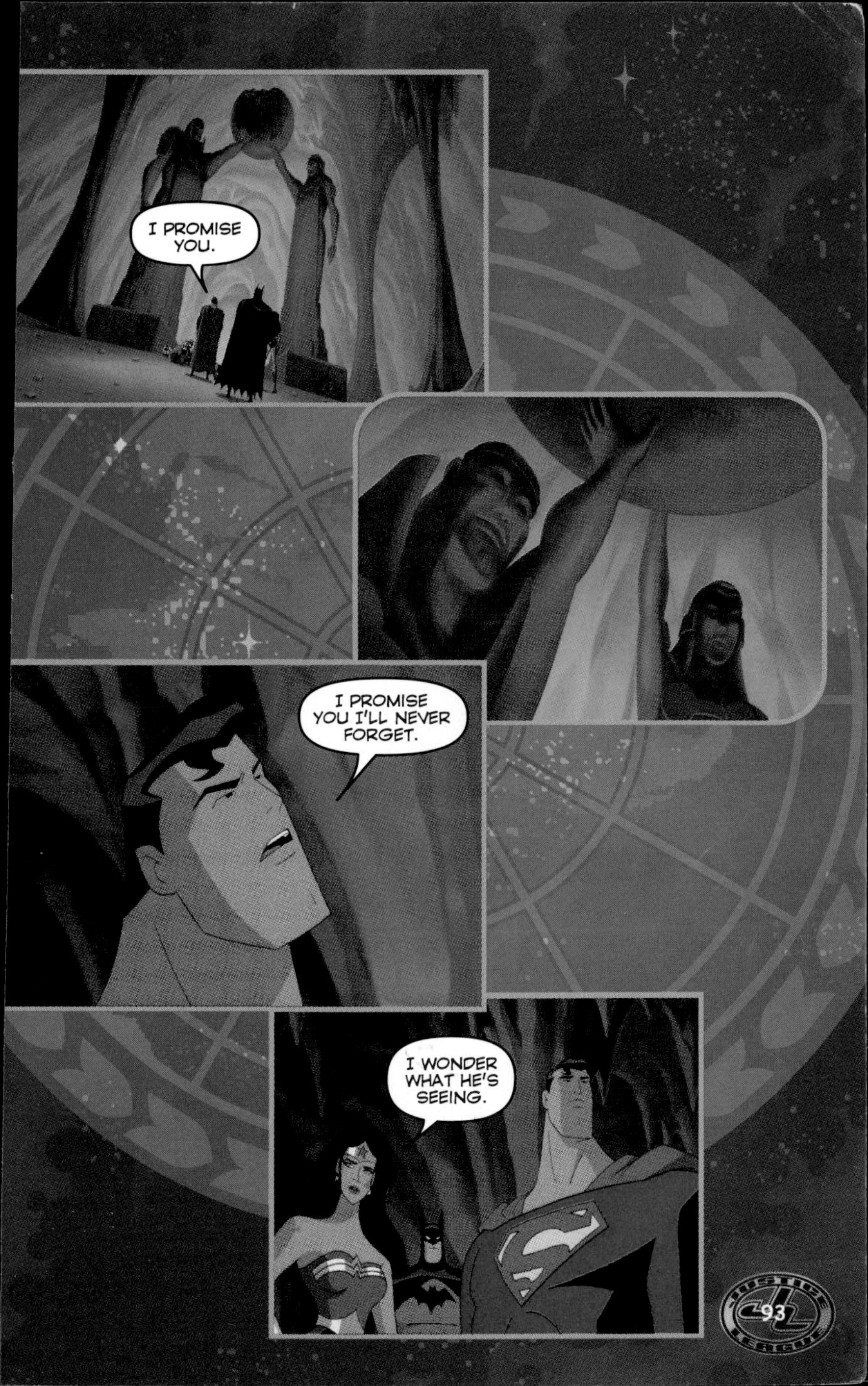
I PROMISE YOU.
I PROMISE YOU I'LL NEVER FORGET.
I WONDER WHAT HE'S SEEING.

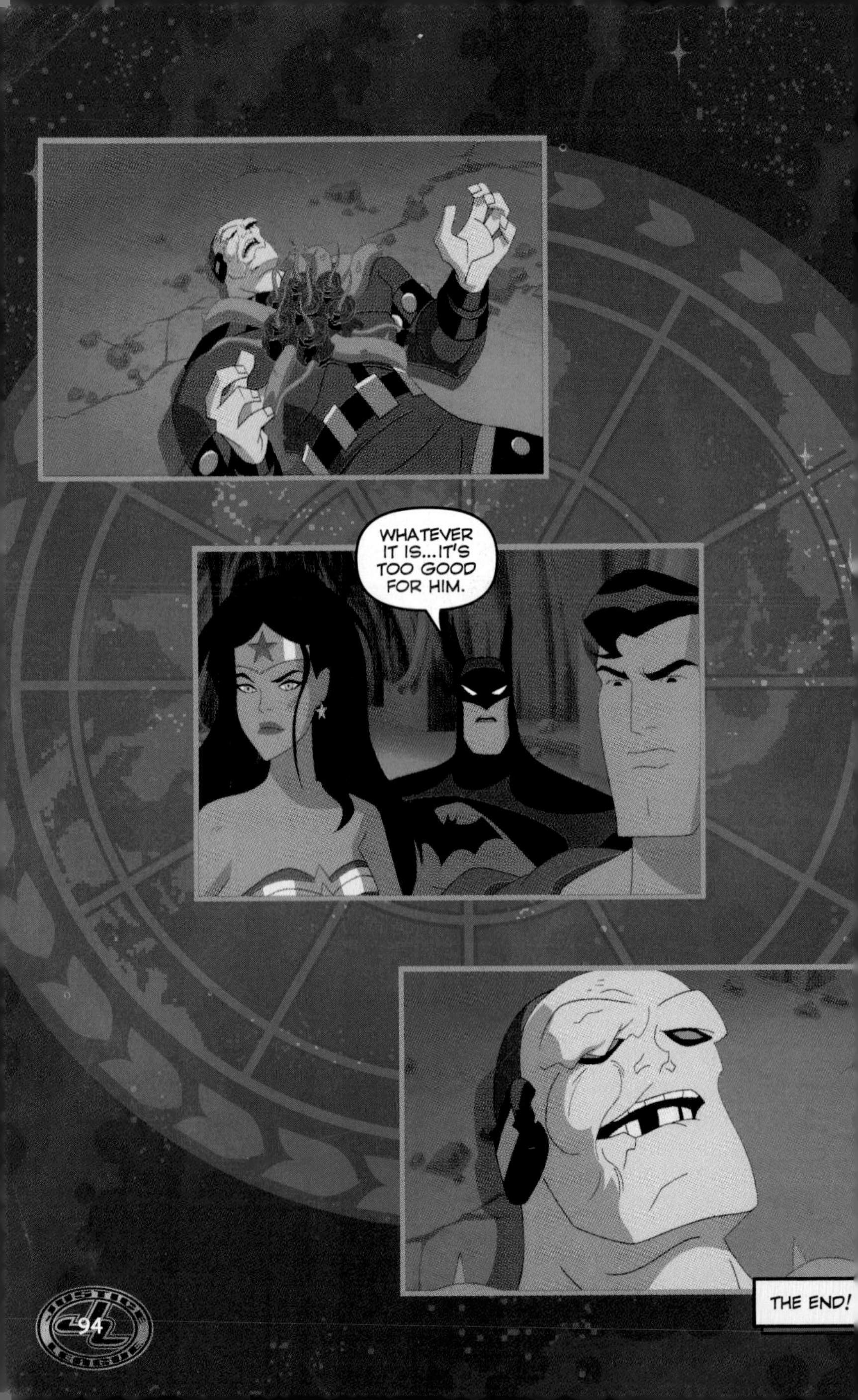
WHATEVER IT IS...IT'S TOO GOOD FOR HIM.
THE END!